ZEHIYA

A NOVEL

BY

MAYRA SONAM PALDON

FOR THOSE WHO VALUE
FRIENDSHIP

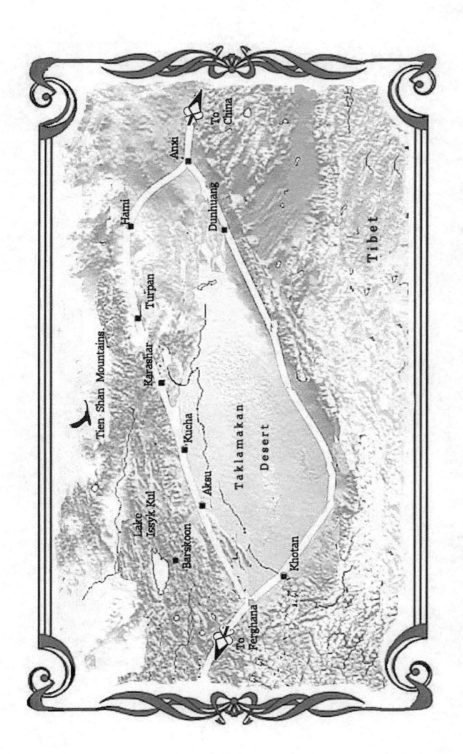

To China

Anxi

Dunhuang

Hami

Turpan

Tibet

Karashar

Tien Shan Mountains

Kucha

Taklamakan

Desert

Aksu

Lake
Issyk Kul

Barskoon

Khotan

To Ferghana

v

1

TIEN SHAN MOUNTAINS
LAKE ISSYK KUL
IN ANCIENT TIMES

Whirling gusts of wind buffeted the girl as she clung by her fingertips onto the sliver of ledge on the near vertical cliff face. Calloused bare toes of her left foot gripped a narrow ridge of rock as her other foot scrabbled to find another secure hold. Her leather trousers slid along the rough surface, protecting the soft skin of her legs. Her arm muscles quivered under her woven cotton tunic, becoming fatigued by the strain of holding her weight. Strands of her long hair, having escaped from the tight leather thong tied at the back of her neck, lifted and swam about her face. Fear simmered in her stomach when at last she felt a jutting rim of rock under her toe. Gasping with relief, she planted her foot solidly upon it.

Birds swooped and chattered in the tops of the tall junipers that swayed in the cold wind near her as she scanned the rock face for the hand holds that she had mapped in her mind when she had studied the crag from below. The problem was that it looked so different now. The roar of the thrashing whitewater river far below filled her ears. Fatigue fogged her mind as she grasped at tendrils of memory trying to pull in the full picture of the route.

"Think!" she commanded herself.

"Zehiya, you must reach to your right, see the rock-hold there?" a man's voice called to her from far below.

Searching in the direction to which he had guided her, she gasped, "Yes, Grandfather, I see it," she replied, grateful for his guidance.

"Once you are there, the climb becomes easy," he encouraged.

Bursting with admiration, Arif watched the lithe form of his sixteen-springs-old granddaughter become smaller as she climbed higher. Tearing his gaze from her, he pulled off his fur trimmed felt hat and searched the blue sky between the tall evergreen trees, looking for the dark shape of the mother eagle who would bring danger if she arrived. Returning his attention to Zehiya, he held her fast in his sight, as though his gaze was a tether that kept her secure.

At last she reached the section of the crag that opened into a gully. The climb was easier now and Zehiya's fear slid away as she scurried on hands and feet to a protected ledge that jutted out below the peak. When she reached the underside of it she raised her head slowly over the edge of the nest of woven branches that was nestled atop. Enchanted, she gazed at two baby eagles nestled inside. Looking at her with anticipation, they snapped their beaks with a high pitched chirping. Zehiya could tell by their size, the length of her forearm, that not yet a moon had passed since they had hatched. Though small and still covered in downy feathers, their talons and beaks were almost as large as that of an adult bird. Struggling to contain her delight, Zehiya stifled the urge to shout down to Grandfather about her accomplishment. The scent of juniper on the frigid air filled her nostrils as she took in a deep breath, composing herself for the sacred action she must perform now, in this significant moment.

Closing her eyes, Zehiya held out her hands in supplication as she prayed, "Oh, great Spirit of the Eagle, I am truly grateful for my success in reaching this nest. Mother of all Eagles, please grant me permission to have one of your children as my own."

Shifting the basket that hung on her back into her lap, she pulled out a freshly killed rabbit. Placing it reverently next to the nest, she prayed, "Mother Eagle, here is my offering in trade for one of your children. I will be her mother now and I will see her grow strong," she promised.

Looking from one eaglet to the next, Zehiya asked, "Which one is mine to take?"

One of the young birds reached out and snapped at her.

"You would like to go with me?" she whispered to the baby, its golden eyes intent upon her.

Reaching into the nest, she gently but firmly folded the wings to the chosen baby's sides, feeling strong small bones wriggle under the feathers. A struggle ensued when a sudden primal fear ripped through the bird, unsure now of this encounter. Zehiya clutched her prize and swiftly wrangled it into the basket. With a slap of the lid she tied the leather thong that secured it tightly.

"Zehiya?" Arif called, from far below. "Hurry now, we do not want to be here when the mother eagle returns."

As she pushed the basket around to her back, Zehiya looked around her and was relieved to see the sky was free of the protective mother eagle with her sharp beak and talons.

Arriving back down to the bottom of the cliff Zehiya let out the breath she had not realized she had been holding. Joy filled her, for she had succeeded in her quest. She laughed in triumph as Arif jogged up to her, his long fur trimmed padded silk robe floated around his tall soft leather boots. The glistening fabric of his robe was dyed in red and gold with patterns of rams horns. Though tall and broad of chest, he moved fluidly up the incline navigating easily over the rocks and boulders. His long white braid bounced on his back and a smile split his equally white beard.

With admiration and relief dancing in his green eyes, he exclaimed, "Granddaughter, you are a wonder."

He took the basket from her outstretched hands feeling the weight of the bird shifting inside. He untied the lid and lifted it slightly to peer in at the eaglet. Zehiya took up her leather belt from the pile of her things she had stored at the base of the cliff and fastened it around her waist. Sitting on a boulder she pulled on her tall soft leather boots, tucking her trouser legs inside, then wove the leather thongs around her calves to hold them securely in place.

"Is it a female?" Zehiya asked anxiously. "The females are the best hunters."

"Indeed a female would be a better hunter than the male, but a male eagle is a good hunter as well. I think this may be a female even so," Arif said, meeting her eyes, the same green as his, but now bluish with the reflection of the sky.

Glancing up at the sky, he said, "We should go now before our luck runs out."

Rising, Zehiya arranged the scabbard that held her sharp knife on her belt, then picked up the basket carefully settling the leather strap across her shoulder so it lay at her back. Untying the thong at the base of her neck she freed her hair and sent it tumbling down her back.

Arif watched his granddaughter as she jogged ahead of him, making her way swiftly down the incline, marveling as the bright sunlight on her hair made it sparkle like fire.

She is so like her grandmother, he thought.

As he followed in her wake, he was seized by a sudden searing pain. Clutching his chest, Arif drew in shallow breaths until the vise-like grip subsided.

Taking in a deep breath he rasped to himself, "You are not long in this world, old man. Give the ancient medallion to her soon, lest she never receive it after you are gone."

Kimizi, the red dun horse, lifted his head from his grazing in a grassy patch at the bottom of the wide gorge by the river, where he was tethered. He whinnied a greeting upon Zehiya's arrival.

"See, Kimizi?" Zehiya said as she lifted the strap over her head and placed the basket on the ground before him.

Kimizi lowered his head to inspect the jiggling basket as Zehiya knelt and opened the lid slightly. He shot backward with a snort when the baby eagle's head popped out snapping its sharp beak.

Arriving in time to watch the spectacle, Arif let out a hearty laugh.

Untying his horse nearby, he asked "What will you name her?"

"Neylan," she answered, as she slipped into her faded blue fleece lined silk robe that had been tied to the saddle, "it means wish fulfilled." Smiling at her grandfather, she said "My wish is now fulfilled."

Arif nodded in approval as he mounted his horse and adjusted his

4

sword hanging from his wide leather belt decorated with gold medallions of falcon motifs. "It is a good name."

2

Lake Issyk Kul sparkled beneath the sun as it hung low over the thickly forested mountain tops. In moments, it fell out of view behind the mountains with a parting gesture of orange and lavender light.

Arif built his homestead a distance above one of the many rivers that spilled into this mammoth lake, beyond the caravansary of Barskoon. Several yurts, round tents made of felt, for himself and his son's family, were clustered in the wide green valley that lay just before a narrow gorge of rock and forest. Log fences enclosed a very large grassy pasture where his many horses, sheep, and goats grazed along the gentle flow of the river.

Originally from the lands of Siberia far to the North, Arif's tribe are the Kyrgyz people. His father and grandfather were master sword makers, handing down their skill to Arif, and Arif to his son, Bagatur.

Bagatur is now a grown man with his second wife, Feray, and four children. Zehiya, his only daughter, came after his first born son, Ugur, with his first wife, who had died when Zehiya was two springs old.

Zehiya is an unusual name for their tribe, being an Arabic name. It is the custom of this tribe that the father choose the names of his children. An Arab merchant, who traveled the Northern trade route through Issyk Kul, came each spring to purchase a selection of Bagatur's beautiful and fine swords. Over the seasons the two men had become good friends. At the birth of Bagatur's second child, a daughter, Bagatur honored his friend by allowing him to name their child, and so he did, naming her Zehiya.

Arif and Bagatur also raised horses and were falconers, both a long tradition of their people. From the talons of their great hunting birds, peregrine falcons and eagles, they received stores of meat from ducks, grouse and rabbit and sold wolf and fox pelts for coats, hats and paint brushes. Their large herd of horses, containing the finest Kyrgyz stock were sought after by travelers and royals alike, who bought mounts for themselves and their armies. With all of this Arif and Bagatur prospered.

As the first stars of night appeared in the sky, Arif and Zehiya trotted the horses up the rise to the homestead. Dismounting, they led their horses to the log corral near the largest yurt. Zehiya tied Kimizi next to the corral then hugged the basket close to her as she bounced anxiously on her toes waiting for Arif to finish tying his horse.

"We should go inside together to show them," Arif said turning to her. "Let us tend to the horses; they have taken us far."

With a sigh, Zehiya nodded. "Yes, Grandfather."

Placing the basket safely by one of the log posts, Zehiya unsaddled Kimizi. Taking a hemp cloth, she rubbed the wet sweat mark on his back. Kimizi lifted his nose in the air, his lips twitching in pleasure as she rubbed until his coat was dry and soft. When Arif had completed drying his horse's back he slid open the log gate to the pasture. They watched as the two horses trotted to the riverbank and drank the cold clear water.

Smoke drifted from the vent at the top of the large yurt, carrying the aromas of mutton and rice on the icy breeze. Hunger gnawed at Zehiya. Arif held the felt door flap open for her and she nodded and smiled up at him as she stepped inside. The air was warm and thick with the aromas of roasted meat, spices, furs, wool and people. The walls of the yurt, made from a lattice of birch poles, were hung with beautiful carpets from Persia, China, and Tibet. Their colorful patterns danced in the flickering light of the butter lamps and the fire-pit.

The faces of her family who were seated on cushions surrounding a matt with the array of food for their dinner placed upon it, turned to look at Zehiya and Arif as they entered.

"Did you find one?" her half-brother, Erdem, asked excitedly, his eyes wide with anticipation.

"Eat your food!" spat her father, Bagatur, at his second son.

Hunching up his burly shoulders, anger smoldering in his eyes, her father went back to his meal and ignored their entrance.

Looking much like her father, with fiery red hair and green eyes, her older brother, Ugur, mimicked her father by glaring at her scornfully then he made a show of ignoring her.

Little Arif, the youngest son, with deep auburn hair and dark eyes, ate slowly. Terror of his father's wrath twisted his smooth young face.

Her stepmother, Feray, who was dressed in several layers of brightly colored floor length tunics of ikat and plant motif designs, secured with a belt of dangling silver medallions that tinkled with her movements, stooped by the fire serving herself a bowl of food. Under her cap decorated with silver and gold pendants that shimmered in the firelight her long dark hair was woven into a long braid that fell down her back. Her skin was the color of the moon and her large brown eyes swam with kindness. She was the mother of Zehiya's two younger half-brothers and was of the Uighur Turkish tribe.

Rising from her task, Feray gestured toward the two empty cushions placed before the mat, saying in a gentle and welcoming tone, "Please sit, you must both be hungry after your journey."

Tears welled in Zehiya's eyes. The joy she had wanted to share, the story of her climb up the cliff. Her triumph, that she had imagined would be greeted with praise, had been swiftly taken away by her father.

"No, I will settle Neylan before I eat," she replied, turning briskly to the door, so no one would see her anguish.

Pushing through the door flap, she burst out into the cold of the night. A crescent moon was rising over the mountains, illuminating the valley.

Bent over the basket she held tightly, she hurried away from the large yurt along the well-worn path. Tears blurred her vision and streamed down her face. Arriving at a smaller yurt, she pushed through the door flap, stopping in the blackness inside. Her eyes soon became accustomed to the darkness. Kneeling on a small worn carpet placed on the dirt floor, she placed her basket down gently and lit a butter lamp. Its soft glow warmed her spirits. Her sorrow melted at the sight of her male Peregrine falcon, Kartal, who was tethered to his perch. Her father's and grandfather's two female eagles sat quietly tethered on their perches, heads flicking at her arrival. Behind them along the yurt wall were three large female Peregrine falcons; her brothers' birds. And at the end of the line of birds was the perch that Grandfather had made for her eagle.

"Look, Kartal," she enthused, as she untied the basket lid. "A little sister for you."

The eaglet was crouched low inside, trembling as it looked up at her. Zehiya looked at the empty meat bowls on the floor that were used to feed the birds.

"You must be hungry," she cooed to her eagle. "I will get you some food."

She hesitated, not wanting to go back to the family yurt and her father. Fastening the basket lid she made her decision.

"I will not be afraid of him. I will not let him keep me from feeding you," she said to Neylan as she rose.

Out into the night she gazed up at the crescent moon and stars, her heart swelled with joy. Flinging her arms wide, she threw her head back and spun making the sky swirl as she sang in glee, "I have found my eagle!"

She skipped a joyful dance along the path.

As she drew near the large family yurt, she heard raised voices from within. Drawing closer she stopped to listen.

"Women should not be wasting their time training an eagle. Our bird-hunting tradition is a man's tradition!" her father growled.

"A man's tradition?" Arif retorted, his voice rising in incredulity. "Your mother was a renowned eagle-falconer!"

Still seated on the cushion Bagatur scoffed, "That was the past. You should not have encouraged my daughter by giving her that falcon when she was a little girl. I should never have allowed it!" he cursed, pounding his thigh with a meaty fist.

"You should have never allowed it?" Arif retorted, his anger broiling. "Do not forget your place, son." Thumping his brawny chest with his fist, he roared, "I am head of this household and I decide what shall be allowed! She is my granddaughter, do not forget!"

In one movement Bagatur shot up. His face inches from Arif's he growled through clenched teeth, "My daughter is not going to raise that eagle. She is going to be married and leave this yurt! The sooner the better!"

Both men turned, startled, as Zehiya barged through the door, "She is my eagle, I found her," she said. "I will raise her and she will hunt for our family."

His face burning with rage, her father glared at her. "Your brother will raise that eagle, not you!" he shouted.

"No! She is my eagle-I will raise her!" Zehiya demanded, stomping her foot.

Lunging toward her, his hand raised to strike, Bagatur bellowed, "You will not! You do not declare what shall be to me!"

Arif grabbed his son's muscular arm to stay its swing at Zehiya. Infuriated, Bagatur pulled his arm free, shoving his father backward. Arif's leg struck the edge of an ornately-carved trunk and he crashed down into the stacks of saddles, blankets, and bridles stored at the side of the yurt. Enraged, he struggled up from the heap and sprang at his son. Searing pain, like a flaming sword slashing through him, stopped his flight. Gritting his teeth, he grabbed at his chest and sank to his knees. Falling on his side, he groaned in pain.

Bagatur looked down at his father in shock.

Feray shouted, "Get the healer, the shaman!"

Bagatur looked at her, uncomprehending.

Crouched at the side of the yurt, her arms clutching her two boys to her, Feray shouted again, trying to break through his confusion, "Get the shaman! Quickly!"

Ugur, who stood pressed against the lattice wall, his eyes wide with terror, rallied himself. Stepping forward, he urged, "Father, we must go find him."

Turning away from the large old man lying on the carpeted floor, Bagatur followed his son out the door.

Zehiya threw herself to the floor, gripping her grandfather's shoulder. "Grandfather? What is wrong?" she cried, shaking him gently.

Reaching across his wide chest he seized her hand.

"Listen, not much…time," he croaked, gasping each breath. "My yurt, in…trunk, a gold…medallion, yours…now. It is…ancient." He took in a ragged breath. "From a great…tribe…long ago. Our ancestors, women…were warriors… strong…like you…granddaughter. My sword…is yours…as well."

Feray knelt at his side.

Turning his gaze to her, he said, through gritted teeth, "Did… you… hear? My sword."

Feray nodded squeezing his shoulder, "Yes, it shall be hers," she assured him.

Arif coughed, choking out the words, "Granddaughter… I am… so… proud…of you," he wheezed, gasping for air. "So like…your… grand…mother."

"Grandfather?" Zehiya shook her grandfather's shoulder firmly, tears streaming down her face. "Grandfather!" She shook his limp heavy form.

Feray wrapped her arms around Zehiya's trembling body, her eyes filling with tears.

"He is gone, Zehiya. He has gone," she sobbed.

3

Clutching the bulky fur she carried under her left arm and a bowl of cold roasted meat in her right hand, Feray shouldered open the door flap of the falconry yurt. In the soft flickering light of a single butter lamp, she gazed down at Zehiya who was lying on the carpet, her body curled around the eaglet basket. Clutched in her hand the gold medallion that her grandfather had bequeathed her glittered.

Kneeling, Feray set the bowl down. Unrolling the fur, she settled it over her stepdaughter. "I have brought you food. You must eat, Little Fire," she urged, using the pet name she had given Zehiya since becoming her stepmother, so long ago. "My Little Fire," she whispered, love swelling her heart.

Zehiya was unresponsive.

With a sigh, Feray rose and went to the door. Stopping, she turned to look back at the grief-stricken girl. Shaking her head in sadness, tears welled in her eyes as she ducked through the door flap out into the clear night.

Zehiya closed her eyes, her body shaking anew with tears. The realization assailed her that her grandfather was gone forever. Her father was taking her eagle away. He would expect her to marry soon and leave her home. The pain in her heart was too much to bear. Sleep finally overtook her.

Her fingers and toes ached as they grasped the narrow and sharp protrusion high on the cliff face. The muscles of her arms began to shake violently from the strain. She was sure she would lose her grip and fall to her death. An ominous dark shadow filled the sky above.

"Zehiya? See the rock there? Go to it and you will be safe." Grandfather's voice called to her, sounding far away.

The dark shadow soared above her as she inched her way to the rock. Reaching it, she scurried up the familiar ravine to the ledge above her. The ledge was empty now, the nest was gone. Suddenly the black shadow fell over her, so close Zehiya instinctively covered her head with her arms. She felt the whoosh of sharp claws slashing the air a hand's breadth from her. Then the form flew away, only to dive at her again. Zehiya screamed, expecting claws that would rip her flesh, yet no tearing came, the form glided away again.

"Zehiya," Grandfather called, "Open your eyes, you must look into the shadow."

"No! Grandfather, it will kill me!" she shrieked.

"Ze...hi...ya..." Another voice, a woman's voice, called to her. "Look into the shadow."

Curled up, her hands over her head, her toes gripping the solid rock of her perch, Zehiya slowly released her arms and turned her head, looking up with one cautious eye. The dark form became lighter and lighter until it was bright white light. Amazed, Zehiya sat up, looking into the light. It swooped down again. To her astonishment, a giant eagle, not of bone and feathers, but of light, hovered before her. Its eyes were bright golden penetrating light, its beak shimmered glassy black. Its feathers glowed rich browns, black and white. Its talons sparkled like stars. Amazed, Zehiya sat transfixed by the sight of this amazing bird, like nothing she had ever seen before.

Then it spoke, its voice was the same woman's voice who had

called to her.

"Zehiya, I am the mother of all eagles."

Zehiya could not believe what was happening. An eagle who spoke? Suddenly all the grief she had felt surged up within her.

"Grandfather is gone," Zehiya sobbed. "What am I to do?"

The Spirit Eagle flapped her wings. "Come, fly with me, Zehiya," the Spirit Eagle encouraged.

"Fly? I cannot fly."

"Oh, but you can, Zehiya. The spirit of the eagle is in your being. Step off the ledge and you will take flight."

Zehiya looked down at the ground far below.

"Come, my dear, take the step and you will fly," the Spirit Eagle assured her.

On trembling legs, Zehiya reached one foot out, into the void. Then she let go, falling, falling into space. Feathered wings instantly sprouted from her arms. Her feet turned to talons, their surface rough like lizard skin, her claws sharp as daggers. From her tail bone, a feathered fan splayed out. Carried up on a gust of wind she soared, laughing in delight.

Wings spread wide, lifted on the wind, Zehiya flew high above the river as it tumbled through the gorge. She could see the sparkling water of the great lake far beyond.

Then she was gliding over the green valley of her grandfather's homestead. Sadness overcame her at the sight of the cluster of yurts that were no longer her grandfather's, for he was gone, now they belonged to her father.

The Spirit Eagle flapped her wings with great strokes next to Zehiya. "You will go on a journey far from your home."

Zehiya looked at the Spirit Eagle, incredulously. "I will leave, to go where? How will I leave?"

The Spirit Eagle banked her wings soaring to an outcropping of rocks high on the hillside and settled on the largest boulder.

Zehiya followed, landing on the boulder below the Great Eagle.

Twisting her head, one shining golden eye fixed intently on Zehiya, the Spirit Eagle answered, "You will leave this place. You have another destiny, Zehiya. You will gather your horse and your falcon, things to aid you in travel, and follow the caravan south. You will tell no one of your leaving."

Incredulous, Zehiya asked, "But where am I to go?"

"You will know when you have arrived," the Spirit Eagle instructed.

"How will I know?"

"You will know," the Spirit Eagle assured. "In addition, you must allow your eaglet, my child, to be given to your eldest brother. She will not survive travel," the Spirit Eagle said, her golden eye boring into Zehiya. "Do you understand this?"

Zehiya nodded in understanding. The pain of losing her eaglet scorched her heart, yet she knew this was true. An eaglet needs a safe and stable place to grow to maturity.

"I will," she sobbed. "I promised to take care of her and so I shall, by giving her to Ugur."

"And you will take my sword that I have bequeathed to you." Grandfather's voice came from afar. "And the medallion. Keep these things with you, they are protection for you."

Hearing his voice, Zehiya called out, "Grandfather?" Tears welled up. "I miss you so."

"We must let go of all things, my precious granddaughter. Nothing can be held on to," his voice said, sounding farther away. "I love you, Granddaughter. My love will always remain."

Zehiya's eyes opened to the gray light of dawn. Then she remembered the dream; it became very clear in her mind.

"Grandfather," she whispered, "and the Spirit Eagle."

Grief boiled through her. Grandfather was gone, forever. Staggering out into the cold of the morning, she saw Kimizi grazing in the distance. On cold bare feet she ran to him. Swinging onto his back, her hands pressed on his neck, she squeezed her heels into his sides.

The earth blurred beneath his hooves as they flew across the valley.

"You will take my sword and the medallion. They are protection for you." Grandfather's words came to her.

"Grandfather! I miss you so!" she sobbed.

"You have another destiny, Zehiya." The Spirit Eagle's prophecy reeled in her thoughts.

Pounding up the rise they spun at the top, with a press of Zehiya's hand on Kimizi's neck. Leaning her body backward as a signal to Kimizi, he stopped, his sides heaving. Zehiya gazed into the valley below at the cluster of yurts that had been her home.

"Will I be able to just leave my home?"

They have taken my eagle and they will give me to a husband for whom I care nothing. Beleaguered by these thoughts, a hot flame rose in her being. Stoked with the fuel of certitude, Zehiya knew, she could do this. She would leave! She would not stay here in this village where her life was not her own. Pulling the gold medallion from inside her robe, she gazed at it in wonder. It was a strange animal. The body of a lion with wings and the head of an eagle. She squeezed it in her hand. Looking up at the sky, now pink and lavender, she noticed a dark form soaring high above.

"An eagle," she whispered, "the Spirit Eagle; it is an omen."

Hugging Kimizi's neck, she breathed in the scent of his mane as he turned his head to nip at her toes with his lips.

"We are going on a journey, my friend, far, far away."

4

The black shadow hovered in the sky, then dropped like a stone, its strong talons killing the rabbit instantly. At the moment of the strike, Zehiya urged Kimizi to the gallop.

"Kartal!" Zehiya exclaimed as she sprang from Kimizi's back. "You are swift and sure, my great falcon!"

Kartal pecked at his prey, his slate grey back shimmered in the sun. His chest and underwing feathers were white with black tips on every feather creating an even pattern. As she lifted the rabbit Kartal had released to her, in exchange for the proffered dried meat she kept in her falconry pouch on her belt, Zehiya nodded appreciatively.

"I will have a fine supper tonight," she said.

The gold medallion she wore around her neck sparkled in the sunlight. Taking in her surroundings, the river in the distance, the forest climbing the steep mountainsides to either side of the gorge, she declared, "This is a good a place to stay the night."

It had been a half moon's cycle since she stole away from her father's homestead. With Kartal secure on the saddle-perch tied onto the pommel, they had ridden up the gorge along a scarcely-traveled route to find the pass. Her plan was to cross the pass, then continue down to meet the caravan, its hundreds of camels under heavy loads plodding along the Silk Road.

"You will follow the caravan south." The Spirit Eagle's instructions played over and over in her thoughts.

Days later, Zehiya secured Kimizi by a stream with grass to eat as she scouted ahead. Kartal circled high above as she struggled up a very steep ravine in search of a route over the mountain. Fighting back tears as thick bushes tore at her clothes and scratched her hands and face; the way became more and more difficult. Knowing she was lost she fought to keep the thoughts that assailed her at bay.

You do not know where you are going. You are so stupid fleeing from home by yourself. You will cause Kimizi to die, a wolf will kill him and you.

"No," she said aloud. "Stop!" she demanded of her mind. Yet it prevailed, the agonizing thoughts spinning round and round.

Pulling the leather belt, with Grandfather's sword in its scabbard, tighter around her waist, she adjusted her blue fleece lined silk robe. Her leather trousers were dirty and worn.

Dark ominous clouds swirled around the mountaintops above. Pushing trepidation away, she clasped a jagged boulder that sat in her path and pulled herself up and over the obstacle.

I should go back, she thought, *Kimizi cannot go up this thicket of bushes and beyond this boulder. I should have gone up that other canyon I passed.*

Yet, if she could find a way over this mountain she may be able to find another route Kimizi could go up and she could meet the caravan heading south. Determined not to go back, she scanned the mountain for a cleft that promised a pass. Then, she noticed a dark shape high above on the steep, rocky, mountainside.

"Cave?" she wondered aloud.

Drops of rain began to pelt her. However resigned that she should simply return to Kimizi, crawl under the felt cloth that she had strung up for shelter and try another way up on the morrow; she could not tear her gaze from the cave- its mystery beckoned her.

"It is not that far," she whispered to herself.

A long climb later, much farther than she had thought it would be, she stood outside the dark opening. Cool air with-to her amazement-a slight smoky scent wafted from the interior.

Kartal flapped onto a rock ledge above her as gusts of wind whipped up the mountainside and whistled through the rocks. Zehiya peered into the opening. Shocked, she flew backwards and fell against a boulder just as a form materialized from the gloom.

To her amazement, a woman stood in the entrance. Long silver-streaked black hair fluttered in the wind surrounding her leathered and handsome face. Her gray felt robe was threadbare and stained. Her stern dark eyes glared down at Zehiya.

"Why do you disturb me? Go away!" the woman scolded.

"I... I am sorry," Zehiya stuttered. "I am lost. I am in search for the route over the pass."

She wondered at this woman, here in a cave in the wilderness. She guessed that the woman was Tibetan, by her features. Having lived near the caravansary, Zehiya had seen people from everywhere in the world.

Kartal clicked and attracted the woman's attention.

Recognizing the thongs hanging from his talons, she said, "Ah, so you are a falconer."

"Yes," Zehiya said, as she rose to her feet. "You speak my tongue?" she asked in wonder.

The old woman looked Zehiya up and down, taking in her strong tall body, her worn robe flapping in the wind and her long tangled red hair spreading out from under her felt hat. Her eyes were a rare green color. The woman had seen this before and the red hair, too, from the Northern tribes. Her gaze fell to the medallion that lay glittering on Zehiya's chest, then to the sword in its scabbard at her belt. It was wide at the hilt narrowing to a sharp point.

"Yes, I speak your Turkic tongue." With narrowed eyes, she asked, "You are of the Kyrgyz tribes, no?" Her tone now tinged with curiosity.

Hunger tightened Zehiya's stomach as she smelled the aroma of cooking rice drifting from the cave.

"Yes, I am Zehiya, of Arif's homestead near Barskoon." Then she amended, "It is Bagatur's homestead now."

With a sigh, she admitted, "I ran away."

The woman's chin lifted. "I see."

Drops began to fall from the dark clouds, turning to a steady shower. The Tibetan woman turned and called over her shoulder, "Come."

Zehiya held her arm up and Kartal landed on her leather gauntlet.

With a swift practiced move, she placed the leather hood, held under her belt, over the bird's head, blinding him.

Sitting on a small rug that was laid on the dirt floor of the cave, Zehiya began to realize how hungry she was. The cave smelled damp, of rock and earth. Zehiya glanced around at her surroundings. She was curious about the cushion placed off to the side. A small table was placed before it, upon which was a thick stack of long, narrow parchment papers. She could see that the pages had black markings, but she could not see them clearly from her position.

Zehiya's story came pouring out between gulping mouthfuls of rice flavored with curry. Her grandfather's death, her father's rage, her brother taking her eagle from her, the Spirit Eagle dream. Zehiya finished her tale with angry tears spilling down her cheeks.

The Tibetan woman listened attentively, then reached over and placed her hand on Zehiya's knee. "It is sad to lose someone you love," she said, softly. "This world is samsara, suffering. Everything is impermanent."

Sitting back, she regarded the girl.

"Dreams are tricky things," the Tibetan woman finally said. "Your dream was indeed powerful; it led you here to me."

Zehiya placed her empty bowl aside. Wiping her eyes with the sleeve of her robe, she considered this.

"But I was told to follow the caravan south."

"Follow it, yes, but join it?" the Tibetan woman asked, her eyes raised in question, "And on the way you have found me."

"Why?" Zehiya asked.

Leaning forward, the Tibetan woman said, "Because, my dear, you need to learn how to control your mind, your emotions and to be the master of yourself and your destiny."

Resuming her seat, she continued, "Now, you are at times happy, then you are sad, then at times angry." Gesturing with a wave of her hand. "You are but a leaf, cast about on the winds of your thoughts and emotions. You are helpless and weak. The Spirit Eagle has sent you to me because, you," she said, leaning forward and tapping the medallion at Zehiya's chest, "are a warrior!"

Sitting back, she continued, "That medallion your grandfather gave you is an ancient one. The union of the lion and the eagle is called a Griffin in your language. We Tibetans call it a Garuda. It is powerful and it is wisdom. Your medallion comes from the Alai Mountains far to the North and East from here. Long ago, in ancient times, this was the home of a great and powerful tribe. The women of this tribe were respected as warriors; they rode side by side with the men in battle." Leaning forward, she hissed, "They were formidable! Feared by all. These people were called the Scythians."

Stunned, Zehiya looked down at the medallion. "Warrior? I have never fought in a battle or with anyone."

"Ah," the Tibetan woman said, tapping her boney finger against the side of her head. "You must learn to win battles from here now-with your wits, your mind. To do this you must understand your mind. You must become master of yourself."

"You will teach me these things?" Zehiya asked.

Nodding solemnly, the old woman confirmed, "Yes, I will."

"Do you have a horse or do you wander afoot?" she asked.

"My horse, Kimizi is tied along the stream below. I fear he may be killed by a wolf," Zehiya said.

Pointing to the cave entrance, the woman said, "There is a small canyon further up the stream. Bring your horse there and cut some small trees with your sword and place them across the narrow opening. You can lead him to grass and water several times a day. We will hear if there is trouble. Your falcon can bring us meat for our supper when you return on the morrow."

Zehiya stood up and for a moment she was unsure of what she should do. Should she stay here with this woman or leave and continue her search for the pass? It was true, she had arrived here in her effort to find the caravan south and the Tibetan woman was right, Zehiya was a leaf on the wind, not master of herself. She was just a little girl who was running away. Her decision became very clear, she would learn what this woman had to teach her. Gathering Kartal on her gauntlet, she straightened her back in determination.

At the doorway, she turned back. "What is your name?"

"My name is Pema," the Tibetan woman answered.

Zehiya nodded, then stepped out into the rain.

"Breathe in; let it fill you way down at the bottom of your belly. Now slowly let your breath out, concentrate on the feeling as it passes out, right at the tip of your nostrils," Pema instructed. "Do not force your breath. Breath in naturally then breath out."

Zehiya sat cross-legged as she breathed in slowly. Down, down into her belly. It felt wonderful. Then, she slowly let her breath out; passing warm through her nostrils to meet the cold air of the cave. Thoughts arose, as she concentrated on the sensation of her breath, yet she paid them no heed.

"Thoughts are just a function of your mind," Pema instructed. "You need not believe every thought you have, nor act upon them. Be a watcher of the thoughts. They no longer control you. Do not be a puppet on the strings of your mind."

It had been three moons now that Zehiya lived with Pema, learning how to master herself and become a spiritual warrior. When she was not practicing the breathing meditation that Pema had called Shamatha, Zehiya was learning the teachings of impermanence and compassion from Pema's ancient text.

Each day when she rode Kimizi up and down the canyon, while Kartal hunted, Zehiya considered the ideas that Pema spoke of. Yet magically she did not have to force herself to understand them-they became self-evident. She became intuitive of Kimizi's comfort and needs. She felt the life-force of the plants by the stream. She would sit by the small pools in the canyon and be mesmerized by the schools of little fish. Life felt more precious and vulnerable now. She felt at peace with all in the world. This feeling was so rich and delicious, she promised herself to remain at peace forever.

Zehiya was amazed that Pema never slept but instead sat up all night in deep meditation, while the girl slept curled on the robe she had brought for her travels.

"You are ready now," Pema declared one morning.

Zehiya looked up from her bowl of rice, a question on her face.

"To go back to your father's homestead. Then onward into your life," Pema explained.

Zehiya swallowed, surprised by this sudden declaration by her teacher. "If you declare it must be so. I will go this morn," Zehiya said, setting her empty bowl aside.

Rising, she picked up her sword, tying the scabbard to her belt.

Pema stood, holding out a bundle. "Here is some food for your journey."

Pema's kind wise eyes looked into Zehiya's. "You have learned much and accomplished what you need to continue on your own. When you are ready, another teacher will appear. This is the way. When the student is ready, the teacher appears."

With a waggle of her finger, Pema admonished, "Yet, you must test the teacher at first, to be sure it is a true teacher and not a fraud. The teacher must be true."

"How will I know the difference?" Zehiya asked.

"You will know. If a teacher asks you to do things that feel wrong, or if you feel very uncomfortable, then either you are not ready for that teacher or they are not the right one for you. In any case, you should not follow that one," Pema explained. "Trust yourself. Your Spirit Eagle will be a great help to you."

Zehiya nodded, sad to leave this woman she had come to trust and admire.

"I give you thanks for all you have taught me," Zehiya said.

Riding away on Kimizi, Zehiya turned in the saddle to look up at the mountainside, bidding her teacher a silent farewell.

5

Zehiya rode Kimizi up the hillside weaving through evergreen trees and around the many rock and boulders that were scattered over the ground. Her mind was filled with thoughts in anticipation of the reunion with her family.

Father will be angry, she thought, *yet, I will be calm and speak to him. I will remain at peace,* she planned. *He will be impressed by my calm.*

Smiling inwardly, she imagined Feray and the boys running to greet her, and her brother, Ugur? She wondered.

He will act as he thinks Father wants him to. She sighed.

The fragrances of the trees and grass were strong in the warm sunshine of the calm afternoon. Reaching the crest of the hill, she reined in Kimizi and sat overlooking the homestead far below. Fear rose in her chest as she took in the scene. The horses were running in panic in the fenced pasture. Their whinnies rose to her and her body stiffened. Standing in the saddle, she looked on as several horsemen herded the horses. The gate was open. She gasped as they drove them out.

Suddenly, her father burst from the yurt, his sword drawn, his booming curses bouncing off the hillsides. Then her brother, Ugur followed, his sword held high as they ran to block the escape of the intruders. The horses scattered as the group of men reined up in front of Bagatur. He charged the first rider, swinging his sharp curved blade. The horse side-passed away as the rider swung his sword, blocking

24

Bagatur's strike.

Zehiya could hear the ring of metal from far atop the hill.

Urging his mount onward, the rider charged again swinging at Bagatur.

Zehiya screamed as the sword struck and her father's severed head fell to the ground, his body dropping in a heap.

Ugur, slowed his steps as the riders encircled him. He spun, his sword held out menacingly in self-defense.

Clutching at Kimizi's reins, Zehiya cried out, "Ugur!"

His body jerked at the impact of the arrows two of the riders shot into him. Then two of the men dismounted and took the gold belts and weapons from the corpses.

"No!" Zehiya cried out as she watched two men drag Feray out of the yurt. The horsemen dismounted and converged on her. She screamed and tried to fight them as they tugged at her robes. Throwing her to the ground, they laughed as the first of them forced himself on top of her.

Kimizi pawed the ground and spun as Zehiya held him tightly, her fear a vise on his reins. Kartal blindly flapped his wings, his talons holding fast to the saddle-perch. Zehiya watched helplessly and in horror as two men threw back the flap and entered the yurt.

"Erdem and Little Arif!" she gasped.

Noticing movement, she saw two small forms appear from the back of the yurt. Clutching his knife in one hand, Erdem pulled Little Arif with his free hand out of the slit he had cut in the thick felt.

"Run!" she urged, watching hopefully as they ran up the rocky hillside and then disappeared.

One of the men appeared, climbing out of the slit that he made larger with his knife. Gazing up the hill, he called out to his men, and waved his arms. Several men, in the group who were encircling Feray's limp body, broke away and hurried toward the yurt.

Zehiya watched in terror as the men disappeared over the hillside after the boys. Anguish clutched her stomach. She waited, easing up on Kimizi's reins and watched as the remaining men went in and out of the yurt, carrying items and tying them to their saddles—the coveted swords and knives her father was so well known for.

Stricken, she wondered. "Who are these men? Where did they come from?"

Then she thought her heart would surely break when the group of men re-appeared with Erdem screaming and kicking being carried over one man's shoulder. Little Arif sobbed as he was carried in the crook of another man's arm. When they reached their horses, each man swung the boys onto the front of their saddle and then mounted behind them.

The man who had Erdem held tightly in front of him, appeared to be the leader of the bandits. He called out orders and the men all mounted and collected the scattered herd. With a rumble, like rolling black thunder, they drove the herd, disappearing down the wagon road.

Zehiya sat, frozen in terror, her heart pounding. The silence that draped over the valley felt like an insult. There below, lay her father's, her brother's and her gentle and kind stepmother's broken and violated bodies. Zehiya gasped, trying to breathe as the reality of what she just witnessed washed over her in wave after crushing wave. Sliding off her saddle and falling to the ground, she curled into a ball. Lying on her side, hugging her knees to her, she sobbed, trying to endure the pain that seared through her.

Choking on her tears, Zehiya suddenly sat up and rubbed her swollen eyes.

"Feray!" she shouted, as the realization dawned on her

Jumping to her feet, she mounted Kimizi. "She may be still alive! I need to help her!" Cursing herself for not thinking of this sooner, she squeezed Kimizi's sides with her heels.

Arriving at the yurt, Zehiya forced herself to go to Ugur, just in case he may still be alive. Averting her eyes so as not to look at her father's decapitated form, her gorge rose seeing the pool of blood around Ugur's kneeling, slumped form. Six arrows protruded from his blood-soaked body.

Leaning to the side, away from Kimizi, she retched onto the ground. Gasping for breath, the taste in her mouth sour, she urged Kimizi onward and over to Feray.

Dismounting, she ran to her stepmother's side and dropped beside her. She shuddered as her knees became wet with Feray's blood that soaked the ground. Steeling herself against the bile that was rising into her throat, she forced herself to scrutinize the bruised and bloodied body. To her astonishment, Feray groaned.

"Stepmother? Feray? It is I, Zehiya," she said, while gently moving the woman's bloodied face toward her.

Feray opened the slits of her swollen eyes. "Little Fire?" She sighed. "My Little...Fire. You must...run...away...bad men," she croaked.

"No, they are gone," Zehiya said, trying to calm the trembling tone of her voice. "I will help you, stepmother, I will help you heal," Zehiya promised.

Feray looked into Zehiya's eyes. "Daughter." She coughed and gasped, "My Little Fire."

Pulling the torn robe over Feray's bloodied body, Zehiya searched franticly in her mind for what she should do first. "Clean the wounds," she said aloud. "Move her to a clean place? But I can't drag her, it will do more harm."

Her body began to shake as indecision clouded her mind.

"Move!" she ordered herself. "Get the salve." Looking at Feray, she said, "I will clean your wounds and make a clean bed for you out here, Stepmother."

Feray gazed into Zehiya's concerned face.

"I am sorry, Little Fire."

Then with a sigh, she closed her eyes. A cold and permanent stillness settled over her.

A suffocating pain whirled in the core of Zehiya's body.

"Feray!" she sobbed, "No! Not you too!"

Collapsing over Feray's body, Zehiya wailed.

Kimizi nuzzled her back with insistent lips. His unusual attention distracted her. Rising, she hugged his neck, burying her face in his mane as she sobbed. As she breathed in his scent, his serene being settled her.

Then the thought came-Neylan, her baby eagle-her family's falcons and eagles. Releasing Kimizi, she ran to the bird yurt. Wrenching the door flap aside, she burst inside. Dumbfounded, Zehiya stared uncomprehending, all that stood were empty perches. All of their birds had been stolen too.

"When?" she asked aloud. "When did they take them? I did not see them take the birds!" she scolded herself. "I sat up on that hill and did not see them take our birds!" She cursed, incredulous. Spinning, she stomped out of the yurt. Clenching her fists, she paced back and forth.

"I did not see them! I did not see them take our birds!" she shrieked.

Gasping for breath with her knees shaking, she covered her eyes as she sank to the ground and wept.

6

A sliver of the moon shone over the ridge of the mountain high above, as it began its ascent into the night. The trill and chirp of night insects was a constant beat accompanying the throaty song of the frogs by the river which rose in a crescendo and then suddenly fell silent, then rose again, one frog, then two, until hundreds joined the chorus.

Pulling her warm fleece lined silk robe tightly against the chill, Zehiya sat staring into the flames of the fire in the pit made of a circle of stones. Flames licked at the rabbit carcass hung on a spit, sending the aroma of searing meat on the breeze.

"Why can I not find the cave?" she asked, speaking to Kimizi.

Tied with a long hemp rope fastened to his halter, the horse ignored her as he nibbled and munched of tufts of grass and an assortment of plants that grew in abundance.

Raising her gaze, she addressed Kartal, who was sitting hooded on the high pommel of the leather covered wooden saddle that was settled over a rock. "It has been a fortnight and I cannot find the cave."

Reaching to turn the spit over the fire, she wondered, "Did I dream that time with Pema?"

The imagery of her family's slaughter, once again, for the thousandth time, began to play in her mind and she stood abruptly in an effort to stop the memory. Pacing, she took up her sword, sheathed in its beautiful scabbard. The moon, now risen to its majestic fullness, illuminated the rich designs embossed on the leather. Drawing the blade, she held it up to shimmer in the moonlight.

"Did I dream of my family's murder?" she cursed, as the pain and rage roiled in her belly, "That Erdem and Little Arif were taken by bandits?" Her heart clenched in fear of their fate.

Executing slow swings of the blade, she answered her own question through gritted teeth. "No, that was real and I will find those men and kill them all! I will save Erdem and Little Arif and... and then..."

She froze, perplexed.

"And then what? Where will we live? How will I take care of them with no father, no Feray?" She wondered aloud, as tears began to well in her eyes. "No! I will find them and I will find a way," she promised, gripping the sword in her fist.

With an angry swing, then remembering what Grandfather had taught her about swordplay, she slowed her movements, executing her strokes careful and precise, as she envisioned her retribution.

Suddenly, Kimizi raised his head from his grazing and snorted a warning. A crack came from the darkness. Zehiya spun toward the sound in the shadows, her sword raised,

"You are a girl!" a voice said out of the darkness.

"Who are you? Come out where I can see you," Zehiya ordered.

"Only if you will not hurt me," the voice, a girl's voice, said.

Swallowing the lump of fear that rose in her throat, Zehiya said, "If you are alone and come in peace, I will not harm you."

Stepping out of the shadows into the moonlight, a young girl stood. Zehiya could see she was dressed in a long thick woolen robe with colorful woven patterns that fell open to reveal necklaces made of silver medallions and beads. Under this an ankle length blue cotton kurta that was split at the sides draped over undyed thick cotton salwar pants, baggy at the top tapering down to tuck into her soft tan leather boots. She wore a turban of fine blue silk with the end hanging down over one shoulder to be pulled across the face when needed.

"I can harm no one," she said.

Looking longingly at the fire, she asked, "May I have something to eat? I have had nothing for days. I would be so grateful."

In amazement, Zehiya lowered her sword. "Come. Sit. I have

enough to share."

The young girl scurried to the fire. Sitting on a rock, she looked up at Zehiya expectantly with dark eyes. The moonlight illuminated her long tangled black hair.

Removing the rabbit from the fire, Zehiya cut the cooked carcass in half with her dagger and proffered a half to the girl.

"It is hot, do not burn your mouth," Zehiya warned.

Watching the girl blow and blow on the meat, Zehiya judged her to be about the same age as herself, though she was a head smaller than Zehiya.

"What is your name?"

Between mouthfuls of meat, the girl answered, "I am called Asrila."

"Slow down," Zehiya commanded. "You will choke."

With a sigh, Asrila slowed her gulping, taking smaller bites and chewing slowly.

"That is better," Zehiya said.

When she was finished with the meat, Asrila sucked greedily at the small bones.

Handing her a flask, Zehiya asked, "How did you end up out here?"

Now closer, Zehiya could see that the girl's clothes had once been elegant and marked her as a person from a prosperous family, yet now they were soiled and her salwar pants were torn.

"We are very far from anywhere," she added.

Lifting the flask, Asrila took a long pull from it. With a sigh, she handed back what was remaining.

"I was with my father. He is a camel driver who takes merchandise from Turpan to Barskoon-that is his route. After dropping off his goods in the caravansary in Barskoon, he then takes a new load of merchandize to Turpan. We live in Turpan, my father and mother and two brothers. My brothers are small-too small to travel yet. I wanted to go with my father this time, to see what he sees, but my mother said no. I tried to persuade her to let me go, but she insisted it was dangerous on the trade route."

Asrila buried her face in her hands. "Father said we would be safe."

As she looked at Zehiya, tears welled in her eyes. "He goes many times back and forth between Turpan and Barskoon. Nothing has ever happened to him."

"Until now?" Zehiya prompted.

With a sob, Asrila nodded. "We were on the camel road back to Turpan. In the gorge, men on horses came out of nowhere. They... they had swords and bows. Father shouted for me to get away, to run away. I jumped off my camel and ran away into the forest," Asrila keened, "I ran and ran and ran. I heard my father yelling and cursing at the men. I then got so far away that I heard nothing. I could not find my way back."

Burying her face in her hands, she sobbed, "I want to go home to my mother."

Kimizi nuzzled the girl's back. Asrila leapt away from the sensation.

"What..!"

Kimizi stepped back and flung his head up with a snort.

Asrila's sobs turned to laughter.

"He is so sweet." She stood and reached to pet Kimizi's soft grey muzzle. Slowly stroking Kimizi's neck, she cooed, "You are a beauty, such a beautiful color; like that of red clay."

To Zehiya, she said, "I thought at first you were a boy." Sitting down again, she asked in wonder, "Why are you out here? What did you mean when you said you would slay them all?"

Zehiya hesitated, then said, "My family...bandits..."

Then she rose, agitated she lifted her sword from the boulder where she had leaned it. Gritting her teeth, she slid the sword back into its scabbard. "One day I will find them and I will kill them."

Resuming her seat, she added, "I am looking for a woman, a friend. She lives in a cave, but I cannot find the cave."

Perplexed, Asrila stared. "She lives in a cave?"

Zehiya nodded.

"Perhaps you and I could go to my home in Turpan. Would you like that? You could help me find my way," Asrila suggested.

Shaking her head, Zehiya was adamant. "No, I must find her."

With a sob, Asrila asked, "How will I find my way home?"

The two girls sat in silence, thinking what to do.

"First, we will find Pema, that is her name," Zehiya said. "We will stay with her for a time. I must speak with her. She is very wise. When I was with her before, she told me how to find the way over these mountains to the camel route, so I know the way. I will go with you to meet one of the caravans and you can go with them to Turpan. I will then return to Pema's cave."

Asrila considered, then slowly nodded. "Very well, I will help you find the cave, and you will help me find the caravan to Turpan."

Days later both girls rode on Kimizi, Asrila behind Zehiya, as they made their way up yet another ravine. Zehiya gazed up at the mountainside.

"There," she declared, "Get off and hold Kimizi here."

Sliding off Kimizi and looking up the rocky, steep mountainside, Asrila asked, "It is up there?"

Nodding, Zehiya handed the girl the reins. As Kartal stepped onto her gauntlet, Zehiya said, "I am sure of it. You wait here until I return." Pointing, she added, "There is good grazing down there for Kimizi."

Zehiya released Kartal to flight and headed up the ravine. Soon she saw the familiar boulder when she first found the cave and which she had passed day after day while visiting Kimizi in his enclosed area. Looking up at the mountainside, she located the dark shadow of the cave entrance. Ecstatically, she leapt over the bounder and hurried up the rocky trail.

As she neared the cave, she called out, "Pema? Pema, it is I, Zehiya."

Arriving at the doorway, she waited. Kartal circled high above.

"Pema? I am sorry to disturb you, but a terrible thing has

happened." Biting her fist to hold back a sob, she struggled to speak calmly. "I am trying to control my thoughts and emotions." She choked back the tears. "I need your teachings."

Zehiya waited but only silence greeted her. *She must be in deep meditation,* she thought, but something felt wrong. She then realized what was amiss-there was no aroma of food.

Stooping closer to the entrance, she peered in. "Pema, are you there?"

As she entered through the rough stone entrance into the interior of the cave, her heart sank. She stood, bewildered and alone, in the cold empty room.

7

Zehiya's fingers gripped the craggy rock ledge. To her horror she felt her grip slipping, slipping, slipping. She desperately tried to hold on, grasping tightly to the thin sliver of rock, her only tether to the earth. Slowly, her fingers slid off their hold, and she screamed as she fell away, careening down into the void.

"Zehiya!" A voice called to her. "Fly! You can fly!"

Zehiya knew that at any moment she would hit the ground and be killed.

"No!" She screamed, "I cannot fly!"

"You must believe. Spread your wings, quickly!" the woman's voice urged.

With her eyes shut tightly in terror and the wind rushing past her ears, she struggled to release herself from the paralyzing grip of her belief that she could not fly. She forced herself to spread her arms wide.

I must, she thought, *I must, I must. I will! Fly!*

Instantly, she felt herself lift up, weightless. When she opened her eyes, she was shocked at the sight of the expanse of the mountains below as she soared high above them. The Spirit Eagle appeared, to her right, large and luminous.

"You see, my dear," the Great Eagle said. "You can."

Zehiya grinned, feeling joy for the first time in she knew not how long.

"What mountains are those? Where are we going?" she asked.

"You must find Pema," the Spirit Eagle replied. "You must cross these mountains. See the pass there?" She indicated with her long beak. "You cross over that and meet the caravan going to the East and South."

Zehiya nodded. "Where am I to go?"

Faint images, like wisps of clouds, paraded in front of them in the sky. She saw large statues of a cross-legged man, his hands and fingers making eloquent gestures. She saw images of red-robed monks seated before low tables, their ink quills moving over parchment. And caves, many caves along a high cliff.

"Is this a real place?" she asked. "Is Pema there? How am I to find this place? What about my little brothers? How will I find them?"

"You will find this place," the Spirit Eagle assured. "You must be steadfast and brave; never give up. Find Pema first."

Lips pressed tightly, Zehiya vowed, "I will find her. I will find Pema. Then I will find Erdem and Little Arif."

"Wake up! Zehiya, wake up!"

Zehiya felt insistent hands shaking her.

"What?" she asked, waking groggily from her dream.

Looking around the stone walls of the cave, she gradually awakened, trying to remember where she was and what happened in the dream she had soaring with the Eagle Spirit. Then she looked into Asrila's concerned face.

"You were screaming," Asrila explained, releasing her grip on Zehiya, as she sat back on the dirt floor of Pema's empty cave.

Sitting up, Zehiya pulled her robe tightly around her, then buried her head in her hands, striving to bring back the dream and the message it held.

Asrila sat, silently watching this strange long-limbed girl with hair

36

the color of fire and a will burning just as hot.

"We must... go..." Zehiya began, as the images of her dream flickered in her consciousness. "Find the caravan... east to your home in Turpan. I will travel from there east and south to a place with caves and monks."

Relieved, Asrila enthused. "We wait here no longer? You will help me go home?"

Zehiya turned her head sideways, looking at this girl with her long raven hair in a tangle, her small delicate form not honed for the rigors of life in the wilderness.

Nodding, Zehiya said, "Yes, I will see you safe. For the next two or three days we will remain here. I will hunt with Kartal and we will smoke as much meat as he catches for us to take with us. Then we will leave this place. We will travel over the pass and find a caravan going east."

8

BELOW THE BEDEL PASS
ON THE GREAT TRADE ROAD
BETWEEN AKSU AND KUCHA

"**B**astards!" The camel driver shook an angry fist at the four horsemen who had charged up from behind then cut in front of the camel-line and disappeared in a cloud dust, leaving chaos in their wake.

Braying and snorting, the line of camels bunched up against each other. Large bundles of merchandise, slung over the beasts' backs, between the two fatty humps, swayed dangerously, sending camels staggering to the side.

"Go, go, go!" bellowed the driver, sitting up in the saddle of the lead camel, kicking furiously with felt-booted feet, simultaneously whipping a hemp quirt, urging the beast forward to straighten out the line.

Finally, the twenty beasts were all straightened out, resuming their former plodding tranquility.

"Those bastards!" the camel driver grumbled.

Laughing, a handsome young man rode up on his horse. His long black hair under a red turban was tied at the nape of his neck, and swayed like horse's tail down his back. The silver hilt of his sword glinted from the belt under his open red silk robe. Road-worn thick cotton salwar pants were tucked into dusty soft leather boots.

"Mother! I could hear you from a league away. What is the trouble?" he called out. His long mustache and narrow beard, confined to only the tip of his chin, framed a bright smile of perfect white teeth.

"A league? Oh, son, you do exaggerate," Kavya, the camel driver, retorted. With a sweep of her hand, she ordered, "Have the men we hired check to see if any loads were loosened!"

With a wave of his hand, the young man booted his mount into the canter and was gone.

"Bastards!" Kavya cursed, her handsome features distorted by a grimace. Her silver-grey eyes scanned the dry landscape for any more trouble. All was calm and serene. Heaving a sigh, she relaxed into the saddle nestled securely between the humps of her Bactrian camel, Delilah.

Removing her dirty headscarf she loosed her dark hair, the highlights of auburn shimmered in the bright sunlight. Running her fingers through the tangles, she pressed her lips in resignation as she gazed at the strands of grey that hung from her fingertips.

"I am growing old, my dear Delilah," she said to her camel. "How many times more will you and I travel this road?"

Delilah turned her head slightly, one eye swiveled back, regarding her mistress who was dressed in a yellow and green cotton and silk woven tunic, bedecked with a silver necklace of medallions, each with red coral at its center, and at her waist a yellow cotton sash held a silver hilted dagger held in an embossed leather sheath. Over this a road weary green woolen robe, its designs long faded by many seasons of sun and wind, draped over salwar pants. Roomy for sitting long hours and many days astride her camel, they were tucked into embroidered black felt boots with corded hemp soles.

Her son reappeared creating a swirl of sand as he halted his mount to a walk beside her. "All is well Mother. Our great fortune in goods are secure."

"Well, it was a good thing we hired six men to guard our string instead of only four; otherwise we may have lost everything just then to that lot," Kavya exclaimed.

"They looked a bit shabby, not the kind that would be brave

enough to go against even four men. But you are correct Mother, it is better we have six men and myself in case we do come upon a more dangerous lot."

Rounding a bend of large boulders piled one atop the other, Kavya squinted, trying to make sense of an object far in the distance below them on the flatland.

"Sahin," Kavya said to her son, as she pointed, "your eyes are better than mine. What is that? Two men riding on one horse?"

Standing in his stirrups, Sahin cast his gaze searching the expanse.

"I see them Mother, in the dust cloud made by that mob that just passed us, you are correct, two men atop one horse. They must have lost a mount to the desert."

Bolting upright in alarm, Kavya shrieked, "Those bastards! They are going to attack the pair! Call the men and go help them!"

The four mounted men that had disrupted them earlier had galloped past the two riders on one horse and now were circling back, bearing down on the vulnerable pair.

"I will help them. It is better that the men stay here, in case more bandits are with this gang and may show up behind us. I can run these four off myself," Sahin said, booting his horse into the gallop. "If it look like I am in trouble, then send some help," he called over his shoulder."

Her heart pounding, Zehiya removed Kartal's hood with a flourish and lifted her arm to release him to flight. Grasping Kimizi's reins, she guided him in a circle, calming his fright at the gang of riders that had just thundered past. Asrila buried her head in Zehiya's back, tightening her arms that encircled Zehiya's waist.

"They have passed. Loosen your grip, lest I die unable to breathe," Zehiya chided the girl.

Raising her head, Asrila gazed into the cloud of sand that

remained in the wake of the gang.

"Look!" she gasped, arm thrust out, pointing.

Zehiya made out the forms of four mounted men coming their way. Gritting her teeth, she unsheathed her sword. "They are coming back for us! Hold tight," she commanded. "They will be on us soon, there is no time to run; we must fight."

"Fight?" Asrila said, incredulous. "We have no chance against those men."

"We have no chance if we do not fight," Zehiya retorted. "I have seen what men do. I will not make it easy for them. Just hold on!"

Glancing skyward, Zehiya saw the form of Kartal circling high above.

"Grandfather, please guide my sword. Spirit Eagle, give me courage," she prayed, urging Kimizi to face the oncoming men.

Raising her sword, she felt, rather than heard, a very clear message.

No thoughts, your body knows what to do.

And her body did know exactly what to do. With a firm kick she charged Kimizi right into the first approaching man, his sword drawn from the scabbard under his grubby robe. Zehiya fixed her gaze on his leathery face, hard and menacing with rotten teeth grinning at her as she swung her sword, sending it into that ugly mouth, cutting clear through severing his neck. Blood sprayed over her as she passed. She heard the thud of his body hitting the ground behind her. The other three men veered off, their faded tunics and soiled robes flapping in the wind as they passed out of reach of her. With his sword raised, one of the bandits circled around and charged at her. Zehiya's sword connected with a loud clang as she parried his first blow. Asrila screamed and held on tightly as Zehiya struggled to guide Kimizi and parry strike after strike from her attacker. Asrila's grip clenched and then her hands slid away from Zehiya and she was gone. Zehiya glanced back to see that one of the men had dismounted and dragged Asrila from the saddle; now he had her on the ground. Asrila screamed and kicked as he tore at her robes.

Gnashing her teeth, Zehiya swung and parried, driving Kimizi into her attacker. Frantically she fought, screaming her rage. She must dispatch this man now, and help Asrila!

Suddenly, a new horseman appeared at a full gallop. He reined in hard, his horse sliding to a stop. Throwing one leg over his horse's neck, Sahin landed on his feet and slid his sword free of its scabbard as he ran to aid Asrila. At the sight of Sahin's charge, Asrila's attacker released her and jumped to his feet drawing his sword. Asrila scurried away, weeping, on hands and knees, as the men's swords clashed above her.

Zehiya caught a glimpse of the arrival of the man in a red turban and sighed in relief that he was not another bandit, but instead had come to aid them. Though encouraged, her arm was growing weak in the fight. Suddenly, she felt strong hands gripping her from behind. The third bandit had dismounted and was tugging hard with a firm grasp of her robe. She could not stop fighting the man in front of her. Besieged, she kicked Kimizi hard, trying to get away from the strong pull of the man on the ground. Kimizi whinnied and reared, hammering the mounted attacker and his horse with his hooves, frantic to clear the way and make their escape. The attacker's horse fell to its haunches in an effort to back away from Kimizi's assault, throwing his rider to the ground. Terrified, Zehiya grasped Kimizi's mane as she felt herself being pulled by the unrelenting man on the ground. Kimizi's mane slithered through her fingers as she slid over the high cantle of her saddle and with a thump, hit the ground flat on her back, the wind knocked out of her, then her head followed bouncing off the hard ground.

Gasping for air and dazed, she did not know where she was. A dark shadow fell over her as the bandit appeared standing above her, evil intent twisted his face as he glared down at her. Memory flooded back and she knew where she was and what she must do. Try as she may, she could not raise her sword, then she realized her sword-hand was pinned to the ground under his boot. She tried to twist away, but her other hand was held fast under his other boot. She kicked trying to land a blow to his groin, but he was too far forward, she could do no damage. She was trapped.

"You bitch," he growled, as he raised his sword high.

His foul stench settled over her. Zehiya turned her face away

42

closing her eyes. She gritted her teeth, waiting for the strike that would end her life, end her pain, end her search for peace.

Yet, the blow did not come. There was a loud thwack, then a groan. She looked up and the man was gone. A thunder of hooves passed by her. She sat up, rubbing the back of her head. The man who had been ready to kill her lay on the ground, an arrow protruding from his bloody chest. In the distance, the last bandit, who had remounted his fallen horse, was racing away at a hard gallop being chased by a mounted archer, with recurve bow drawn. His arrow loosed and found its target in the bandit's back. The fleeing man toppled from his horse with his foot trapped in the stirrup. His frightened horse dragged his body mercilessly over the rocky ground. Never slowing, the archer stowed his bow in its quiver and charged his horse faster to catch the bolting horse. Edging alongside, he leaned over and grasped the reins urging the horse to slow, then to pony behind him. The bandit's body fell away from the stirrup, limp and lifeless.

Zehiya watched as the archer turned and headed for her. Then, she turned her attention to Asrila, just as the man in the red turban was helping the shaken girl to her feet. The bandit he had fought lay dead, his blood soaking into the earth.

Dazed, Zehiya slowly rose to her feet, holding her throbbing head. The archer trotted up to her. Stopping before her, he gazed down at her quizzically.

"By the gods, you are a girl!" he laughed. "Are you injured?"

"No, I am not injured!" she spat, pulling her hand away from her head, offended by his laughter.

Looking into his broad sun darkened face, she flinched. One side was normal. The other was pulled into a grotesque expression by a gnarled scar that ran from his chin, along the jaw to his ear.

"Who are you?" she asked, avoiding his face, looking into his dark, almond-shaped eyes that twinkled with mirth.

"My name is Jangbu," he said.

Noticing the gold medallion that had come out of the folds of her robe at her breast, he added, "You fight well, for a girl."

"A girl? Well if that be so, indeed, she does," came a voice behind her.

Concealing the medallion back inside her robe, Zehiya turned to the man in the red turban. His arm was wrapped, protectively, around Asrila's waist as they made their way to join her.

Gently, he lowered Asrila to sit on the ground. Turning to Zehiya and Jangbu, with a huge smile, he said, "I am Sahin."

Zehiya stared at Sahin. She was struck speechless by him. Never had she seen such a handsome man. His skin was the color of cream, his hair black as midnight. She shuddered as he gazed down at her with sparkling silver eyes.

Wrenching her gaze from his strong lean form in embarrassment at her obvious attraction, she forced herself to look back at Jangbu, who was now dismounting his horse.

"You men saved our lives. I thank you," she said.

Seeing her sword lying in the dirt, she picked it up, wiped the blood and sand off it with the end of her robe and slid it into its scabbard.

At the tinkle and clang of camel-bells in the distance, they all turned to watch as a string of camels and six mounted men approached. When the procession came near, the camel driver waved and called to them.

"Son, did you kill those bastards?"

"And that," Sahin said, with a bow and sweep of his arm, "is my mother, Kavya."

Zehiya suddenly realized that she had forgotten all about Kimizi. But there he stood, in the distance nibbling at scarce tufts of grass. Leaving the group, she jogged over to him. At her approach, he raised his head with a whicker. She threw her arms around his neck and hugged him hard.

Running her hands over his body, she asked, "Did you come out of that unscathed, my boy?" With a sigh of relief, she stroked his neck. "You did, my boy; you did."

"He is a fine horse. Where did you get him?" Jangbu asked.

Not hearing his approach, she turned, startled.

Now that he was off his horse, she could see that he stood no taller than she. Powerful forearms were visible from the wide sleeves of his dusty red and black felt robe. He held the reins of his horse loosely in his strong hands.

"I...we...my family raises... used to raise... horses," she stuttered. "Where is my gauntlet?" she asked, in an effort to change the subject.

Seeing it a short distance away lying on the ground, she strode over to it and picked it up. She then searched the sky for Kartal as she pulled and flexed her fingers into the thick leather. Not seeing his dark form, she placed the thumb and forefinger of her other hand in her mouth and let out a piercing whistle and then another.

Jangbu watched with interest as a falcon appeared, lighting on her outstretched arm.

"You are full of surprises," he said, with a nod of approval.

"What is your name? Where are your people?"

She stared at him, not wanting to answer. "My name is Zehiya," she said, reluctantly.

Turning away, she retrieved the hood from under her belt and gently slid it over the falcon's head, then guided him onto the saddle-perch. With Kimizi's reins in her grasp, she led him away from Jangbu's questions, to join Asrila and Sahin.

"We must get those bodies off the road, it is best if no one sees them in case they are from a larger band," Kavya was saying as Zehiya approached.

Jangbu arrived a moment behind her, leading his horse.

Kavya stared at Zehiya in disbelief. "Why, she is just a girl. Son, you neglected to tell me that this is a girl. I had thought, surely, this was a man, seeing the way he...she fought."

Looking Zehiya up and down and then at Kimizi and Kartal perched on the saddle, she added, "She is tall, and with a falcon, no less."

"And who is this?" Kavya asked, with a wave toward Jangbu.

"I am Jangbu, Lady," he said, with a slight bow, "of Amdo, in the land of the snows."

"Well, you showed up in the nick of time," Kavya said, approvingly. "Where did you come from?"

With a gesture to the rising landscape beyond, he said, "I have a camp up there, where my horses are secured. I saw those four riders heading east. Then, I watched as they circled back to attack these two."

He gestured toward Zehiya and Asrila. "Attacking two riders on one horse? Well... if I did not help them, I would have to call myself a coward."

With a bow, he added, "You are correct, Madam. We need to hide these bodies." Pointing toward his camp, he said, "We can drag them up there and leave them concealed behind the rocks. I am sure no one will see them so far off the road. The buzzards will reduce them to bones in little time."

With a nod of approval, Kavya said, "We will keep their saddles and gear and sell them. You keep their horses Jangbu, do what you wish with them." Then with a wave to Zehiya and Asrila. "You girls are coming with us." To Asrila, she inquired, "What is your name girl?"

"I am Asrila."

"Sahin, help Asrila up to ride with me," she ordered. "My Delilah will carry us both."

9

THE OASIS OF KUCHA

Zehiya craned her neck, looking up in awe as they passed by the feet of the two towering Buddhas carved of stone. Their serene presence stood nine stories tall, two sentries of peace and wisdom, welcoming all through the western gate of the thriving oasis city of Kucha.

They made their way through the busy streets to the large livery. Completing the business of unloading the camels and placing their bundles of ware into a locked storehouse, then leading them and the horses to a corral. They paid the hired men and the livery master and set out for the marketplace located in the center of the town.

"Those idiots at the livery had better treat my Delilah and the rest of my stock well," Kavya grumbled, as they entered the crowded marketplace.

"I am sure they would not dare to incur your wrath, Mother. Do not have concern," Sahin said, with a wave of his hand. "Enjoy this fine day."

Glancing back at Sahin, Kavya laughed. "Oh, son, where did you get your constant sunny disposition?" She shook her head with a snort. "Not from me, must be from your blessed father." With a whisper to herself, she added, "Wherever he may be."

"You leave your stock with them each time you pass through

Kucha?" Jangbu asked.

"Yes, we do," Sahin answered, strolling alongside Jangbu. "And they are always well taken care of. Fear not for your horses, for they will be well tended and safe from theft."

Noticing the furtive glances and the manner in which the crowd in the market made a wide berth for the lot of them, what with swords and bow, and a tall fire-haired girl with a falcon perched on her gauntleted hand, Sahin added, "I think the livery master would fear our wrath more than Mother's."

Jangbu chuckled. Zehiya looked over her shoulder. Glancing at Jangbu, her eyes slid away from his disfigured face to rest on Sahin's. She smiled. He gave her a wink. She turned away quickly, so he would not see her blood rise, turning her face as red as her hair.

Sahin's gaze rested on Asrila, as she walked in front of him, alongside Kavya. She was petite and perfect, with her long black hair, tied at the nap of her neck, swaying with her hips.

Strolling through the marketplace, Zehiya had never seen such an array of fruits and vegetables piled high in mounds. Though she had been at the market in Barskoon, this oasis of Kucha was many times larger and offering much more variety. There were plums, peaches, grapes and melons. There were almonds, rice and wheat. Like Barskoon, there were people of many tribes and faraway lands. Chinese, whom she had seen in Barskoon, though not as many as here in Kucha, and those of the Turkic Uighur tribe. But there were others too: Tibetans, like Jangbu, and some travelers who were tall and broad, light skinned with yellow or red hair and green eyes, like herself. She did not think they were of her Kyrgyz tribe, because something about them seemed different. She looked at Kavya, wondering for the hundredth time, of what tribe she was from. She decided she would ask her when the time was right.

"All of this food—I am so hungry," Asrila said, gazing at the mountains of melons they passed by. "I need a bath," she added, looking down at her dusty and dirty robe.

"Indeed, we all do," Kavya assured, stopping before a stall. Purchasing peaches for all of them, she handed them out, one by one.

Zehiya bit in greedily, sighing at the juicy sweetness of the fruit.

"There is a bath house in the inn we always go to when here in Kucha," Kavya said, between mouthfuls of the luscious fruit. "But first, you girls need proper clean clothes. We shall go to the clothes market before the bath house."

Turning to Jangbu, Kavya invited, "Jangbu, pray tell me that you will remain with us here in Kucha? I do so appreciate your helping us with the unpacking of the camels and loading our merchandize into the storage room."

"We women," she said, indicating Zehiya and Asrila with a jerk of her chin, "shall have a bath."

Looking at Sahin and back to Jangbu, she continued, "After you men have your baths, you shall join us for a fine meal-the best in Kucha."

With a glance at Zehiya, Jangbu bowed. "You are gracious, Madam, I would be most honored to remain here."

Sahin laughed, slapping Jangbu on the back. "Good man."

Raising her foot out of the warm water, Zehiya watched the droplets fall away spilling into the pool, the sound echoed in the domed ceiling bath house. Zehiya let out a sigh of contentment, reveling in the aromas of the fragrant herbs and scrubs that cleansed her of the dirt and grime from the road. For a moment, she had forgotten her pain, her loss. She let her head fall back into the warm comfort of the bath water. Her hair, an undulating nimbus, spread out around her. She felt at peace. Images of Sahin paraded in her thoughts: his smile, his handsome face.

If he were to ask me to marry, I would say yes. She confirmed in her day dream. *We would travel the road with Kavya...*

Oh stop! She chided herself in her mind. *I wish not to marry, remember?*

But the thoughts stubbornly returned. *But, with Sahin, I would be so happy, if he were my husband...*

Asrila was talking with Kavya across the pool and Zehiya raised her head out of the water to listen.

"The bandits attacked my father's camel-string. He told me to run. So I ran and ran. I was lost. But then I found Zehiya, in the wilderness," she was saying.

"Those Bastards," Kavya, said, shaking her head, her long hair a wet shiny shawl draped across her shoulders and down her back. "Well, my dear Asrila, as it happens, I know your father."

Asrila stared at Kavya in awe. "You do?"

"We camel drivers on this route between Turpan and Barskoon know one another," she assured. "If he is alive, he is either in Barskoon looking for you or he has returned to Turpan. We are continuing on to Turpan with our next load. We will take care of selling some of this load here in Kucha over the next few days. Then we will buy more goods here to take to Turpan. We will send word on the morrow, on the next caravan to Barskoon, this is how news travels along the camel route. In a short time, he will know that you are safe with Kavya, and on your way home to Turpan."

Looking to Zehiya, Kavya asked, "And you, my falconer-how did you come to be in the wilderness, all alone, with your horse and falcon?"

Zehiya stared at Kavya, pain rising from her heart welling up as a lump in her throat.

"I...it was...terrible...what happened..." she trailed off.

Her stomach clenched. Water sluiced down her body as she stood, clambering out of the bath. Her wet feet slapped on the stone floor as she ran into the dressing area. Looking frantically around, she saw a pot and hurried to it. Just in time, she crouched over it, retching up the peaches. Heaving over the pot again, with nothing left inside her, she felt a warm, strong hand on her back.

"Poor child," Kavya's voice was soft and soothing, "Tell me when you can."

Asrila and Zehiya could not believe the beautiful clothes that Kavya had bought for each of them.

Asrila put on the ivory-colored cotton undershirt, then pulled on a pair of dark blue, wide-legged, silk salwar pants, tied at the waist and ankle. She held out the intricately woven tunic, marveling at the indigo and red designs dyed into the fabric and the detailed embroidery around the sleeves and around the neck. After pulling it over her head, she took up the long red and blue ikat dyed silk sash, winding it around and around her waist, tucking in the end to hold it securely. Over this, she slid into an exquisite padded silk robe of cobalt blue with gold-embroidered designs of flowers and leaves. On her head, she wound the azure and gold silk making a small turban. The effect was dazzling.

Asrila ran her hand over the clean cool fabric. "Oh, it is so beautiful," she exclaimed.

Then, she slid her feet into the supple leather boots, tucked her salwar cuffs inside and wound the leather thongs around her calves to hold them up.

Zehiya pulled on an ivory cotton undershirt, covering it with a cotton tunic dyed in green and yellow persimmon motifs and with richly embroidered geometric designs in black thread around the neck. She tucked her gold medallion inside the tunic, so it would remain hidden. Then, she slid on thick emerald cotton salwar pants, tying them at her waist and the ankles. Over this, she fastened a wide leather belt. Sliding her sword scabbard onto the belt, she marveled at how one complemented the other-together, they were regal. She slid on a thick vest that was richly embroidered with multi-colored horses. She shook her head in disbelief at the fine leather boots. Sitting on a cushion, she pulled them on, a broad smile on her face.

She looked at Asrila, who sat on a cushion watching Zehiya dress.

"They fit perfectly, they are the finest boots I have ever owned," she exclaimed, as she tucked the pant-legs inside.

And lastly, she slid into the most exquisite outer robe: dark green silk with black embroidered patterns and trimmed with fleece. A wide heavy cotton belt with patterns in red, green and gold, was also included to be used around her waist to close the robe over her sword. And lastly, she pulled on a fox-fur hat.

Asrila looked her up and down. "It's a bit warm for the season?"

Zehiya shook her head, then spun, making the embroidered hem of the robe fan out. "Oh, it is perfect for the nights and travel on Kimizi. True, the hat is warm for the days, but these warm days will not last forever."

Zehiya asked Kartal, who sat on his perch on the saddle that was draped over a barrel, "What do you think?"

Asrila laughed. "He can't see with that hood on, silly. Why don't you take it off so he can see you?"

"I only take the hood off for hunting. He will see when I take him hunting on the morrow."

"Are you ready girls?" Kavya called from the other room of their suite. She swept in without waiting for a reply.

Zehiya and Asrila gasped, looking at each other, then back at Kavya in disbelief. Kavya regally stood before them in a long flowing robe of purple padded silk, trimmed around the collar and down the lapels to the floor with luxurious sable fur. Subtle designs embroidered in silver thread floated on the material. The auburn tones of her hair were accented by the purple silk and dark brown sable. Under the robe was layered an indigo-dyed shirt and tunic over a skirt of woven ikat silk. A solid silver belt was wrapped around her waist. A short dagger in a silver scabbard embossed with flower designs, peeked out from under a vest of purple with embroidery in silver thread. On her feet were supple leather slippers.

"Close your mouths, my dears. Did you think I lived in filthy travel clothes?"

Looking Asrila and Zehiya up and down, she smiled. "You two girls look beautiful."

To Asrila, she said, "My dear, I would have you in a tiara rather than a turban, your beauty is such; yet in two days we will be on the camel road to Turpan, so a turban will serve you best."

Asrila bowed slightly. "No, please, Madam, this is beautiful; I am so grateful."

"There is no formality between us now-call me Kavya."

Kavya turned and went back into her room, returning with a length of green silk.

To Zehiya, she said, "The fox-fur hat is for you to put away in your bag, for when the cold returns."

Wrapping the silk around and around Zehiya's head, she continued, "This is better for the warmer days now."

Stepping back, Kavya inspected the turban. The green silk against the red of Zehiya's hair was striking.

"You are most unusual, my dear," Kavya marveled.

"Thank you, Lady... I mean Kavya, for these fine clothes. I know not how I can I repay you," Zehiya said.

With a dismissive wave, Kavya said, "Repayment is not necessary. God granted me a safe journey and grand profits. I can afford to be generous. Besides," she added, looking pleased, "it is a pleasure to shop for young ladies."

Turning with a whoosh of her robe, she bade them, "Come now, I am starving."

Zehiya hesitated, "Madam... I mean Kavya...?"

Kavya turned back, a question on her face.

"Kartal? Will he be safe here, alone?"

"Oh, yes, he is safe here." she assured. "All of our belongings are guarded."

Sahin and Jangbu were deep in conversation when the three women entered the public dining area of the inn. The aromas of roasting meat and spices made Zehiya's mouth water. The room fell silent as all turned their attention to Kavya gliding across the room, tall and regal. Seeing them approach, Sahin rose, followed by Jangbu, who stared at Kavya in disbelief.

"Ah, Mother, transformed before us all. You are as beautiful as a queen," Sahin said, with a bow.

He smiled to Asrila as he gestured toward the cushions placed before a low table.

"Please be seated, ladies."

As Zehiya, Asrila and Kavya made themselves comfortable on the low cushions, Zehiya could not take her eyes off Sahin. He was dressed in layers of shirt, tunic, vest and robes of ivory white. His wide cotton salwar pants were tucked into soft leather boots. His curved sword, its scabbard cleaned to a shine, hung from the wide cotton sash that was embroidered with woven designs in gold thread under his flowing robe.

Forcing her eyes away so as not to be openly staring at him, she turned her attention to Jangbu. He wore a clean felt robe dyed deep red that was trimmed with a spotted leopard pelt. A wide woven silk belt in red, green and black designs tied the robe closed. Dark cotton salwar pants were tucked into black felt boots which were trimmed at the top with gold embroidered designs. His long black hair was woven into a single braid down his back. She wondered at the strings of coral and large amber beads that hung around his neck to his belt. Noticing that he was looking straight at her, his eyes moist and kind, she willed herself not to flinch at his hideous scar and grotesque distorted face. She gave a quick, polite little smile and looked away.

Sahin clapped for the attendants, who scurried over, bowing.

"Bring your best mutton, rice, vegetables and those tasty wheat cakes-the ones made in the shape of a flower."

"Yes, at once," one of the attendants said, as he departed.

"And jugs of rice wine," Sahin called out after him.

The man turned, acknowledged the request, and disappeared into the kitchens.

"What were you and Jangbu in deep conversation about, Son?" Kavya asked.

Glancing at Jangbu, Sahin answered, "Ah, well, we were discussing the similarities of the doctrine of the Buddha and that of Jesus Christ."

Eyebrows raised, Kavya asked, "And, what have you discovered?"

Jangbu answered, "There are similarities in requirements of proper behavior. Yet, in the Buddhist teaching, there is not the concept of a divine person—a personality god. We have no one in our history like a Christ, a son of God. All are sons and daughters of Buddha. There is no separation between Buddha and oneself, as all have Buddha nature within. Buddha means awakened one; the Buddhist practices are the path to awakening to our own Buddha nature."

"Is one better than the other?" Asrila asked.

With a slight bow, Jangbu answered, "The Buddha once explained that there are many paths because there are many types of people. I think we each must choose which seems best for us and leave others to their own choice. Who are we to judge another's path?" he said with a shrug, "Or even care?"

"Tell that to the Mohammedans," Sahin said, wryly, smiling at Asrila.

To Sahin, Zehiya asked, "You are Christian?"

Tearing his gaze from Asrila, he nodded, "Yes, my mother and I are indeed—we follow the Nestorian faith."

His gaze then returned from her back to rest on Asrila.

Noticing Zehiya's sword-hilt peeking from under her robe. Jangbu said, "That is a fine sword you have, Lady; may I see it?"

With a twinge of pain at Sahin's attention toward Asrila and not herself, she slid the sword from its scabbard and leaned over, placing it into Jangbu's outstretched hands.

Jangbu took the hilt in his one hand and rested the blade on the sleeve of his other wrist, so as not to stain it with the oil of his hands.

His attention briefly drawn away from Asrila, Sahin inspected the blade from over Jangbu's shoulder. "It is excellent. Where did you get this fine weapon?" Sahin inquired.

"My grandfather bequeathed it to me. He was a master sword-maker. And my father, after him," she replied.

"Where?" Jangbu asked.

"Barskoon," Zehiya answered, then fell silent, pain tightening her chest.

Kavya stiffened. With her eyes raised, she asked, "Barskoon? Your family... sword makers and falconers?"

Reaching over Asrila, Kavya grasped Zehiya's hand, holding it tightly. "I know of your family, Zehiya." With a squeeze of her hand, she assured, "We will speak of this later."

Surprised, Zehiya asked, "You know? How?"

"Yes, I know, but we must not speak of this here, at this moment."

Just then the food arrived. Platters of roasted mutton, steaming rice and vegetables were placed before them. Jugs of rice wine landed noisily on the wooden table.

Releasing Zehiya's hand, Kavya reached for the wine, filling Zehiya's cup.

"Drink. You must not think of this now. You must eat, you will need your strength."

Picking up the cup, Zehiya tasted the sweet sharp liquid and felt it warming her belly. She began to feel dizzy.

Pushing a plate heaping with food before Zehiya, Kavya ordered, "Eat." Sahin looked at his mother questioningly.

She shook her head slightly, indicating that they would talk later.

Pulling a plate of food before her, Kavya cursed under her breath. "Those bastards!"

10

Kimizi's hooves drummed the sand as the two galloped away from Kucha. The sun peeked over the mountains to the east. The morning air was cold, but with the rising sun, the new day promised to become hot. Zehiya's beautiful green robe flapped on Kimizi's flanks as she gasped, choking back the tears that welled up inside her. Kartal gripped the saddle-perch with his sharp talons, his feathers ruffling in the wind.

"Why?" she pleaded. "Why her and not me?"
The dam broke. Tears blinded her as they galloped, widening the distance from Kucha, and Sahin.

"Why can he not look at me like that? Why am I not as pretty as she?"

Bending low over Kimizi's neck she urged him on—faster.
Do not hurt Kimizi, it is not his fault you are in pain, a voice inside cautioned her. She noticed the sweat on his neck and chest and slowed him to a walk.

"Oh my friend, I am an idiot," she said, reaching past Kartal to rub and gently pat her horse on the neck. "You will run for me to your death."

She slid off his back and led him by the reins.

"I will get water for you. The man in the market told me there is a river this way," she assured him.

Sometime later she found the river and waded in to let Kimizi drink. He sucked greedily at the cool water. When he lifted his head, his belly full, she swung onto Kimizi's back and they continued on with deep sadness remaining a heavy shroud over her. After some time traversing sand dunes they crested the top of a rise and Zehiya was surprised at seeing huge red rock formations ahead that sprang up high into the sky.

"I bet that there is prey in those rocks for Kartal," she said aloud.

Sadness returned to her-even hunting was useless. Despondent, she continued on with a vague sense she could find a cave in the rocks just big enough to crawl into and remain all night if need be.

No one would miss me, maybe I will never go back, she thought, feeling miserable.

They arrived at the base of the rocks that opened like a great gate into a canyon. Zehiya marveled at the unusual designs and shapes that covered the multicolored stone towering high above her-seemingly carved by a sculptor's hands using a millennia of rain and wind as their tool. The one canyon became many as they drew further into the maze. In her wonder of this place she lost all sense of time and her thoughts of Sahin and her misery faded away.

Kimizi stopped suddenly, his head high, ears perked. Kartal's head swiveled. His hood was fastened, blinding him, yet he was hearing something.

"What is it?"

She strained to listen. Then there was a clicking sound, like falling rocks. Zehiya spun, looking up the walls of stone that seemed to rise forever, but no rocks were falling. A tapping sound began, softly then growing louder. A shiver went up Zehiya's spine. Kimizi began to jig sideways; she could feel his anxiety growing.

"We will leave now, we need not stay in this strange place," she said, trying to sound calm, as she turned him back the way they had come, holding him in with a firm grip on the reins, lest his fear rise to panic.

Inexplicably, a strange ball of mist appeared before them. Kimizi stopped with a snort, his legs braced. Zehiya felt him tremble. She held him firmly and watched the strange ball of fog rise up and up, to the top of canyon wall and disappear.

"This is a strange thing, but not harmful," she encouraged.

Suddenly a loud BOOM rumbled through the passageways. Kimizi leapt in fear. When he hit the end of the tight reins, he struggled, terrified he tried to flee. Gripped by terror, he grunted and spun, then reared and lunged, throwing Zehiya off balance. Kartal let go of the perch and fluttered away blindly. When he hit the cliff face, he fell to the ground.

"Kartal!" Zehiya screamed, twisting to see where he had gone. Gaining a bit of slack in the reins, Kimizi pitched his head down. With a squeal, he humped his back and bucked hard, throwing Zehiya off him. Free of her, he bolted through the passage and was gone.

Zehiya landed solidly with all of her weight on her side on top of her sword. With a groan, she rolled onto her back. She slowly got to her feet, gasping at the throbbing pain. She limped over to Kartal. Kneeling next to him, she gently ran her hands over his wings and body, feeling for any injuries. He trembled under her touch, the shock of the fall still coursing through him. With a sigh of relief that he was uninjured, she turned her attention to the pain in her hip which was growing more insistent. When she prodded the area, she was relieved that it was just a very bad bruise and not a broken hip bone. She then discovered her dagger was gone. She looked frantically about, then saw it lying in the dirt. She retrieved it and secured it in her belt. Sliding her sword scabbard away from the injury, she pulled her gauntlet from her belt and pulled it on. Gently she guided Kartal and he stepped onto the gauntleted hand, the familiarity calming him.

Looking around her, up at the cliffs, all now silent, she limped as she followed Kimizi's tracks.

"Well, Kartal, that was a first. Kimizi has never done that before," she said, with a shudder.

Tears threatened. "No!" she demanded. "I will not cry."

Hours later, trudging along the barren landscape, hot and thirsty,

Zehiya cursed, "Where did he go?!"

"Kimizi!" she called out, for the hundredth time, in frustration.

Only the wind answered.

Exhausted, having been searching so long with no result, eyeing the sun that was low over the barren hills she felt a foreboding squirmed in her hungry belly.

"It will be dark soon," she worried.

And the night would be cold. She was grateful for her new warm robe, though now the beautiful green was soiled with dirt and sand.

What if he is lost? What if someone finds him and simply takes him? The thoughts assailed her, tears pressed behind her eyes.

Stealing herself from the urge to cry, she said to Kartal, "We cannot go on into the night. We must find shelter."

The form of cliffs rising up to a flat top plateau appeared in the distance, Zehiya was sure she could make out dark shadows along the walls.

"Cave entrances?" she wondered.

Arriving at the base of the cliffs, she did indeed see an entrance to a cave up high on the cliff. A path to the entrance snaked up through boulders and rocks.

Absently, she licked her lips to no avail, her tongue was as dry as dirt. For the hundredth time she cursed herself for not thinking of bringing a water bag along.

"I will have to find my way back on the morrow and find water along the way," she said, miserably to Kartal. Stroking his back, she felt the feathers stiff under her hand.

"I hope you are not too thirsty, my friend."

Her legs felt heavy as she trudged tiredly up to the cave entrance. She peered warily inside the dark interior and listened for any movement inside. Sure the cave was empty, she entered. She sighed in relief at the coolness inside. The dim light of dusk filtered through the entrance as she settled Kartal on a large rock. The stone room was large, and further back from the entrance it was very dark. Zehiya slid off her robe and set it aside. She then pulled a piece of dried meat from the bag she carried on her belt and offered a piece to Kartal. He ate it in two gulps.

She had neglected to bring food for herself. When she had left Kucha that morning, she had been forlorn about Sahin and wanted to get away, not thinking of her needs, or even Kartal's.

"Stupid, stupid, stupid girl!" she cursed herself as she pulled her dagger free. Tears welled up, and pain. Pain in her side, pain in her heart.

"You are stupid!' she cursed, blinded by her tears as she sliced the last piece of Kartal's meat into smaller pieces, "and ugly."

"Ouch!" she cried, cutting her finger.

Hot anger shot through her. Bolting to her feet, she stormed around in a circle, dagger clenched.

"I am a stupid girl!" she wailed, her finger throbbing as the blood dripped from the cut. "Ugly hair, stupid red color. My legs and arms are too long. I am ugly and stupid! No wonder Sahin doesn't want me! "

Then, with no thought, she swiped the blade across her forearm. Red blood sprang from the shallow wound that was created. She stared at it, dismayed. Inexplicably, she cut herself again, further up her arm. She stood, frozen, staring at her work. Her arm stung with new pain. Her knees felt weak. She sank to the floor as a strange sleepy calm covered her like a warm blanket.

11

Jangbu trotted Rinzen, his coal-grey mare, at a swift pace across the barren ground. They had been out most of the day.

"Where did she go?" he asked Rinzen, in exasperation.

The sun hung low now on the horizon.

"Mmm... we have only a few hours until dark," he said, becoming worried.

Scanning the desert he noticed a small cloud of dust rise in the distance. He halted Rinzen, staring at the cloud as it seemed to move across the land. Booting Rinzen into the gallop, he headed for it. Then, he saw the horse at a hard gallop, trailing the cloud of dust.

"Kimizi," he gasped, urging Rinzen faster. "By the gods, he is rider-less!"

In moments, they were closing in. Kimizi's head shot up, seeing them. Jangbu kept Rinzen at the hard gallop to collide with Kimizi's path. When they appeared on Kimizi's left with thunderous hooves bearing down on him, Kimizi swerved to the right, kicking back at them in fear.

Jangbu urged Rinzen to catch up. She knew this game and without further cues, bolted after the gelding. Coming up on Kimizi's side, Jangbu leaned sideways, grasping at his reins as they flopped on his neck. With gritted teeth, he grabbed, once, twice, a third time, until he felt them tight in his fist. Pulling up, he leaned back in the saddle, slowing Rinzen as Kimizi jumped and reared against the restraint.

Jangbu eased up, slackening the reins a bit to release the pressure that was causing Kimizi to fight. The release gave the gelding time to think, no longer feeling trapped he slowed, matching Rinzen's gait until they were at the walk. When Kimizi relaxed Jangbu halted Rinzen.

Kimizi blew hard out of his nostrils and shook his whole body. His saddle jangled and slapped loudly. He hung his head low, in exhaustion. Jangbu leapt out of the saddle. Keeping hold of Kimizi's reins, he stroked the horse's neck which was slick with sweat.

"There boy, that is good-settle now," he soothed as he inspected the saddle for signs of blood. Relief washed over him because there was none. *Yet, she may be lying injured somewhere.*

The thought assailed him.

Unhooking the flask from his saddle, he poured some of it into his cupped hand, then held it under Kimizi's muzzle who, lapped it up with his thick tongue.

With his hemp rope now tied around Kimizi's neck, Jangbu mounted Rinzen, then headed back in the direction from which Kimizi had run.

"Come along now Kimizi, let us find your mistress."

12

Zehiya opened her eyes to the dim early morning light. She clutched her robe tightly around her against the cold. For a moment, she forgot where she was, then the memory flooded back.

"Oh," she groaned, sitting up and burying her head in her hands, remembering.

She made out the dark form of Kartal, perched on a rock, hooded and silent. Noticing her robe was on, she remembered falling asleep, but not putting her robe on after... she... had...

At the stinging sensation on her arm, she pulled her sleeve up, exposing the dried bloody slashes.

Shaking her head in disgust, she moaned, "Stupid."

Resisting the urge to cry, she got to her feet, loathing herself. "Stupid girl," she muttered, feeling pressure in her bladder, wondering which direction to go to relieve herself.

She headed to the back of the cave, then stopped, startled, at the large object blocking her path. The form of a huge stone foot materialized before her as the sun had just crested the hills to the east illuminating the interior of the cave. Slowly she gazed up, making out a hand, the fingers in a gesture she did not understand, then carved swirls of robes, and a chest, until, at last, she stared in dismay into the serene face of the Buddha, eyes lowered, regarding her with a compassionate gaze.

Feeling a wave of awe and calm overtake her, she turned away from the huge figure to search for a more suitable and less sacred, place to satisfy her more and more urgent need.

As she exited the cave, she stood for a moment, shielding her eyes from the glare of the sun. She took in the view of the land which tumbled away from her high perch into the distance. Clutching her robe closed against the cold morning air, she proceeded to a group of boulders in the distance.

After a short time, Zehiya stumbled over the rocky path that lead back to the cave. Licking her lips, her tongue dry and thick, she longed for water. Entering the cave, she stopped, staring perplexedly at the form of a monk in a saffron robe seated on the floor of the cave who was contemplating Kartal.

At Zehiya's entrance, he twisted to look at her.

"Ah," he said, "now I understand." With a gesture toward Kartal, he inquired, "Your falcon?"

Dismayed, she stared at him. "Where did you come from?"

Even though he was a young man the monk rose slowly and stiffly to his feet. With a deep bow, he said, "So sorry, Madam; I am Tsang." Gesturing toward the rear of the cave, he explained, "There are passageways linking the many caverns that are carved along this cliff."

Folding his hands into his sleeves, he straightened, making himself tall. "Yet, the more astute question is, where did you come from, Madam?"

Zehiya stood frozen-unsure.

"Oh my, forgive me," the monk said, gesturing toward the floor of the cave. "Please have a seat, Madam. What is your name?"

"Do you have water?" Zehiya asked. "I... we have had no water for more than a day."

Tsang stiffened. "Oh, pardon my rudeness. You must therefore be hungry as well? Madam?"

Gesturing for her to remain, he disappeared into the back of the cave. Zehiya followed, stopping at a small doorway behind the Buddha statue. Peering through it she could feel a cool breeze of air that carried an earthy scent.

Caves? she wondered, walking back toward the entrance, looking out at the bright morning. *With monks and a Buddha?* She remembered her dream with the Spirit Eagle. In the dream she had images of saffron-robed monks seated before low tables, ink quills moving over parchment. And caves! Many caves along a high cliff.

The monk had said there were many caves here. Could this be the caves where Pema is? Is she here, in one of these caves?

Startled out of her reverie, Zehiya turned as the monk entered the cave from the back exit, carrying a tray with cups of tea and bowls of rice. A flask was slung over his shoulder. Placing these before her, he sat and settled himself.

Sipping from his cup of tea, he watched with interest as Zehiya gulped from the flask. She rose, filling her cupped hand before Kartal. He swept the water with his lower beak, bringing up grateful mouthfuls. After he finished all the water she offered, Zehiya then resumed her seat, saying to Kartal, "That is all for now, my friend."

She drained the tea cup and began devouring the rice.

"Please, Madam, you must eat slowly or surely you will choke," Tsang implored.

Zehiya looked up at him. Nodding, she took a breath, chewing more slowly. The tea and rice tasted like nothing she had ever eaten-it was delicious.

Sitting cross-legged, hands on his knees, Tsang asked, with a smile on his leathery face, "How did you come to be in this cave, Madam?"

Swallowing her last mouthful, she answered, "I became lost, unhorsed in the canyon."

"Unhorsed?" Tsang inquired, with a tilt of his head.

With a sigh, Zehiya explained, "I rode out from Kucha. I entered the canyons, where there was a strange fog and loud sounds. My horse panicked and bolted. I...we," gesturing to Kartal, "were unhorsed and my horse ran away."

Standing, lifting her sword in its scabbard, Zehiya said, "I must go now and find him."

Dismayed, Tsang said, "A sword?" Tapping his lip with his forefinger, he considered. "I did not see the sword; I saw the falcon. I did, indeed, see the falcon. Yet the sword did evade my attention."

Standing, Tsang bowed, "Madam, you cannot leave."

Fastening her belt, Zehiya winced, having forgotten the bruise on her side.

"Why not? I am going. I must find my horse."

"You cannot," Tsang stated, more urgently.

Zehiya stared at him. "Why... not?" she asked, slowly.

"Because your sadness is very great, Madam. I must help you."

Zehiya glared at him. "What do you know of my... my... anything?" she challenged.

"Madam, please, sit," Tsang implored. "Tell me why you hate yourself?"

Stunned, Zehiya froze. "What do you...how do you..." she trailed off.

"Madam," Tsang invited, his tone soothing, "Please sit—just for a time?"

Zehiya sat, adjusting her sword and crossing her legs, regarding him. She felt safe with him, yet remained cautious. Then she realized.

"You heard me last night. That is how you know," she said.

"Last night?" Tsang asked. "No, I knew not of your presence here until this morn when we just met."

Folding his hands in his lap, seated before her, he explained, "It does not take a sorcerer to see that you loath yourself, Madam. I can see it well, because of my many moons in quiet meditation."

Looking into her eyes, he continued, "Sometimes I can hear what people are thinking."

With a chuckle, he added, "Oh, well, that is not so difficult, I suppose. People mostly think the same things, over and over and over." He laughed.

His laugh was infectious. Zehiya could not help smiling.

Picking up his cup, he sipped, then stared, dismayed, into its empty interior. Setting it down, he regarded her.

"My name is Zehiya," she offered.

"Ah, Zehiya," Tsang bowed from the waist. "Why do you hate yourself?"

Zehiya stared at him, dumbstruck.

Tsang went on, "To hate oneself is an error. To hate anyone is very bad karma. Yet to hate oneself..." he trailed off, thinking. A tear rolled down his cheek. "...is so... so cruel. So wrong."

Zehiya felt her tears welling behind her eyes. She took in a breath, bracing herself.

With a look of compassion that seared through Zehiya, Tsang reached over, placing his gentle hand on her knee. "You must become a friend to yourself, Zehiya. Be your own best friend and value yourself."

The dam broke and Zehiya could not hold back the sobs.

Tsang sat patiently waiting while the girl wept.

When she quieted, he asked, "Do you know how to meditate?"

"Yes, I do. I had... have a teacher," Zehiya said, wiping her eyes.

Eyebrows raised, Tsang enthused, "That is very good! Who is this teacher?"

"Her name is Pema," Zehiya replied and told the story of accidentally finding the cave and staying with Pema for three moons.

Then she remembered that she was in caves – these caves.

"Do you know her? I was looking for her..." Zehiya took a breath, the pain of Pema's disappearance sharp in her heart. "I found the cave, but she was gone..." she trailed off. "Is she here? " she asked, hopefully.

Tsang shook his head. "I do not know your teacher." Raising his finger, he continued, "Yet, it is most likely she was on retreat when you found her. Her retreat ended and she returned to her home or..." With a shrug, Tsang said, "Who knows where she has gone."

Zehiya's heart sank.

A shadow filled the entrance to the cave. A large eagle landed. Folding its wings to its sides it stood with glistening gold eyes regarding Tsang and Zehiya. Squawking it then turned and soared away on the wind. Zehiya stared, incredulously, at the disappearing bird. She never knew of an eagle acting that way.

Unless... The Spirit Eagle? Is there something she is trying to tell me? she wondered.

"An acquaintance of yours?" Tsang inquired with his palm up, gesturing toward the large bird. Without waiting for an answer, he went on. "I would go east on the trade route to Dunhuang to search for Pema. She is on her way there. There are a very many caves at Dunhuang. There are monks as well as practitioners there. Perhaps you may catch up with her at one of the Buddhist temples or monasteries along the way."

"Where is Dunhuang?" Zehiya asked.

"You must first travel to Turpan, then to Hami and then to Anxi. At Anxi, you take the road southwest to Dunhuang."

"Oh," she said, dismayed, "why do you think I will find her there?"

Tsang shrugged, glancing at the sunlit cave entrance. "The eagle told me."

"She...the eagle told you?" Zehiya gasped.

Nodding, Tsang lifted his cup and sipped. He looked into it, perplexed, it was empty. Shaking his head slightly, he set it down.

"The eagle also told me that you are descended from an ancient warrior people." With a chuckle, he added, "Well... we all are, are we not?"

He looked up, tilting his head as if trying to hear something.

"Ah, your friend has arrived."

"Friend? What friend?" Zehiya asked.

Tsang rose to his feet and looked out of the cave entrance.

"That one." He pointed.

Zehiya jumped up to look out. There, proceeding slowly along the road, was a rider with Kimizi being led along behind him on a rope.

"It is Kimizi, my horse. And Sahin?" She squinted, trying to make out the rider. Sahin, looking for her? Quick as a flash, she saw herself riding alongside Sahin all day back to Kuchu. He would tell her how he had worried about her.

The rider came closer and Zehiya's heart dropped.

"It is Jangbu," she said, disappointed.

Tsang looked at her quizzically. "Not a friend?"

Hands folded, Tsang regarded the approaching figure of Jangbu intently. "The mind is funny," he said. "It is always picking and choosing—pulling, desiring, grasping the desired object. Shunning, pushing, avoiding the undesired object; ignoring the neutral object." He sighed. "We cannot simply see what is right in front of us, stripped of all our grasping concepts."

She looked at Tsang. "You speak just like Pema."

"Ah," Tsang intoned, "then, my dear, you had better find her."

Shaking his head solemnly, he said, "Otherwise, you will remain forever in samsara, in suffering."

She turned from him, gathering up Kartal. "Thank you for the tea and food."

Halfway down the path, she turned to look up at the serene monk standing in rocky opening.

"I will look for Pema in Dunhuang," she called to him. "I will find my teacher."

Tsang raised his hand in farewell as he faded back, disappearing into the cavern.

13

"Jangbu!" Zehiya's voice rang out, as she scurried down the steep path.

Jangbu halted, scanning the hillside. There, he saw her, Kartal on her arm, sword at her side and fire for hair. His heart soared. She was safe.

"Oh, Kimizi!" she threw her arms around the horse's neck after placing Kartal on the saddle-perch.

"Where did you find him?" she asked Jangbu.

With a twinge of pain that she did not greet him in such a fashion, Jangbu said, "I found him running hard, near the canyons."

Running her hand down her horse's legs, she asked, "Is he injured?"

"He is fine, with strong legs—very good stock," Jangbu assured her as he dismounted and untied his water bag. After taking a swig he offered it to Zehiya, asking, "What happened to you? Why was he in such a panic?" Looking up at the cave, he added, "How did you find this place?"

Eyeing the molten sphere of the sun rising higher, Zehiya said, "There is much to tell." Taking the end of her turban, she wrapped it around her face to protect her light skin from the burning rays. "It will be very hot today."

Mounting Kimizi, Zehiya repeated, "There is much to tell."

Jangbu swung up into the saddle, saying, "Very well." He looked into her eyes. Feeling himself tumbling into their emerald sea he looked away and straightened in the saddle, adding "We have a long ride back to Kucha. You can tell me along the way."

"Then a loud boom came from the recesses of the canyons and he threw me and bolted," Zehiya recounted.

The late morning heat was scorching. Sweat ran down Zehiya's sides and back, soaking the shirt under her tunic. Winds out of the north dried her clothes quickly.

"Those canyons are called the 'mysterious canyons'," Jangbu explained. "Many people of Kucha tell of strange experiences there. Most never go them near, for fear of possession by mischievous spirits."

Leaning over and stroking Kimizi's neck, Zehiya said, "I have never seen him so afraid."

Jangbu halted and untied his flask, offering it to Zehiya. She took a small sip, the water was hot but thankfully wet, then handed it back.

"Does he mind that hood on his head?" Jangbu asked, nodding toward Kartal.

Shaking her head, she replied, "He was trained to wear it when he was very young. It keeps him calm and when it is taken off, he will seek out the prey I choose for him."

"How?" Jangbu asked, quizzically.

"I will show you at dusk before we enter Kucha. This is when the prey will come out of their dwellings," she said, animatedly, feeling good to be once more on Kimizi's back with Kartal at the pommel.

She studied Jangbu furtively. The first thing she noticed was that he sat a horse well with a relaxed but straight posture and a light hand on the reins. She liked his mare who was the color of coal—a color rarely seen, with long sturdy legs and a strong compact body. Jangbu and his horse were connected in the same way she and Kimizi were. Jangbu was a true horseman.

"What is her name?" Zehiya asked, gesturing toward Jangbu's mare.

"Rinzen," he said, giving the mare a gentle pat on her neck. "It means she is smart, always thinking. Mares collect knowledge. Indeed, it is the eldest mare who leads the herd. The old mares know where the water is, where the grazing is, where danger lies. They hold all the experiential knowledge of the herd."

Zehiya looked at him in amazement. "How do you know this? Not many people know this about horses. Grandfather taught me, about the old mares in our herds."

Sadness rolled over her, the memory of her family, their horses, her home, now gone.

"My brother and I raise horses," Jangbu replied, "We live in Amdo, in Tibet. Every three springs I travel to the Ferghana valley to buy a fine stallion and some mares to improve our stock."

"Alone—all that way?"

Shaking his head sadly, he said, "I was traveling with my friend, Norbu." With lips pressed, he steeled himself against the memory. "He was killed along the way."

"How?"

"We were attacked by bandits who were after our pack camel and silver. We stampeded our string of horses and let go of our camel, who carried provisions, water and fodder for the horses, to get away." Gripping the pommel of his saddle, Jangbu shuttered. "He fell." With a grim chuckle, he went on. "One of the best horsemen I have ever known, and he fell. His horse stumbled and threw him."

With the pain of the memory flooding back he could not stop the tears that trickled down his face.

"Broke his neck; it was very quick. One minute alive, the next dead." Wiping his face, he said, "Life is impermanent. We never know when it will be over for us." With a wry laugh, he added, "Yet, we go on, day after day, thinking that we will live forever."

Bent over her own tears threatening to spill, Zehiya held fast to her emotions—the memory of Grandfather's passing, then that of her father and brother. And Feray, poor, dear Feray. And she must find Erdem and Little Arif.

"Oh, but I have disturbed your mind," Jangbu said apologetically, seeing the expression of grief on her face. "I am sorry. Let us forget this sad story. It is a beautiful day and we are alive and well."

Sitting up straighter, Zehiya composed herself. "Did the thieves steal your silver?"

"Yes, I threw what we had remaining at them. They rode off with our camel and silver laughing." He shook his head in disgust, "My friend lay dead, and they laughed."

"Were they the same men who attacked Asrila and me?" Zehiya inquired.

Jangbu shook his head. "No—not the same men. It is an unfortunate thing that there are so many bandits along the trade route."

"Will you find the men who attacked you and caused your friend's death and kill them?" Zehiya asked.

"Kill them?" Jangbu asked, in wonder.

Shaking his head, he laughed. "They are long gone. Revenge will serve me nothing—just more pain and suffering. Their karma will catch up with them," he assured. "Like those men we killed who attacked you, they are dead now and will harm no one ever again."

Zehiya bowed her head in deep thought, considering Jangbu's statement.

They rode side by side in silence.

"Kavya told me of the slaying of your family by bandits," Jangbu said, softly. "I am sorry if I have caused the memory of your sorrow to rise with my story."

Zehiya stared at him, remembering. "Kavya told me that night, at the inn, that she knew. But how? How does she know of it?"

"Word travels this route," he said. "You witnessed the murder of your family?"

Lips pressed tight, holding back the pain of that horrific day, Zehiya nodded. She coughed as tears burst through the barrier.

"I am so sorry," Jangbu said, softly.

Composing herself, she stared into the distance, her eyes hard.

"I was up high on the hill and saw them, I saw everything. They did not know I was watching." Looking at Jangbu, she said, "They took my little brothers. They are just young boys. My wish is to find them

74

Zehiya

and to rescue them and kill those men who killed my family."

Jangbu reined up in shock. "Find them?"

Zehiya reined in Kimizi and regarded Jangbu. "Yes, find them and get my brothers back," she spat, hot anger rising.

"Zehiya," Jangbu said, keeping his voice calm and gentle, "you will never find your brothers. They are most likely in Samarkand or even on their way to Bactra by now, or else they are being taken to India."

Zehiya's gaze seared into Jangbu. A tight knot formed in her chest as she gasped unable to breath. Realizing now how vast the spaces of this land was, she knew he was right. She would never find them, she knew Samarkand was very far to the west and Bactra even farther. The knot tightened. Tears began to well in her eyes.

"What will become of them?" she asked.

"They will be sold as slaves," he replied, bluntly. "Most likely a wealthy household or a merchant will procure them, however it will not necessarily be a bad life for them," he assured her.

Wiping her tears, she asked, "They will not be harmed?"

Shaking his head, Jangbu said, "They are small boys, so they will not be put in the work gangs. They will probably be house slaves or a merchant's slave. If they are lucky, they will be able to stay together. They may also be separated—of this I will not mislead you."

She looked into his half handsome, half grotesquely misshapen face, and the sight of his deformity disturbed her. She slid her eyes away.

"I must let them go?" she wondered.

"Let them go to their own fate," he said, nodding solemnly.

Urging Kimizi to walk on, she considered and made a decision. *Then I will find Pema.* After riding for several hours in silence, Zehiya wondered aloud, "Now you have no coin, Jangbu? How will you pay for food and fodder?"

"Ah, coin," Jangbu said, smiling. "I hide caches along the way, from Amdo to Ferghana," he explained, "Collecting them on my return. That was why I was in the rocky hills when you were attacked; collecting the cache I had hidden there."

Zehiya nodded in approval. "That is a smart thing to do."

"I have been lucky that I have never been robbed at the beginning

75

of my journey before I could hide my caches. Norbu and I, two armed men traveling on horseback was not an inviting target." With a shrug, he wondered aloud, "I know not why two armed men with a string of six horses was more of a temptation."

They rode on as the sun made its slow hot arc across the sky. When it was finally on the decent toward the tops of the distant hills, they topped the rise that lay at the outskirts of Kucha. Zehiya halted. Jangbu watched as she took Kartal onto her gauntlet. He flapped his wings against the tresses, then settled on the thick leather. The shadows on the land stretched out dramatically, painting dark patterns. Then Jangbu saw a movement.

Zehiya saw it too. Removing the hood from her falcon, she raised her arm up, releasing him to flight. Jangbu watched in admiration as the predator rose high in the sky, his tress bells tinkling on the silent air. Kartal soared, making a circle over the land. Suddenly, folding his wings against his body, he dropped like an arrow.

Jangbu stiffened. *Surely he will crash to his death at that speed,* he thought.

Kartal struck his target in a blur and flutter of movement on the ground. Zehiya, not able to contain her delight, made a "Whoop!" as Kimizi leapt into the gallop towards Kartal.

Jangbu and Rinzen sprang after them. In moments, Jangbu reined up next to Zehiya, who was standing over Kartal, reflexively fishing in the bag at her belt for the dried meat. Finding it empty, she crouched next to him as he tore at the fresh kill.

"There, my friend, have your fill," she said.

Looking up at Jangbu, she shrugged, "This one is for Kartal. I have no more meat to give him."

Gazing in the direction of Kucha, she asked, "Is Kavya angry with me?"

"No." Jangbu chuckled. "I think she feels she has found a daughter in you."

Zehiya looked at him in surprise.

Jangbu nodded. "It is true, she was desperate for you to be found."

"Why did Sahin not join you?" she queried tentatively, not

wanting to show her disappointment, sharper now at this new revelation.

He shrugged. "He had business in Kucha that could not wait."

By the name of Asrila, Zehiya guessed in her thoughts, anger and sadness clutching her heart, making her face hard and twisted.

Gazing at the sun's fading light of reds and oranges in the sky above the distant hills, Jangbu said gently, "Jealousy is a poison; it is best to have good thoughts and set free that person so desired. And you will be set free by wishing them only happiness."

Surprised at his words, Zehiya watched as Jangbu rode on ahead.

14

"Her name is Leyla" Kavya said. "She is a Bactrian camel. Though she is very big and strong; she is sensitive. Her heart is gentle, it can break very easily. If you say a bad word to her or mistreat her, she will lie down and refuse to go on."

Seated in the saddle, securely wedged between the two humps of Leyla with Kartal perched on the wooden hand-hold of the pommel, Zehiya cooed, "I promise, I will never mistreat you, Leyla."

Leyla swung her head back arching her long neck. Her soft eyes swiveled under long eyelashes as she let out a low bellow. Startled, Zehiya leaned back. Kartal squawked and flapped his wings.

"There, you see?" Kavya laughed. "She likes you. She knows you are a good person."

Zehiya settled against Leyla's fatty hump and swayed with the camel's long strides, as she gazed up at the steep barren hill illuminated in the cool light of the full moon. She pulled the medallion from inside her robe, turning it over and over, admiring how it glistened in the moonlight. Feeling its weight in her hand, she thought of Grandfather and what he had said. *You are of a great warrior people. What warrior people?* she wondered. Twisting to look back over her shoulder, she searched along the string of horses to find Kimizi. There, she saw him, walking contentedly in the line.

Good, she thought, with a sigh. *He deserves a rest.*

She noticed Jangbu on Rinzen, at the end to the line, making sure that none strayed.

Many days had passed since her return to Kucha. Kavya and Asrila hugged her tightly when she and Jangbu arrived back at the inn, expressing their fear for her safety. As much as she wanted to dislike Asrila for taking all of Sahin's attention, she liked the girl, who was warm and sincere.

"We are sisters now," Asrila had declared, holding Zehiya's hand tightly. "You must come home with me to Turpan. You shall live in my parent's house and we shall become your new family."

Placing an arm around Zehiya's shoulders parentally, Kavya drew her aside. "The story of the murder of your family traveled swiftly. Many knew your family—they traded with your father and grandfather."

Turning Zehiya toward her, her hands resting on her slim, strong shoulders and looking into her eyes, Kavya said, "You are alone in the world now. I can see that you are not one to settle into the drudgery of married life. You will come with me, my dear." Tears welling in her eyes, Kavya declared, "as my daughter."

With a wave of her arm, she promised, "You will live in my great home in Turpan. Learn from me, Kavya," she said, tapping her chest. "I am the best camel driver to travel the great trade route." Looking lovingly into Zehiya's green eyes, she promised, "You will become rich!"

Zehiya felt unsure at this. *Did she want to be this woman's daughter? Yet Kavya was so kind and Zehiya had no home. This was good luck, surely.*

And Sahin? He had smiled his beautiful smile, professing his joy that she had been returned to them alive and well.

The memory made her dizzy. Now, Kavya joined her string of camels with a larger caravan of three hundred camels and a hundred horses and forty donkeys. They were a seven days journey out of their last stop—the Kingdom of Karasahr, and onward to Turpan. The days were stifling hot, making it necessary to travel at night. Leyla took careful steps up the rocky path. Hour upon difficult hour passed as they trudged up the route, over the mountains toward Turpan. The rumble of the wagons at the end of the caravan, carrying silver from the mines in these mountains, could be heard all along the line of camels, horses, and donkeys that carried the immense wealth of the West in the form of gold, jade, spices, and nuts to be traded for the wealth of the East, silk, ceramics and tea.

Images of their stay in Karasahr, the oasis many days travel eastward from Kucha, along the trade route at the base of the Tien Shan Mountains, paraded through Zehiya's mind, assuaging the weariness and boredom draping over her like heavy cloak.

Bright markets and all manner of fine foods. The memory of the aromas and flavors made her hungry now and the musicians who played music of lutes and drums in melodies she had never heard before.

"It is true," Kavya laughed.

Wakened from her dreaming, Zehiya straightened in the saddle to listen.

"Your mother was of the northern tribes?" Asrila asked. "And he stole her? No one came to rescue her?"

"No one came for her," Kavya explained. "It is customary to steal a wife. My father was of the Uighur tribe of the South. He had been traveling in the Kyrgyz tribal lands near the Altai Mountains." With a wave of her hand, she scoffed, "I do not know why he was traveling in those lands. It was dangerous for him as the Uighurs and the Kyrgyz were then—as now—enemies. Yet, he had seen my mother while she was tending sheep. He was instantly besotted with her."

Leaning back in the saddle, she said, conspiratorially, "My mother was very beautiful. One day he rode into the village of his enemies and took her—right in front of her parents' yurt! He threw her over the front of his saddle and rode away."

"This was custom?" Asrila asked, incredulous.

With a solemn nod, Kavya said, "Yes, a man can simply steal a woman from her home and she is married to him." With a flick of her hand. "Just like that, one day a girl, the next a wife in a man's yurt."

"Can she run away and go back to her home?" Asrila asked.

Shaking her head, Kavya said, "No, she is his wife. No one would take her into their home, even her parents."

Kavya gazed at Asrila. "My dear, your family is Assyrian?"

With a look of surprise, Asrila said, "Why yes. How did you know?"

"In truth it was a guess. Your beauty and features are that of the

Assyrian people," Kavya explained.

"Mother," Sahin called, as he rode up to her camel on his fine black horse. Walking his horse alongside them, he smiled to Asrila, who was seated behind Kavya on the large saddle, made for two riders. "The pass is ahead," he said. "We will be stopping for a rest on the other side."

"Ah," Kavya sighed. "Very good. I so wish to be off this saddle."

With a smile to Zehiya, Sahin wheeled his horse, booting it into the canter toward the back of the line. Zehiya's heart lurched at his attention. Not able to resist, she turned to watch him go. With a knowing look at Zehiya, Kavya said, casually, "My son Sahin is very handsome. Is he not?"

Asrila giggled. Zehiya looked away, ashamed at being caught.

"His father was very handsome as well."

"Is his father in Turpan?" Asrila asked.

Leaning back, Kavya chortled, wryly, "If he is, I know not where."

Zehiya looked at her quizzically.

"His father was a most handsome man. The most handsome man I had ever laid eyes on."

Closing her eyes, as if to see more clearly, Kavya continued, "Long ago, I met him on the first camel drive that I made without my father, from Turpan to Barskoon. You see, my father taught me how to drive camels and to transport wares. Sahin's father was on route with several other merchants from a faraway land. He called it Ja-pan. He rode a magnificent horse and wore beautiful silks. He had a long sword. His hair was as black as a moonless night; his braid went clear down his back." Looking at Zehiya, she said, "I was captivated by him. I could not take my eyes from him."

"Did you marry him?" Asrila asked.

Kavya twisted to look back at Asrila and laughed, "Oh, my dear, I dreamed he would marry me, yet he did not. He was on a journey to Samarkland and then to India. He did leave me with a most wonderful gift though—a beautiful son."

All fell silent as Kavya's words trailed off.

As the sky toward the east pushed the dark of night away with a rose-grey hue that promised another day of the searing sun, the weary caravan slogged over the pass.

A shout of alarm came from far in the front of the procession. Zehiya rose up in her saddle as Sahin and Jangbu galloped by them toward the shouting.

"What is happening?" Zehiya asked Kavya.

"We will find out soon enough," Kavya said, her face working with concern.

Sahin appeared, trotting up them, with a grim expression, as he gasped, breathless, "Bandits—a caravan from days ago. It is ugly. Be prepared," he warned.

As they came to the saddle of the pass, a wind carrying the stench of rotted bodies assailed them. In moments, Zehiya saw the first one, a heap of mangled flesh, torn and half eaten by buzzards. She could make out the white of bone under the caked black of dried bloody flesh. More soon appeared. Naked corpses lay in various states of decay, their flesh hanging off bone.

Zehiya wrapped the end of her turban around her face to smother the smell of rot. She fought back waves of nausea as she passed body after body.

"Horrible. Let us move faster through this," Kavya called out as she laid her whip on Delilah's flank. Delilah leapt forward. Zehiya held on as Leyla followed. Soon they were slowed by the camel string ahead of them in the line.

Sahin appeared from the gloom.

"We will stop a league ahead," he called up to his mother. Then, he said, his voice catching in his throat, "They killed every man. They took every camel and horse."

At last the caravan came to a halt for all to rest and to eat. With a groan, Leyla dropped to her knees, then lowered her hind quarters to lay her belly on the hard ground, allowing Zehiya to dismount.

Dizzy and sick, Zehiya placed a hand on Leyla's side to steady herself. Forcing herself to stand straight, she adjusted her sword on her belt, then took Kartal onto her gauntlet. Feeling pressure to relieve herself, she decided to find Kimizi first and then a place to sequester herself. Approaching Kimizi, she noticed Sahin and Jangbu, their heads close together, whispering. She could only hear the urgent murmur of their conversation.

They turned, noticing her.

"Is something the matter?" she asked.

Glancing at Jangbu, who gave a slight nod, Sahin said, "That previous caravan was killed to a man. They may be content for a time since their last haul of goods. Yet we must still be vigilant. We do not know how many they may be."

A shiver ran through Zehiya. "I shall ride Kimizi then."

"You will be better served by Leyla's height," Sahin said.

Unsure, she looked to Jangbu.

"I will protect him, if anything should happen," he assured.

"Come Zehiya," Sahin said. "I will escort you to wherever you were headed."

With a blush, she hesitated, "I was just going to find..." her words trailed off.

"Ah, I see," Sahin said. "I will assure your privacy. It is not wise for you to go off by yourself in these mountains. There could be a scoundrel behind any boulder."

With a gesture, he bid her. "This way?"

Walking alongside Sahin, Zehiya could feel the power in his stride and could smell his sweat. She concentrated on each step she took, for fear she might swoon and stumble.

Why do I feel this way when he is close? She wondered. *It is... painful. Is this love? I love Kimizi and it is joy. Is loving a man different?*

He turned his eyes away as she skirted behind a group of small boulders. When she emerged, he was standing with his lean form swaying as he gazed at the moon, still bright, hanging low over the horizon in the light of dawn. Turning to her, he said, "Beautiful, is it not?"

She nodded. "Yes it is very beautiful. I love seeing the moon on the horizon as the sun rises."

"Such ugliness committed here," he said with a wave of his hand. "It is a marvel that beauty can still exist."

His gaze lingered on her for a moment.

Scurrying feet shivered up her back. Suddenly Kartal felt very heavy on her gauntleted hand. Her knees felt weak.

"We should return and have something to eat," he said, with a gesture toward the caravan.

"I cannot eat," she said, swallowing the lump in her throat so she could speak.

"You must force yourself; you will need your strength," Sahin said.

As the two of them walked in silence, Zehiya's thoughts were all a tumble. *Maybe he does want me?* She pondered. *Perhaps not Asrila, perhaps me?* Then she felt shame rise up from her belly, tightening at her throat. *You have just witnessed the remains of the murder of perhaps fifty men and all you can think about is Sahin?* She scolded herself in her thoughts.

Arriving at their camp, Kavya was bent over a ceramic bowl mixing flour with water. Asrila was tending a small fire.

"Ah, there you are," Kavya said, as Zehiya arrived. "Milk Leyla, my dear."

Leyla stood compliantly as Zehiya milked the camel's teats into a milk-bag. Returning to the fire, Zehiya sat and watched Kavya cook hand-formed cakes over the fire, searing them with a protective crust. Then she placed them into a small hole she had dug in the ground and covered the cakes with clean sand. One by one she placed coals from the fire atop the sand and sat back to wait for them to bake.

Sahin arrived with Jangbu, setting down a bowl of dates and an oiled cloth filled with goat butter.

Soon the cakes were ready. Kavya took them out, blowing and dusting the sand off.

They ate slowly, dipping the hot cake into goat butter, forcing the food down, sickened by the horrid scene they had encountered. Each mouthful was washed down with frothy camel's milk.

"Those bastards," Kavya said, scornfully, between mouthfuls. "I do hope we are not headed for the same fate as that caravan."

Shaking his head slowly, Sahin replied, "I am sure they will not attack us so soon after their previous conquest."

"So many bandits," Asrila said, shaking her head.

"It was better along the trade route long ago when Tibet was powerful and had a King," Jangbu said, taking a sip from his cup of camel's milk.

Nodding, Sahin said, "I have heard that said. It is becoming so dangerous now..." He trailed off, considering. "With the peasants rioting in Chang-an, it is becoming more difficult to acquire tea, silk and china." Shaking his head, he added, "I am not sure how long trade will be profitable from the East."

With a dismissive wave of her hand, Kavya said, "There will always be trade, yet, if the trade slows, we will remain as the last of the traders!" she promised.

"Or," Sahin offered, "we can move to Kashgar and trade the western route through Samarkand."

Kavya considered this. With a nod of approval, she said, "You are shrewd, my son—yes, that would be the better course if need be."

15

TURPAN

As she couched low over Kimizi's neck, his hooves flashing like lightning over the earth, Zehiya whooped in glee. Rinzen edged up alongside them, then sped ahead, Jangbu raising his fist to celebrate his victory to come.

"It is not over yet!" Zehiya called, through gritted teeth. "Come on my boy," she urged Kimizi. "You can beat her!"

Kimizi surged and Zehiya bent low, shocked at his power; from where it came, she knew not. Her hips followed his rapid strides. They were as one. In moments, they gained on Rinzen and Jangbu, then pulled alongside. Zehiya glanced over at Jangbu, his face contorted in a grimace of disbelief. Slowly, they gained the lead. The thunder of hooves was deafening. The goal was not far now—in seconds the tree by the river blurred past Zehiya. Jangbu was a few footfalls behind.

She allowed Kimizi to slow down, then circled him back at a trot, her fist raised in victory, her red hair all a tumble down her back, her face flushed and her green eyes wild with joy. Jangbu gulped back his heart as it leapt in his chest, stunned by her savage beauty.

The greater prize is her joy, he marveled.

Breathless, she gasped, "That was marvelous!"

"Indeed!" Jangbu said, "Kimizi is impressive."

Swinging down off the saddle, Zehiya hugged Kimizi's neck, unconcerned about the hot, salty wetness of his sweat on her face.

Breathing in his strong scent, her heart burst with love. Kimizi blew hard through his nostrils, then lowered his head with a sigh.

"He is indeed!" she agreed.

Dismounting, Jangbu led Rinzen to the riverbank, taking his time so the mare could cool down.

Exuberant, Zehiya strode alongside, leading Kimizi. Rather than avoid looking at the twisted side of Jangbu's face, she regarded it, finding the courage to study the flesh.

"How did you get that scar?" she asked.

Absently fingering the thick knotted skin that ran from chin to ear, he said, "A horse kick."

Eyes raised, Zehiya exclaimed, "Big horse!"

With a shake of his head, he chuckled. "Small horse. Big kick!"

Zehiya burst into a laugh.

Side by side, they fell silent, gazing across the undulating flow of the river, lost in thought, as the horses sipped at the cool water.

"Will you practice sword strokes with me?" Zehiya asked, breaking the stillness.

Surprised at this request, Jangbu looked at her in dismay. "Sword strokes?"

Checking her irritation, she replied, "Yes, sword strokes. I need to practice."

"Why? You are off the road. Kavya has adopted you as her own. You are under her protection now."

"No one is ever free from danger," she retorted, her blood rising.

Remembering the murder of her family, Jangbu said, "Of course, you are right." He heaved a sigh. "There are evil people who will do us harm at any time and at any place."

Dropping Rinzen's reins, he drew his sword.

"Then let us begin."

Startled, Zehiya asked, "Now?"

Eyes raised, Jangbu replied, "Why yes, now; the present moment is always the best time."

With a grin, Zehiya dropped Kimizi's reins and drew her sword. Stepping back, she held it up, ready. Quick as a snake-strike, Jangbu leapt to her side and slapped the side of his blade on her hip as she clumsily tried to parry; then he was behind her. She spun, blocking his next strike. Copying his move, she leapt to the side, attempting, yet not succeeding to landing a strike home.

"Good try," he encouraged, as their swords clanged and tinged.

He pressed forward, striking again and again as Zehiya struggled to parry the blows of his sword. There was no way out—her arm was tiring.

"Hold strikes!" Jangbu called out, backing away.

Zehiya bent over gasping for breath. "How,.. how do... I..." Taking in a breath, she calmed herself. "How do I escape from that?" she asked.

"I will show you when we practice again," he said, sheathing his sword. "Yet, for now, let us return to Kavya's home. I am starving!"

Nodding in agreement, Zehiya asked, "Will we practice on the morrow?"

Jangbu looked at her with a grin.

"Very well. On the morrow," he replied.

The city of Jiaohe, located outside of Turpan, sits atop an islet plateau that rises up in the middle of a river that splits around it like a moat. Its high walls on all sides act as natural defenses.

Crossing over the bridge through the southern gate Zehiya's and Jangbu's horses' clop-clopped up the baked-brick paved street through the maze of dwellings, each carved into the earth, as they searched for the entrance of Kavya's home.

"Here it is," Zehiya exclaimed triumphantly, pulling up in front of a gated entrance.

"I can never find it so easily," Jangbu said, shaking his head, "even though we have been here for more than a moon."

Looking around him, he marveled, "I have never seen a city such as this."

Opening the carved ornate wooden gate, Zehiya said, "You have never gone off the trade route?"

Leading his horse into the courtyard behind Zehiya, he replied, "No, I was always in a hurry to return to Amdo with our horses."

Kavya swept from the doorway of her abode. Her light-blue silk robe swirled around her bare feet. "Ah, you have returned," she said.

Taking in the sweaty condition of the horses, she looked from Zehiya to Jangbu. "Running from bandits?"

With a chuckle, Jangbu said, "Race."

"And you won! Tell me this is not true," she enthused, placing her arm around Zehiya.

"How did you know?" Zehiya asked.

"Why, by that smile on your face and the joy exuding from your heart, my dear," she said. "Now, tend to your horses, then come in quickly. We are to have the midday meal shortly."

Entering the large, cool and airy earthen room, Zehiya and Jangbu each took a seat on one of the various cushions placed in a circle on the fine Persian carpet covering the packed-earth floor. Zehiya practically swooned at the aromas of the feast of fresh baked bread, honey, goat butter, roasted mutton, and dates, that was arrayed on the thick clean cotton mat placed in the center. Rays of sunlight shined through the windows carved out of the walls, casting all in a golden glow. She smiled at Sahin who sat across from her, her heart skipping a beat as his warm silver eyes settled on her, returning her smile.

Turning his attention to Jangbu, Sahin asked, "Brother, will you assist me after our meal?"

"Of course, my bother. What can I do for you?"

"I am negotiating the sale of our load of frankincense with a trader in Turpan who is a surly cuss. Your warrior presence will impress him and I will have a better chance of a fair deal."

With a grin, Jangbu said, "In truth, I am a peaceful fellow, yet, it would be my pleasure to assist you. I will wear all my weapons just to complete the illusion."

"Here is tea," came the sing-song voice of Asrila.

As if standing on the back of a swan, she glided into the room, carrying a tray of china tea cups. A white sari that was decorated with flowers embroidered in indigo thread, hugged her shapely figure. Her long shiny black hair was braided in four braids that swept alongside her head, joining at the back, then falling gracefully down to her waist. Her perfect skin glowed like the moon. Her dark eyes sparkled with warmth and kindness.

"Asrila?" Zehiya said, looking up from the bread she was hungrily dipping into butter before devouring it, stifling her surprise at the girl's presence, for they had escorted Asrila to her home when first arriving in Turpan a moon ago. Zehiya had not seen nor heard of the girl since then. "It is so nice to see you; it has been too long," she stammered. "What is that you are wearing? I have not seen a gown such as that."

With a furtive glance at Sahin, Asrila placed the tray on the mat.

As she passed a cup of hot tea to each around the circle, she replied, "This is called a sari. It is the dress of the country of India. Sahin gave it to me as gift." Standing, she swirled. "Is it not beautiful?"

Struggling to hide her jealousy at how graceful and beautiful this girl was, Zehiya said, "Yes it is, indeed." Her throat was tight in the realization that she would never be as beautiful and elegant as Asrila.

Wrapping a piece of bread around a date, then dipping it into butter, Kavya announced, "We have delightful news."

"Perhaps we should wait until after our meal?" Sahin suggested.

With a dismissive wave, Kavya finished chewing the tasty morsel. "No, no, it is wonderful news."

Everyone stopped eating, all attention rested on Kavya in anticipation. Nestling the fine porcelain tea cup in her palms, she said, "Asrila's father has returned to Turpan."

"Good news!" Jangbu said, with a laugh.

"Is he well?" Zehiya wondered.

"Yes, he is lucky to be alive," Asrila answered, wide eyed, as she seated herself. "He did suffer bruising, as the robbers had beaten him, but luckily, a merchant came around the bend during the attack. He had two others with him, armed with swords and bows. The bandits ceased their attack and fled." Looking into each face around the circle in turn, she added, "And so, they were not able to rob him. He lost nothing."

Jangbu clapped his hands. "This is wonderful news."

"Did he look for you?" Zehiya asked, gripping her cup of tea between her palms.

"Oh yes," she replied, twisting her fingers in her lap. "He looked and looked. He was very angry that I ran so far. He feared I was eaten by wolves." Quieting her hands, she went on, "He continued to Aksu to store his wares and to hire men to aid him." With a sigh, she said, "He looked for a fortnight." She looked at Kavya with a smile. "Then word came, sent from Kavya. He told me he was elated at the news." With a quick glance at Sahin, she added, "He arrived four days ago."

Setting down her tea cup, Zehiya's appetite returned, she reached for more bread. Dipping it in butter, then honey, she chewed slowly, savoring its sweetness.

"Yet, that is not the great news," Kavya said, finger raised. With a slight bow to Asrila, she went on, "Of course the news of your father's return is good news, no doubt—yet there is more."

Asrila let out a little giggle.

Kavya looked at her, charmed. Slapping her hands on her knees, Kavya said, "Sahin and Asrila are to be married!"

Zehiya choked. The bread turned to stone in her throat.

"Sahin has asked Asrila's father to accept his offer of marriage to Asrila and he has accepted!" Kavya said with glee. "All the negotiations for dowry have been completed and the date is set."

With an open palm gesture toward Asrila, she declared, "I will soon have another daughter." To Zehiya, she added, "My dear, you will have a sister!"

Thumping Sahin on the back, exuberant, Jangbu said, "Congratulations, brother!" With a small bow of his head to Asrila, he said, "May you have many fine children, my Lady."

Zehiya struggled to hide her shock. Her cheeks burned as she pushed down the torrent rising within her. Forcing a smile, she looked from Sahin to Asrila.

"Congratulations. My... wish... is for... your happiness."

Reaching to take Asrila's hand in his, Sahin replied to Zehiya, "Thank you for your good wishes, little sister."

16

"**Y**ou are ugly, ugly, ugly!"
Zehiya stormed back and forth along the shoreline of the river below the high cliff walls which were on the eastern side of the Jiaohe plateau. Kimizi, tied to one of the peach trees of the riverside orchard, made a low grumble, uneasy at her behavior. Only he was present to witness her rage.

"Why am I cursed with this ugly red hair? With arms and legs that are too long? I am too tall. I clump around like an ox! I will never be as beautiful as Asrila." As her unbearable pain turned her hot anger to icy grief, she buried her hands in her hair.

Gripping tightly, her head bent, pulling at her locks, she moaned, "Little sister! Little sister! How could I have thought he would want an ugly, stupid girl like me!"

Releasing her grip, she let her hands fall to her sides as she gazed up at the stone cliffs towering above, tears rolling down her face.

Shaking her head slowly, she cried out, "Why?"

Pacing again, she searched for a way out of the pain, the searing knot in her chest, the sick feeling in her stomach—her shame.

Sliding her dagger from its scabbard, she grasped the sleeve of her green robe, baring the soft white skin of her arm. Chin trembling, she drew the knife slowly across her arm.

Through gritted teeth, she swore. "You are an ugly, stupid girl. Why would anyone ever want you?"

Bright blood oozed from the stinging path of the blade. Knees growing weak, she staggered to a sturdy tree, near Kimizi. Crumpling to the ground, pulling her knees to her chest, a calm settled over her. She surrendered to the overpowering pull to fall asleep.

She crouched low over Kimizi's neck as they thundered across an icy plain. Her heart was a cold, hard lump her chest. She needed to get away. Kicking his sides, she urged him on, faster and faster. Suddenly, Kimizi stumbled. Shocked, Zehiya leaned back and pulled up on his reins, trying desperately to help him regain his footing, yet it was of no use. Weightless, her body pitched from the saddle. Behind her, she heard the horrid thump and crack of Kimizi's fall. At any moment, she would feel the impact of her fall to the earth. Yet, it did not arrive.

Dumbfounded, she realized that she was in flight. Looking from right to left she saw that her arms had turned into wings. Soaring above the land, she searched for Kimizi. Far below, she saw a mass of red in the white frosty landscape. It must be he. Diving, she was by his side in an instant. His sides heaved as his eye swiveled to look at her.

With a gasp, she cried, "Kimizi!"

Her wings now turned back to hands, she slid them over his body. With horror she felt his broken and shattered bones under his soft coat.

"Oh no!" she cried. "No, not you. Kimizi, no! Please!"

Then she noticed blood oozing from many cuts on his legs.

"Who did this?!" she gasped.

"You did," a voice came, from the sky above.

Startled, Zehiya looked up. Shielding her eyes from the bright light. "Who are you?" she called out.

"Have you forgotten me?"

The light grew brighter. Squeezing her eyes shut, Zehiya pressed her hands to her face.

"I cannot see. It is too bright. Please, tell me, who are you?

What do you want?"

"What I want, is for you to remember me. Do you see how you have destroyed Kimizi?"

Looking back at Kimizi's shattered body, the blood from the cuts forming a steaming pool on the frozen earth, Zehiya cried, "How? How did I do this?"

With a flutter, the sparkling form landed on the ground in front of Zehiya.

"You!" Zehiya said, in surprise, shielding her eyes from the shimmering light of the Spirit Eagle.

Piercing gold eyes bore into Zehiya. "Have you so easily forgotten who you are?" Looking down at Kimizi, the Spirit Eagle said, accusing, "Do you so easily destroy your freedom?" Looking back into Zehiya's tearful eyes, she asked, softly, "Are you so filled with hatred for yourself?"

The words were hot searing daggers in Zehiya's heart. Wrapping her arms around herself, she bent over, gasping for breath, as she wept.

"I never wanted... It was my fault..." she sobbed, "I should have been home... to help fight them off...the men...maybe... if I had... my family would still be alive."

"My Zehiya," the Spirit Eagle said, soothingly, "you know that is not true. You would have been raped and sold into slavery or killed."

Hugging herself tightly, Zehiya wailed, "Why do I live and they all died?"

"There is no answer, yet you do live." the Spirit Eagle said. "You must cherish the gift of life you have been given."

"Come with me," the Spirit Eagle invited, spreading her wings.

Side by side, they soared above the plateau city of Jiaohe.

"There." The Spirit Eagle pointed with her beak.

In an instant, they were in the open and airy main room of Kavya's house, yet no one seemed to notice her and the Spirit Eagle. Sahin was bargaining with two men seated on cushions around the floor matt. Before them were piles of silver and gold coins. Asrila appeared, sliding in quietly and gently placing a cup of tea before Sahin and each man. He looked up for an instant, giving her an appreciative nod, then returned his attention to his guests. Without a word, Asrila padded silently out of room back into the kitchen

Zehiya's stomach clenched as the realization washed over her. *I could never be a wife like that for Sahin. Asrila is perfect for him. She would be happy as his wife and he would be happy with her. I could not live a life like that!*

The Spirit Eagle looked at her, nodding in approval. Spreading their wings the two took flight away from the house.

"So, you see?" the Spirit Eagle said, as they flew high above the earth.

Amazed, Zehiya said, "I thought I wanted only him, that his love would bring me peace and happiness, yet if I had ended up as his wife, I would have been terribly unhappy. Being a wife to him is not what I want at all!"

They soared over a rise clearing the tops of Juniper trees, a legion standing straight and tall covering the steep ravine of the Barskoon Gorge. The two glided above the river that tumbled toward Lake Issyk Kul which was far in the distance. Finally they arrived at the familiar cluster of yurts nestled on the hill top that swept down to the green pastures along the shore of the river where horses and sheep grazed contentedly

"Home? I am home?"

Below she could make out Feray standing by the large yurt, calling out.

Zehiya and the Spirit Eagle landed lightly near Feray.

"Little Fire," Feray called, "come away from the shore."

Zehiya turned to see a mass of fire red hair, like a halo, around the white face of a little girl flitting over the green grass. Zehiya was mesmerized by her.

"Feray! Look what I have found," the little girl sang, waving her little hand, in it a large hawk feather.

Feray knelt to catch the charging girl in her arms.

"Oh, Little Fire, how beautiful," she said, admiring the stripes of browns, blacks and copper of the feather. "It is a tail feather. It is good luck to find such a feather."

Zehiya knelt down, the moisture of the grass cool on her knees, not able to tear her eyes from the beautiful child with green eyes that sparkled with glee and fire for hair. She longed to pick up the little girl in her arms and to hold her.

"She is precious, is she not?" a familiar voice said from behind Zehiya.

Looking up, Zehiya was stunned to see Grandfather standing there, his form made of shimmering white light.

"Grandfather? Oh, how I have missed you," Zehiya said, as she rose to her feet.

Suddenly the girl screamed. Deep cuts appeared on her arms. Rivulets of blood dripped onto the ground as the little girl shrieked in pain and terror.

Shocked, Zehiya turned to Grandfather, who shook his head in sorrow.

Zehiya leapt toward the girl. "I will heal you, little one," she cried out, yet as hard as she tried to grasp a hold of her, the girl remained out of reach.

Frantically, Zehiya called out, "Help her! She will bleed to death!"

"Yes, she will surely die," Grandfather said.

"Grandfather, I can heal her." Zehiya turned to him, pleading. "Help me reach her."

"It is you who inflicted these wounds on that poor child. How can you heal her?"

Zehiya froze, bewildered. "I caused those wounds?"

"Yes, Granddaughter, you caused those wounds. Do you not remember?" With anger rising in his voice, he pointed at the terrified child. "How could you harm her? How could you do harm to yourself? How could you call yourself ugly?" Now with deep sorrow in his eyes, he said, "Do you not know how much we all loved you? How much I loved you?"

"I..." Zehiya stared at the beautiful little child, now fading away as a mirage. A deep sadness washed over her as realization dawned. "I do not know why..."

Sinking to her knees, a great weariness overtook her. "I did not realize what I was doing," she said, looking up into Grandfather's face.

Softening with compassion, he seated himself on the ground before her. Taking her hands into his, he said softly, "Granddaughter, you must promise me that from this day forward, you will care for yourself as you would your own child or as you would your best friend."

Looking at his hands of sparkling white light, she asked, "I am to become my best friend?"

He nodded solemnly.

"If you do not, who will? If you cannot love yourself and be kind to yourself and stand up for yourself, who will? If you cannot be a friend to yourself, how can you be a friend to anyone else?"

Feeling a great resistance to this idea, Zehiya shook her head. "I do not know... I do not know how to do this."

A sparkling finger under her chin raised her face up to look into his. "Learn how," he encouraged. "Promise me this?"

"Yes, Grandfather," she said, hesitantly. "I promise I will try... I will learn how."

Instantly, she was in flight again, the Spirit Eagle by her side.

"Have you forgotten the reason you took this journey?" the Spirit Eagle asked.

Looking down below them, she recognized the now familiar plateau of Jiaohe. They soared past the dwellings dug into the earth, and to Zehiya's surprise, there at the northern tip stood a temple, its carved wood and tiled roof swept up at the corners like wings reaching to the sky to greet them.

"A temple? Here?" Zehiya asked.

"Yes, a temple of Buddhist monks and nuns," the Spirit Eagle confirmed.

"Pema." Zehiya remembered.

17

Zehiya awoke with a shiver. The sun, low in the sky, cast the peach grove in shadow. The scent of earth and green leaves, warming to the day's sun, filled her nostrils. She looked over at Kimizi, who stood with a lowered head, snoozing. Slowly, she got her feet under her and rose. Seeking Kimizi, she hugged him fervently.

"You are alive! My dearest Kimizi. I will never let harm come to you."

Releasing him, she realized that her dagger was not in her belt. After a brief search of the area she found it lying on the ground. Reaching down to retrieve it, the sharp sting on her arm made her wince. She pulled her sleeve back to reveal the dried blood over the cut she had inflicted upon herself. The image of the little girl, screaming in pain came clearly and Zehiya felt ashamed.

"You stu...pi..." Zehiya stopped herself.

Looking at Kimizi, she said, "No! I am not! I am not stupid!" Her eyes grew hot. "I am not."

Pain clutched Zehiya's heart at the memory of the dream that now flooded back to her. "Grandfather."

Tears welled inside her as she remembered. "I will learn to become my own best friend, I promise you that I will!" she declared.

A delicious sense of freedom washed over her as she realized that she no longer wanted to be a wife to Sahin.

"Zehiya!" a voice called from the distance. "Zehiya?"

Kimizi raised his head and with nostrils flared, he whickered.

"Over here!" Zehiya answered, recognizing Jangbu's voice.

"Ah, there you are," Jangbu said, trotting up on Rinzen.

A look of concern clouded his face at the sight of her red swollen eyes and disheveled hair. "What is the matter? Are you alright?" Glancing around, he asked in alarm, "You have not been attacked?"

"No, no," she said, a chuckle rising in her voice at his concern. "I am fine, really. I just fell asleep and had a... a sad... dream."

Bewildered, she asked, "How did you find me here?"

Relief turning his expression into a smile, he replied, "Well, I found Kimizi's tracks and followed them. I have a gift for you."

"A gift?" she asked.

Swinging down from the saddle, he untied a long bundle from the cantle. Holding it out to her, he said, "For you."

She took the linen-wrapped bundle. It was longer than her arm and two hand-widths wide. She could feel that there was something sturdy inside, yet it was very light in weight.

Kneeling, she placed the bundle on the ground. Jangbu knelt down across from her, an expression of pure glee in anticipation lighting his face. Zehiya unfolded the wrapping and gasped.

"Oh! It is...so..." Looking into Jangbu's face, the right side, that of a handsome young man, with a huge grin. The left side, twisted, pulled down taut by the gnarled scar, making the whole incongruous and grotesque. She forced herself not to look away, but to meet his dark kind eyes.

"Beautiful," she said, as she ran her fingers over the leather quiver which was embossed with swirl designs. Lightly, she brushed her fingers over the stiff white fletching of the twelve arrows in the pocket at the front of the quiver. She then slid out the short recurve bow. She held it up and inspected its laminated parts. The underside was made of black horn, the middle a lighter wood and the backside was dried sinew. At each end were wrapped extensions, called siyahs, of carved bone.

"It is not as powerful as a man's bow," Jangbu explained. "You need a light bow to build the strength to pull back the string. It is short, which is best for shooting from your horse."

"Where did you find it?" Zehiya marveled, as she inspected the tight wrapping of the siyahs.

"I came across it in the market, at a bowyer. It had been the bow of a traveler's son. His boy grew stronger so needed a new heavier bow," Jangbu explained. "Here, let me show you how to pull the string over the end."

Taking the bow, Jangbu secured one end in the arch of his foot and bent the middle of the bow with the side of his knee, pulling the loop of the sinew string over the end of the siyah.

"There," he said, handing it to Zehiya as he stooped to free an arrow from the bow quiver.

Zehiya tested the string, trying to pull it. It took all her might to pull back only a hand's distance. She frowned.

"Do not worry, you will become strong quickly," he assured. "And here is this." He handed her a carved ring made of black horn with one side flat and elongated.

She took it, turning it over and over. Then she looked at him in question.

"It is a thumb ring," he explained.

Taking the ring from her, he slid it onto her thumb with the flattened side resting on the pad of her thumb. This act caused his throat to tighten and his heart to pound. Jangbu swallowed hard, stepping back away from her. Regaining his composure, he took the bow gently from her.

"You draw the string with the thumb ring," he explained, as he seated the nock of the arrow onto the string. With his thumb hooked around the string, he drew back to his nose, aiming at the tree. "You let the string slide from the ring. The ring protects your skin from the release of the bowstring."

The bow made a soft thwang and released the arrow to flight.

Twack! The arrow struck its mark, buried deep into the bark.

They ran to inspect the shot, both kneeling at the base of the tree. "It is not powerful enough to shoot far, but at medium range, you can do some damage," he said, with a chuckle.

Zehiya looked from the impaled tree to Jangbu.

"Why?" she asked.

"Why? Why what?" Jangbu asked, perplexed.

"Why did you give this to me?"

Jangbu looked steadily into her green eyes. "Because you need a weapon that can protect you from farther away than a sword. You are a good fighter, no doubt about that, but you are still weaker than most men. One day you will lose."

Raising the bow in the air, he said, "Learn to be proficient with this, and you will be much safer." Rising to his feet, he added, "Besides, I think you will enjoy the practice of this skill, knowing you as I do."

Taking the bow from Jangbu's outstretched hand, Zehiya returned to the quiver. Placing an arrow onto the string, she imitated Jangbu's example. Hooking the string with the jade ring, she pulled with all her might, aimed as best she could and released the arrow. She then watched it wobble in the air then fall, skittering along the ground and stopping before the tree.

She looked at Jangbu in exasperation. "I can't do this, I am no good at it."

"Practice. You need to practice," Jangbu encouraged, taking an arrow from the bow-quiver and holding it out to Zehiya. "Every archer has to practice and so must you."

Zehiya sighed as she secured the nocked arrow-end onto the string and pulled. She released, letting out her breath as the arrow followed the same path as the previous one.

Jangbu, walked to a tree and sat, leaning his back against the rough bark.

"You practiced to learn sword-play, did you not?" Jangbu inquired.

As she nocked her third arrow, she said, "Grandfather placed a sword in my hand when I was five springs old. It was play."

"Well then, you will experience great satisfaction as you improve your skills with the bow. We have a bit of time for your practice until dark," he said. "On the morrow, there will be time for more practice."

With a smile at his planning her practice schedule, she nocked another arrow. "Very well. I have always admired archers. It is well that I learn this skill." Releasing the arrow, she watched in mild admiration as the arrow did not wobble but flew in a smooth arc, landing at the base of the tree. She looked over at Jangbu.

"Better! See? You are already improving," he laughed.

Shaking her head slowly, a smile curving her lips, Zehiya nocked another arrow. As she pulled and released, she asked, "Is there a Buddhist monastery or temple here, in Jiaohe?"

"Why, yes, Kavya told me that there are both, at the northern end of the plateau. Why?"

"Will you take me there and show me where it is? I am looking for... someone. She may be there," Zehiya said, as she concentrated on her next shot.

"Yes, I will take you. We will go on the morrow," Jangbu replied, intrigued.

18

Zehiya gazed about in wonder as they rode into a maze of dome-topped structures made of stone, on their way to the Buddhist temple the next morning. At the tops of the domes were tall thin spires that rose into the clear blue sky.

"What are these?" Zehiya wondered aloud.

"They are stupas," Jangbu answered.

Zehiya reined in Kimizi and waited for Jangbu and Rinzen to come alongside.

"What are stupas?"

"They usually are reliquaries for the remains of an enlightened being; like a monk, nun or practitioner that has achieved enlightenment, or the Buddha Sakyamuni or Padmasambhava," Jangbu replied.

Zehiya regarded the structures around them. "There are so many, there must be hundreds of stupas here; can they all hold the remains of enlightened beings?"

"Stupas are built also as a symbol of the enlightened mind. Their presence create a sphere of peace and harmony. They also subdue negative forces, like war and famine. They bring health, prosperity and wellbeing to the community," he explained.

Jangbu considered the forest of structures. "It appears that they are built in groups of quincunxes. And the entire maze is made up of these groups," he continued, "my guess is that there are most likely one hundred and five stupas here."

Zehiya stared at him. "What is a quin...cu...?"

"Quincunx; five stupas per group," he replied. "The quincunx, the shape they are positioned in, is an ancient configuration that represents an ordered world." Pointing he explained, "The five points, five stupas, create a cross with the outside corners making a square. This shape symbolizes the ability of an individual to ascend from the four physical elements to the fifth one—enlightened mind. The number one hundred and five represents deliverance of the spirit from suffering."

Zehiya shook her head slowly, incredulous. "How do you know these things?"

Jangbu shrugged as he urged Rinzen onward. "I heard these principles explained once; I do not remember where."

Rounding the last stupa, they exited the maze to see the ornate roof and carved frontage of a temple in the distance.

"We will tie the horses there," Jangbu said, raising his chin to an area off to the side.

With the horses watered from a trough and tied on a rail for visitors, Zehiya arranged her sword on her belt. Jangbu considered her, with a mild look of amusement.

Zehiya glared at him. "What?" she asked, more as a challenge than a question. "I go nowhere without it," she answered, without waiting for his inquiry.

"As you wish," he said with a smile.

Zehiya admired the many stone Buddhas that greeted them from niches carved into the front of the temple as they mounted the stairs to the entrance. A Chinese monk, dressed in a simple, clean saffron robe, appeared in the doorway as they reached the top. Hands folded in salutation, he bowed low.

"Greetings, may I be of assistance?" he inquired.

"Good Monk, we are in search of someone. Perhaps you know of her?" Jangbu began.

The monk raised an eyebrow in question.

"Her name is Pema," Zehiya said.

The monk glanced at the sword at Zehiya's side, then took in her tall stature and hair, blazing red in the sunlight.

"A nun?" he asked.

Unsure, Zehiya considered. "A practitioner, of that I am sure," she said.

"I am most sorry," the monk said, shaking his head slowly. "There is no one of that name here."

"I know her!" came a craggy voice from inside the doorway.

Startled, the monk turned just as the stooped form of an old woman in a long undyed hemp robe, its color faded and its hem thread bare, with long gray hair woven into a braid down her back, shuffled from the doorway. She leaned heavily on a crooked cane that made a loud thunk with each step.

"Who is asking?" she croaked, her deeply-lined face glancing back and forth from Jangbu to Zehiya.

With a flicker of irritation, the monk said, "Sister Sonam, these people are in search of this Pema—I know not of this person."

With a dismissive wave of her gnarled hand, Sister Sonam scoffed, "And why would you, monk? Do you know of all who visit this place?"

Taking a visibly slow deep breath, the monk bowed stiffly to Jangbu. "Then, I leave you in the care of Sister Sonam."

With twinkle in her eye, the old nun chuckled as she watched the retreating form of the monk.

Then turning to Zehiya and Jangbu, with a wink, she whispered, conspiratorially, "I am teaching him patience." Placing her hands one atop the other on the top of her cane, she straightened as much as her bent back would allow.

"So you are looking for my friend, Pema?"

"Is she here?!" Zehiya asked, hopefully.

Sister Sonam looked Zehiya up and down. "She was here but has departed two days ago. What is your name, girl?"

"Two days?" Zehiya groaned, her heart sinking.

"This is Zehiya," Jangbu said, with a gesture. "My name is Jangbu."

Sister Sonam regarded him, then she turned, calling over her shoulder as she clunked away, "Come with me; we will have tea and you can tell me why you are looking for Pema."

Zehiya and Jangbu followed the old woman into the temple. The aroma of sandalwood and frankincense hung thick in the smoky interior. Reverently, they shuffled past the great altar with hundreds of butter-lamps flickering below a great golden Buddha that rose to the ceiling. Several monks sat on cushions, their faces serene in deep contemplation, unconcerned by the passage of these strangers. Exiting a small doorway behind the altar, they followed Sister Sonam through a courtyard. The stench of rotten fruit and burnt grain hung in the air as they passed smaller buildings. They arrived at an old wooden door. Sister Sonam pushed it open with her cane, releasing a cloud of thick sandalwood and patchouli incense smoke that wafted out into the light. She ducked inside.

"Seat yourselves," Sister Sonam directed, as she settled herself on a short bench before a stone fire-pit at a side wall of the small dwelling. A shaft of sunlight filtered through the smoke hole in the roof above it casting the interior in a soft glow. Hot coals burst into flame as Sister Sonam placed chips of dung on them.

As she poured black tea from the pot she took from the rack placed above the hot coals into a silver cup, Sister Sonam asked, "Do you carry a cup with you, as we Tibetans do?"

To Zehiya's surprise, Jangbu produced a silver cup from the fold of his red felt Zhuba-style robe.

"Ah," Sister Sonam said, "I thought you were a lad from the Land of Snows. From which part of Tibet is your family?"

"Amdo," Jangbu said, placing his cup into the old woman's outstretched boney fingers.

Sister Sonam regarded him thoughtfully. "I have heard of a man from Amdo, with a scar. Are you that same man?"

Jangbu shrugged. "I am sure there are many men from Amdo with a scar."

"Indeed, yet this man is renowned," Sister Sonam replied, looking inquisitively into his eyes as she handed him his cup filled with dark green tea. "Not butter-tea, I am afraid it is too hot a climate here." With a nod to a niche in the stone wall, she added, "There, you will find a cup for your friend with fire for hair."

Seating herself on a worn cushion, Zehiya leaned forward anxiously. Her medallion, swinging out from the fold of her robe, caught the flicker of firelight.

"You know Pema? She had been meditating in a cave in the gorge of Barskoon. Is your friend this same Pema I am seeking?" Zehiya asked.

Sister Sonam poured tea into Zehiya's cup. Handing it to the girl, she gazed for a moment at the medallion as it glittered, then looked into Zehya's deep green eyes.

"Yes, the same, however she did not mention a girl such as you. How do you know of her and why do you seek her?"

Absently taking the cup, Zehiya told the story of her finding Pema in the mountains while lost, then searching for her and finding Pema had gone. Sister Sonam sipped the green woody tea as she listened attentively to the tale.

"The monk in the caves outside Kucha said she has most likely gone to Dunhaung. Has she gone to Dunhaung?" Zehiya asked, hopefully.

Nodding slowly, Sister Sonam said, "The monk is correct. My friend Pema is indeed now headed for Dunhuang."

Zehiya slumped, deflated. "I missed her. She was here all the time I was... was..."

"Distracted?" the nun asked, eyes raised.

Zehiya nodded slowly, dispirited, as she gazed into her cup, the tea now grown cold. "I must go to Dunhuang then," she declared.

"It is far. And dangerous. You must join a large caravan," the nun warned. Then with a nod to Zehiya's medallion, she asked, "May I see it?"

Zehiya looked down at the golden glitter, then pulled the leather thong over her head, saying, "My grandfather gave this to me. He said it belongs to an ancient people. The women were warriors."

Taking the heavy gold piece, Sister Sonam turned it slowly in her hands, inspecting the carved form. "My people, the Tibetans, call this creature a Garuda. Your ancestors made this medallion. It is of the ancient tribe known as the Scythians from the Altai Mountains far to the north of Turpan." Looking Zehiya up and down, she said, "Your ancestors—tall, skin like milk, hair like fire. The women were renowned warriors; feared by all.

"Pema told me this as well," Zehiya said. "Yet, that was in ancient times. What good to me is the knowledge of it?"

"You have that warrior blood coursing through you. Your grandfather wanted you to know of it—that you are a strong woman, from an ancient line of formidable women." She handed back the medallion. "He knew you would need this knowledge of your heritage. Yet, Zehiya is an Arabic name, is it not?" Sister Sonam inquired. "How did you receive this name?"

"My father had a good friend who was a merchant from Arab lands. He called him his brother. When I was born, my father gave the honor of naming his first born to his friend. This is a custom of our people," Zehiya explained. "My name means 'radiant person'."

Sister Sonam nodded. "And so you will grow to be." Glancing at Jangbu, she continued, "I am sure of it."

19

Jangbu kept his distance as he watched Zehiya striding ahead of him. He could feel the hot waves of anger radiating from her.

"Two days! She was here—right here, and I missed her!" she hissed in a whisper to herself, wanting to scream her rage, yet wanting no one to hear.

"You, you..." she clenched her fists, "Stup... stu..."

The image of Grandfather and the Spirit Eagle came into her mind. She gritted her teeth. "No! I am not." Her anger cooled as she began to think. "I... I have... have... been delayed on my quest. Now, I realize, my attraction was... was..."

She trailed off, searching for a word other than stupid.

"Mistaken," she whispered, triumphantly. "As my best friend, I will not call myself bad names," she declared. The clenching of her heart eased. She slowed her pace, taking in a long, deep breath and letting it out slowly. Calm descended over her.

Feeling the change in her demeanor, Jangbu quickened his pace, striding up alongside her.

"So, you have a quest, I see," he said, casually.

Arriving at their tethered horses, she wrapped her arms around Kimizi, burying her face in his mane, breathing in his horsey scent. It calmed her more and gave her strength. She turned to Jangbu.

"Yes, I missed my friend because I was... was... occupied with other matters." she said. "Now I must go to Dunhaung. Is it far to

109

Dunhaung?"

Jangbu snorted. "Is it far? Yes, it is far, very far! It is on the doorstep of China."

"Well, I must go," she said, determined.

"You cannot travel there alone!" Jangbu exclaimed. "What about Kavya? She would be heartbroken to have you leave. And Sahin's wedding? It would be disrespectful to not attend his wedding."

"I am going to practice my archery now," she said, swinging up into Kimizi's saddle. "Then I am going to take Kartal hunting. I will think on this matter, yet I am going."

Jangbu shook his head as he alighted on Rinzen's saddle.

"I will come help you with your bow practice," he said. "You will need to improve quickly if we are to survive the journey."

Zehiya stared at him. "We?"

"Yes, we!" he retorted. "Do you think I will let you travel in a caravan all that way alone?"

2O

Hami

Kartal was just a dark speck in the blue sky as shades of dusk, in pinks and lavender, began to appear over the hills to the west. He cocked his wings back and fell like a javelin. In the stillness only the wind fluting over his plummeting body could be heard. With the sound like the clashing of Ibex horns, Kartal hit his prey. With an ecstatic whoop, Zehiya and Jangbu charged down the rise to reward him for his capture of the hare.

Zehiya sprang off Kimizi and ran to Kartal. Stooping before the raptor, she proffered a piece of dried meat, drawn from her falconry pouch. Kartal took it greedily and surrendered his catch.

Holding the hare up, inspecting its size, Zehiya inquired, "Is it much farther to your friend's home?"

Sitting atop Rinzen, Jangbu looked to the faraway patch of green grass, inspecting his six horses, who were grazing contentedly. He had sold the four horses that had belonged to the bandits as they were of common stock; the silver they brought was of more value.

"His estate is on the eastern edge of Hami. It is not much farther now." Casting his gaze to the deepening of lavender hues to reds, he considered. "I think it would be best if we camped here, allow the horses to eat all night long, then we will arrive at his home midday on the morrow. Better that we not arrive in the dark of night."

"Very well, we will feast this night," she agreed, holding up the hare.

Zehiya sat contemplating the patterns of the stars; how the pattern her life had changed. She once had a family. She was destined to lead a life very much like Feray; living in a yurt homestead, raising children and breeding the great horses she loved beside the river that flowed to the great lake Issyk Kul.

A pop from the crackling fire brought her out of her reverie. She followed its smoke drawn away on a soft breeze. *Like my life,* she thought, *drawn away on a wind of events.* She shook herself. *I was to be given to a man as a wife, I know not what my life would have been.*

Her attention was drawn to a whicker from Jangbu's small herd of ten horses. She listened intently, then relaxed back to her musings when all fell quiet again. *Jangbu's horses are beautiful,* she thought, *he calls them Sogdian horses.* She wondered at the offspring her family's horses and these would produce. Then with a stabbing pain in her heart she remembered; her family's horses are all gone, stolen.

She looked at the mound that was Jangbu sleeping next to their saddles and bags. He was as still as a stone, yet now and then she would hear a murmur rise from his deep sleep.

Memories of her last days in Turpan came flooding in, as they often did during these many days on the road, in moments when she was idle.

Asrila was beautiful in her sparkling wedding gown, silver discs dangling from her head scarf. She was a goddess and Sahin was handsome and elegant in white robes.

They were made for each other, she thought.

Then she smiled at the memory of what had occurred after the Nestorian Christian wedding ceremony. She was standing in the courtyard when Sahin had wandered out to get some air. Seeing her, he sauntered over.

"Congratulations on your marriage. Asrila is a wonderful girl," Zehiya said, as they stood side by side gazing up at the stars, visible from the small courtyard. She could smell his scent mingled with sandalwood and rice wine.

"Sister, no longer little, you have grown," he said, with admiration. Then he turned to her. She looked at his glowing form, able to see his handsome face in the starlight. His voice was deep yet smooth.

"Zehiya, never think you are not a beautiful girl, now becoming a woman. You must value yourself. It would be tragic for you to waste your life married to the wrong man." With slight bow, he concluded, "Be sure the man you marry is worthy of you."

Then he left her.

Tears welled in her eyes at the memory. She grimaced at the thought of all the pain she put herself through thinking that Sahin thought her to be ugly, yet, in fact, the opposite was true.

"Stu...pi..." she whispered, and stopped herself. With a sigh, she amended, "Mistaken."

She picked up a small stone and tossed it into the fire, watching the sparks scatter. She wrapped her robe tighter around her and pulled down her fox-fur hat against the chill of the night.

Then she shuddered at the memory of Kavya.

"You are going away?" she had asked, incredulous. "Why? Where?"

"To Dunhaung. I must find my friend, my teacher, Pema," Zehiya had explained.

"Pema? Your Buddhist teacher? Why, there are many teachers right here," she had said, with a wave of her hand toward the north. "A great temple right here!"

"I must find Pema," Zehiya insisted. "She is my teacher, I must find her."

Tears welled in Kavya's eyes. "It is a dangerous journey."

"Jangbu is going with me," Zehiya assured.

Kavya looked Zehiya up and down. "Jangbu? Do you love him? Are you going to marry him?"

Shocked, Zehiya said, "Love him? No, he is a friend and nothing more."

Kavya took Zehiya's hands in hers. "I had hoped you would stay here as my adopted daughter and learn the trade."

Squeezing Kavya's hands, Zehiya said, "I would have no greater honor than to be your daughter. You have been so kind to me. Please know, dear Kavya, that I have come to love you, yet, I must go."

Holding tightly to Zehiya's strong hands, Kavya nodded, tears rolling down her face. "Then promise me you will return to visit me. Know that you have a home here, with me, with us, always," she said.

Nodding emphatically, Zehiya swore, "I will return, I promise!"

Burying her head in her knees now, alone by the fire under cold stars, Zehiya wept. So many leavings, so many losses.

"You must focus on what you have," Jangbu said.

Zehiya's head shot up to see Jangbu sitting next to her. She could make out his profile in the starlight.

Wiping her eyes, she asked, "Do you ever weep for the loss of your friend?"

Picking up a stone, he tossed it into the fire. A small flame shot up, the stone breaking away a piece of dung, exposing it to the cold night air. "Yes, I did weep. His death was a shock and caused deep sadness, yet I strive to stay in the present moment." Turning his attention to look at her, he continued, "When my thoughts carry me away to the past or into an imagined future, I shake myself, and return to the present, because the present is where my life is."

The flame disappeared, burned away to only wisps of smoke carried off by the wind. Gesturing to the fire, he said, "Our lives are short, I do not wish to live my life in dreaming of a past, gone, and wondering of a future to come. My life is in this present moment, it is here I strive to remain. And, yes, grieving is part of that, yet I strive to keep grief from overwhelming me, taking me away from what exists in the present moment."

Wiping her tears, she said, "You sound like Pema."

"It is the basic teaching of the Buddha," Jangbu said.

"This staying in the present is difficult because my mind constantly wanders," Zehiya complained.

"Ah, yes, it does indeed," Jangbu said, "however you have noticed it does so. Do you realize that that is the first step on the path, to see that this is so?"

"How do I keep it from wandering? How do I stop it?" Zehiya asked.

"You don't. You cannot." Jangbu chuckled. "The practice is to simply observe how your mind functions and be aware. You must train in this as you train in your bowshot or sword—a little every day."

"Train?" Zehiya asked.

"Meditation," Jangbu answered.

"Oh, of course. This is what Pema taught me." Zehiya sighed in frustration. "Look, how I have already forgotten."

"At the beginning we all forget. This is normal. Simply begin again and again," Jangbu said. "Would you like to meditate now?"

Zehiya straightened, crossing her legs. "Yes, I would."

Settling himself, he asked, "Do you remember how?"

"Follow my breath? Ignore thoughts?" she asked.

He nodded, slowly. "That is a good place to begin."

The night settled over them as they sat silent and still.

21

Sunlight illuminated the sea of green broad leaves as Zehiya, Jangbu and Ozturk, a Uighur Turk, rode between the rows of the melon field.

"The crop looks good," Jangbu said to his friend. "This is a new field?"

"Indeed," Ozturk said.

The embroidered designs on his waist jacket were bright in the sun. Under this, he wore a loose-fitting white cotton shirt. On his wide leather belt he carried a dagger in a decoratively carved sheath.

He glanced at Zehiya, mounted on Kimizi, Kartal perched on the pommel, her bow strapped within easy reach behind the cantle, her sword and dagger at her side, her hair afire, illuminated by the bright sun. He then turned his attention to Jangbu, with a wave toward the mountains, piled one upon the other rising high in the distance, their snowy peaks glistening. He continued, "We built a new system, diverting more water from the mountain runoff to expand into these new fields."

Under his white cotton turban, his dark eyes squinted into the distance as he fingered his long black mustache. Then, burying his fingers into his beard, scratching his chin, he considered a barren area farther to the south of the green expanse.

With a smile stretching his leathered face, he said, "We will expand over there next season."

Urging his white horse onward with his strong legs, dressed in cotton salwar pants that ballooned out from high, supple-leather boots, he called over his shoulder, "Come, let us return to the house for the midday meal, you must be hungry."

The courtyard of Ozturk's estate was all a bustle with workers coming and going to the fields. Zehiya watched as two men led horses to a corral, tying them to the railing as a rider inside the ring schooled a young horse.

"How does he come along?" Ozturk called to the trainer, trotting up to the corral.

With a wave the man called back, "He is a fast learner—a good horse."

To the men watching at the railing, he asked, "Which pasture have you placed my friend's horses?"

"They are in the eastern pasture, Master."

With a nod, Ozturk turned to Jangbu and smiled, then ordered, "Make sure they are looked after well. When my friend returns from his journey, I want them fat and ready for travel." Dismounting, he said, "Take our horses and water them."

One man took his reins. Another ran to take Rinzen from Jangbu. He stared agape at Zehiya as Kartal wrapped his strong talons onto her gauntlet and she lowered him from his perch.

Handing Kimizi's reins to the man, she asked, "Can you give him a handful of grain? He has been on the road long."

"Yes, Mistress," he said with a bow.

"Papa!" Two small boys ran from the tall, arched doorway of the house, flinging their arms around Ozturk's legs. Their dark brown eyes danced as they shrieked and giggled in glee when he walked on, unperturbed, with them attached, one to a leg, bare feet clinging atop each boot.

Jangbu and Zehiya shared a smile as they followed their host into the large, airy house. Carpets from Persia and China softened the cool stone floors. The aromas of roasting meat, baked flat bread and spices mingled on the cool breeze, softly blowing through the open-shuttered windows. Cushions were placed around a mat on the floor, upon which was a feast, of bread, honey, dates and melon.

From the next room, a small, handsome woman with several black braids tied to the back of her head, spilling down to the middle of her back, appeared carrying a platter of roasted meat. Behind her, a young girl, with willowy, long limbs and huge dark eyes cast to the floor demurely, appeared. She cradled a pot of tea.

"Welcome," the woman said, cheerfully, her light skin moist with perspiration.

Zehiya stood hesitantly, with Kartal perched on her gauntlet, his hooded head swiveling back and forth.

"There," Ozturk said, pointing to a trunk at the side wall.

The boys followed, watching in rapt attention as she urged Kartal to leave her arm and sit on the wooden top.

"You have a falcon?" the boys questioned. "But you are a girl; girls do not have falcons."

"Baran, Doruk, sit!" Ozturk ordered. "This is no way to treat a guest in our home."

The two boys slunk sheepishly to their seats.

Ozturk's wife bowed to Zehiya. "I am Afet and this is our daughter, Talya."

With a slight turn and bow to Jangbu, she said, "It is so good to see you again, Master Jangbu. Please sit and make yourselves comfortable." Producing a small fan made of thin slats of wood, she fanned her face, adding, "The day is hot, have you traveled far?"

Seating himself, Jangbu answered, "Afet, it brings me joy to see you looking so well. Yes, we have just arrived from Turpan."

Motioning Talya to serve tea, Afet seated herself.

"Please eat, you must be very hungry," she invited, with a gesture toward the feast.

"My good friend, Jangbu, is leaving his latest purchase of horses with us for a time," Ozturk explained to Afet, as he reached for a morsel of roasted meat, wrapping it in a piece of flat bread.

"Why?" Afet asked, perplexed, her cup of tea held aloft.

"We," Jangbu said, gesturing to Zehiya, "must go to Dunhuang to find Zehiya's friend. It would be faster if we were not encumbered by the horses. As well, I wish them to be safe. We will join a caravan that is going east."

Chewing slowly in thought, Ozturk swallowed, then said, "You have missed the caravan going east. They left two days ago."

"We will join the next one, there should be another in a day or two." Jangbu said.

Shaking his head, Ozturk said, "No, maybe in a fortnight or maybe a moon."

"So long? Why?" Jangbu asked, incredulous. "There are many caravans going east, they leave every few days."

"Not anymore," Osturk said. "The uprisings in China have grown larger. The peasants have had enough of Tang rule. Not much is coming out of China for trade now. Not much is going there either."

Jangbu considered, "We can catch the one that left two days ago if we leave on the morrow, or the day after."

Ravenously devouring a slice of melon, Zehiya swallowed, then declared, "The day after."

All turned toward her with surprised looks.

"Kimizi is tired, he needs rest," she explained, reaching for the platter of meat. Afet stared in amusement as Zehiya voraciously wrapped a piece in bread.

To Zehiya, Afet said, "You must be tired as well."

Nodding, she said, through bites, "It would be good to rest for a day or two."

The group fell into concentrated silence as they continued to eat.

When everyone was sitting back full and content, Afet rose.

"Zehiya, come with me now and I will show you to your room," she said.

Looking at Jangbu, Zehiya hesitated. At his slight nod, she rose from her cushion. Retrieving Kartal, she followed Afet out of the room.

"Where did you find her?" Ozturk asked, as soon as the women were out of earshot.

With a chuckle, Jangbu finished his tea. "Outside of Kucha, in a battle for her life against four bandits."

With raised eyebrows, Ozturk asked, "You saved her?"

"Well, she was holding her own fairly well, yet she did need assistance," Jangbu explained.

"And her people?" Ozturk asked.

"All dead," Jangbu said.

Looking at the empty doorway through which the women had exited, Ozturk said, "Sad."

Jangbu nodded solemnly.

"A good thing she is so beautiful," Ozturk said, ruefully.

With a laugh, Jangbu punched Ozturk's shoulder.

Reeling back on his cushion, Ozturk howled in glee, slapping his knee. "A rare one, a warrior," he chortled.

Then, leaning forward, becoming serious, he said, "Now my friend, take heed. As you are well aware, the roads to the south are thick with bandits. Yet, reports are coming in of a new danger. Khitan warriors have been sighted in the Gansu."

"The Khitan? Who? Yelu Khan?" Jangbu asked. "Why?"

"Word has come that the Prince of Kashgar, Satuq, has murdered his father the King. He had converted in secret to the Mohammedan religion against his father's will," Ozturk explained.

Jangbu sat stunned. "He killed his father for the throne?"

Nodding his head, Ozturk said, "For the throne and he now has an army of Mohammedans to force all in Kashgar to convert to their faith. There is word of many killings. So Yelu and his army of Khitan warriors are heading there to stop the Prince who is now the King."

Jangbu scratched his scar absently, deep in thought.

"Yelu wishes to stop the Mohammedan army now, so they will not continue to sweep through the trade route towns forcing all to convert to Islam," Jangbu surmised. "The Prince and his Mohammedans will then have taken control of the trade route and will grow rich on the taxes, thus increasing their power."

"Yelu will be collecting conscripts along the way to swell their ranks," Ozturk warned.

Sitting back, growing pale, Jangbu said, "And we are heading right in their path." Sitting straighter, Jangbu asked, "The caravan. Are they attacking caravans for supplies?"

Shaking his head slowly, Ozturk thought for a moment, then said, "No, so far I have heard of none attacked. Their sights are on Kashgar."

Brightening, Jangbu said, "If we can reach the caravan, we should be safe."

"Yet, if you do not..." Ozturk trailed off. Raising a finger, he amended, "They will need supplies for their army, it is possible he would raid any caravan for what his army needed, replacing their tired camels as well."

Jangbu slumped, shaking his head. "If we find ourselves in the path of Yelu's army or a forward scouting party, they will press me to their service as a conscript and..." His stomach clenched, he looked into Ozturk's eyes. "They will press Zehiya into their service as well."

Nodding somberly, Ozturk said, "Take my small pack camel, she can carry two water bladders over the sands; you will need these. She is old, yet is able to cover the miles. If you can stay out of the way of any of Yelu's scouts or his army and make it on your own to Anxi, then you will be on the road to Dunhaung and you will have succeeded."

Slapping Jangbu on the back, he brightened. "And you will, my friend. I am sure of it. You have good karma. Come, let us see to your Sogdian horses. You can tell me all about their fine breeding."

Afet gestured for Zehiya to enter the small room. Sunlight filtered in through the window brightening the space. Large cushions for sleeping lay against the wall, atop a worn carpet that covered the stone floor. A small low table was set against the opposite wall.

"You may rest your falcon here," she said indicating the window sill. "He will not fly away, if placed here? I thought he may like the fresh air."

"This will serve for now," Zehiya said. "I will bring my saddle in later for him to rest on his perch."

"He is beautiful," Afet said, marveling at the bird. Reaching her hand out, hesitant, she asked, "May I touch him?"

"Why, yes, if you would like," Zehiya said.

Gently stroking the soft breast, Afet said, in wonder, "The feathers are so soft." Then, she cooed, "You are a beautiful one."

Looking up at Zehiya, she asked, "Will you take his hood off now?"

Shaking her head Zehiya said, "Not until we hunt."

Afet looked at Zehiya in surprise. "He wears the hood all the remainder of the time?"

Nodding, Zehiya explained, "He is trained to it, since he was a baby. I will take him hunting today."

The sound of the horses' whinnies and men calling to one another from the corrals drifted into the room. The familiar sounds carried Zehiya back in time: images of her family's horses, running, whinnying in the paddocks—her father's gruff voice calling to her brother.

Her heart clenched. The sword swung. Her father's head rolled to the ground, blood spurted from his headless neck as his body toppled down like a felled tree, thumping onto the earth.

She gasped at the vivid memory. Biting her fist hard to hold back the pain and terror, she staggered. Reaching out to the wall for support, she closed her eyes tight. Her brother, slumped in a pool of his blood. She gulped back the flood of tears surging up. The torn and bloodied body of her step-mother, Feray.

She could hold on no longer. "No!" she cried, slumping onto the cushions.

Shocked, Afet stepped back and asked, "Dear, what is wrong?"

Her head buried in her hands, Zehiya gritted her teeth, trying to stop the images parading through her mind. "No, no, no..." Looking up at Afet, she sobbed, "I am sorry to display this in your home. I am so sorry. I cannot bear the pain." She convulsed, drawing her knees up to her chest, covering her face with her hands she sobbed, "My family is gone. They are all..." she gulped, "murdered."

Sinking down next to the girl, Afet put her arm around Zehiya's shoulders, pulling her close. Zehiya could smell the aromas of spices and sweat. Her warm soft body reminded her of Feray and the painful realization that she would never see her stepmother again seared through her.

"They are all dead; I will never see them again," she wailed.

"You poor dear," Afet whispered, soothingly, holding Zehiya tightly and rocking her. "It is alright, I am not offended. You need to cry. You cannot hold in pain like this."

Zehiya wiped her face as the pain subsided. Feeling the girl calming, Afet released her. "Better now?" she asked.

Nodding, Zehiya said, "Yes." Gulping in long deep breaths, she let them out slowly. "Yes, I am better now." Rising to her feet, she said, "It just came over me."

Nodding sagely, Afet said, "Painful memories will arise like that." Looking Zehiya up and down, she offered, "Would you like a bath? I can have your clothes washed as well."

Zehiya felt her knees go weak. "Oh, yes, that would be wonderful."

With a nod, Afet asked, "Will your falcon be well while you are gone?"

Lifting him from the window and placing him on the low table, Zehiya said, "He will be safer here. I will get my saddle for him—then a bath?"

"Come then, I will show you the bath-house," Afet said over her shoulder as she turned away.

"You rest here and I will return, my friend," Zehiya whispered to Kartal. Then a new, sharp, pain arose in her. Her heart clenched at the memory of Neylan, her beautiful baby eagle. Gone. Taken from her. She took in a long deep breath and turned away from the sorrow to follow Afet.

Zehiya stopped at the doorway. Turning, she stared at Kartal. Stepping back into the room she gazed out the window watching the men and horses; the clop of hooves and the men's voices and laughter. The sky was a clear blue. The sweet fragrance of jasmine wafted in on the hot breeze. She considered all of this.

Dropping down on one knee before Kartal, stroking his soft breast, she said, softly, "I have you, my friend. And I have Kimizi. I have Pema. I have..." she thought for a moment, contemplating. "I have Jangbu and the Spirit Eagle, and I have Grandfather."

She stood. Taking in a breath of air, feeling it travel down to her belly, she sighed, "I have life; I have this moment."

She looked down at Kartal once more and then she turned and strode out.

22

"I am no good!" Zehiya cursed. "I cannot hit anything with consistency!"

Storming to the target, she stooped and picked up arrows that had missed, scattered on the ground.

"You must be patient and just keep practicing," Jangbu said, observing from a safe distance with his arms folded, like a warrior's shield, across his chest.

Zehiya spun around, arrows clenched in her fist. Stomping back to the shooting line, she muttered, through gritted teeth, "Patience—be patient."

"You should shoot one hundred arrows a day," Jangbu added.

She glared at him. Turning back to the target, she nocked an arrow and yanked on the string, releasing. The arrow careened wide of the target. Her anger boiled watching the errant shaft. Nocking another, she began her angry pull on the bow.

"Slow down," Jangbu said, "slow down and draw smoothly. Slow and smooth, smooth and accurate."

Zehiya let out a breath, trying to shake the anger that had its claws buried deep.

"Wait!" Jangbu ordered.

Zehiya lowered her bow, her jaw clenched. "What?"

"Come with me!" Jangbu ordered.

With a huff, Zehiya followed him to a nearby tree.

"Sit," he ordered, as he sat himself down and leaned against the trunk of an apple tree in Ozturk's orchard.

Zehiya settled herself on the ground with her legs crossed.

"Let us breathe for a bit and settle," he said.

Zehiya let out a long breath, then breathed in slowly. Closing her eyes, she let out her breath, more slowly, then breathed in, feeling the warm air travel down, filling her lungs. The claw loosened its grip. Her muscles relaxed. Relief filled her as her tension eased. She took in another breath and listened as a bird chirped and then another. She heard the trill of several more. The leaves in the trees rustled in the breeze, cool on her skin. The claw slid away. She could smell the aromas of earth and the woody scents from the tree.

"It is common to judge one's performance when practicing to improve one's skill at any endeavor," Jangbu began. "We characterize every experience we have and by doing so, we miss what is really happening—what our experience really is."

Zehiya opened her eyes and asked, "What do you mean—'characterize'?"

"We name the experience. Yet the name is simply an idea; our idea. If you hit the target it is 'good,'" Jangbu said. "If you miss, it is 'bad.' If you have a particular experience while meditating, it is 'peaceful,' or 'distracted.' We must investigate WHO is creating these ideas."

Zehiya shook her head, "If I hit the target, it IS good; if I miss, it IS bad and it is I who knows these things—what is the folly in this?"

"All of these ideas are characterizations that stop your experience, your true experience," Jangbu explained.

"Well if I miss the target, my true experience is I am a poor shot and I need to improve," Zehiya retorted, her irritation rising.

Jangbu leaned forward. "If you miss the target, yes, you realize that you have missed it, it is a miss and you are striving for a hit. To berate yourself by the added judgement of the result, the characterization, brings added meaning; it bogs you down and clutters your mind. But, these are simply ideas; your ideas. But who is this YOU—or I? Come," Jangbu said, rising and striding toward the shooting line.

Zehiya followed.

"String an arrow and stand in your shooting stance," Jangbu said.

Zehiya stood her left side toward the target, with her feet apart. She raised the bow in her left hand, her right thumb and two fingers around the arrow's nock securely on the string.

"Release your breath and then breathe in slowly and relax," Jangbu said, "and again, relax. Raise the bow and aim at the target drawing back smoothly. When you are ready, release the arrow by letting the string slide from your thumb ring," he instructed.

Zehiya drew the string and released an arrow, which landed just wide of the target.

"Now relax your mind. Do not be concerned about what just happened, and loose another, aiming again for the target."

Ignoring her thoughts berating her for the unsuccessful shot, she felt the cool breeze on her face. As she slowly drew her bow again, she became aware of the bunching of her muscles, the sensation made her feel strong and confident. The string slid from her thumb ring. She watched as the arrow hit the target just wide of the center.

"Now," Jangbu said, "do not get carried away with thoughts of this result just loose another arrow while striving for your goal."

Zehiya took in a long breath and let the next arrow fly; it hit closer to the center mark.

"Now, you stay here and continue your practice," Jangbu said.

"Stay?" Zehiya asked.

"I must help Ozturk until the sun sets. Do not regress into characterization. Yet if you do, just ignore the thoughts and begin again; be patient with yourself," Jangbu said.

Striding away, he stopped suddenly and then returned to Zehiya.

"There is another thing," he said. "Patience means accepting what is; not the same as enduring what is. Usually when we say 'be patient' it is understood to mean we try to calm down and endure. This is not what I mean by patience—I mean embrace, accept, what is happening." Jangbu thought for a moment, then continued, "I like to think of it as the gesture of inviting one in for a cup of tea. You are in acceptance of what is. Though it is not acceptance as in approval of what is. It is a subtle but important distinction. This attitude allows space to work with what is happening. Do you understand?" he asked.

Zehiya stared at him blankly, "I...I will think on it," she said, finally.

"I will see you at supper," Jangbu called over his shoulder as he strode off toward the house.

Zehiya watched as Jangbu's form disappeared among the trees.

Returning her attention to the target, she drew her bow, letting the arrow fly. It went wide, missing the target. As the judgements on her performance arose, she ignored them. Loading another arrow she focused on the center of target and with a smooth intake of breath she drew the bowstring to her cheek, then on a slow exhalation she let it slide off the smooth surface of her thumb ring. This arrow hit almost dead center. Resisting the urge to jump and cheer, she drew again, feeling the ground under her feet. She felt a sense of elation by the scent of earth and trees filling her with each breath. Lowering her bow, she marveled at the sensations.

"I have been missing what is all around me by being lost in my thoughts," she said aloud.

Then she drew her bow again, releasing the arrow to flight.

23

The hillside shone in the full moonlight. It looked as if a million stars had fallen to the ground. Zehiya stared transfixed at the display of glittering light, it made her feel weightless and disoriented. She held onto the pommel of the saddle to steady herself. Kimizi and Rinzen's plodding hooves over the barren ground was the only sound in the night. Kartal slept soundly on his saddle perch, head swiveled back nestled in the soft feathers on his back.

"It is as if we have entered another world," she said, breaking the silence that had fallen over them for the past several hours.

"Indeed," Jangbu said.

He held the rope that was leading the pack camel behind him in his hand loosely. "Though I have been through this area many times, it never ceases to amaze me."

"What is it?" Zehiya asked.

"Crystals," Jangbu said. "The entire hillside is made of small clear crystal stones."

Zehiya pulled her green robe more tightly around her and cinched her belt. "Getting colder," she said. "The nights are much colder here in this flat rocky desert than on the grassy steppe we traversed after Hami."

"Yes and it will be dawn soon. It gets colder closer to the dawn and then it will become hot again," Jangbu replied.

"Where will we spend the day?" Zehiya asked.

"There are mountains a league from this crystal pass. In fact, they are not really mountains, like in Tibet, they are more like high hills. A maze of hills. When you come upon them from this flat desert, they appear as mountains."

"Is there water there?" she asked.

"Yes, I know of a spring in one of the canyons between the hills."

Reaching beyond Kartal, she gently patted Kimizi's neck. "I bet you wish we were back in that sea of grass, my friend. Do you think that we will meet up with the caravan in the hills ahead?" she asked Jangbu, hopefully.

"It is possible," he answered. "Yet it is more likely that we will come upon them on the other side. They will not want to linger in the trap those hill provide for attacks by bandits."

Rocks rattled under the hooves of the horses as they traversed the well-worn route. The forms of pointed peaks appeared ahead.

The earth rose to embrace Jangbu and Zehiya as they rode between the barren hillsides. Zehiya looked up and watched the rays of the rising sun illuminate the rim of the ragged dry hill tops in deep red then becoming golden light.

A shadow appeared from a rocky ledge inside a canyon. It spread its wings, riding high on an eddy of wind, then breaking away, soaring over Zehiya and Jangbu.

Eagle. Zehiya confirmed. *An omen?*

"Stop," Jangbu hissed, in a whisper. "Did you hear that?"

Zehiya strained to hear, searching for sounds. Kimizi snorted, side-stepping uneasily under her. She patted him to calm him. They sat listening, hearing only silence and the soft moan of the cold breeze.

"Maybe nothing," Jangbu said, still whispering. "Let us go on. There is a secure place I know just off the path hidden from view, and there is a small spring there. We can stay there until tonight."

Jangbu urged Rinzen onward. The camel pulled back for an instant on its lead rope then relented and followed. Jangbu stopped again. Zehiya came alongside. They stared at the pathway ahead. As the dawn brightened, large boulders appeared along the path and up the steep rise of the hillside.

Zehiya felt uneasy. She unhooded Kartal and released him into flight. They watched as he soared ahead of them over the boulders and then caught an upward draft. Nothing else moved. Releasing her breath, Zehiya squeezed Kimizi's sides. Jangbu took the lead. They relaxed, relieved, as they passed the boulders and were on their way. Zehiya yawned, the urge to sleep draping over her. Her eyelids began to droop.

She sprang up, realizing that she had fallen asleep for a moment. Ahead, Jangbu shouted. She tried to comprehend the sight. Ropes flew out of nowhere, a lasso tightened across Jangbu's chest. He kicked Rinzen madly, trying to get free. Two men appeared, one swinging a rope toward Rinzen. She fought hard against the rope around her neck. Jangbu held tight to his saddle, fighting the pull of the rope. The camel bellowed, as two of the men grabbed its lead rope. They wrestled with the terrified creature, its head held high as it backed away from them.

"Run!" Jangbu shouted. "Get away!"

Zehiya froze, unsure. With a thwap, she felt a lasso brush her side as Kimizi stepped sideways, seeing the rope coming at them before she did. Two more men appeared, one swinging a lasso aimed for his neck. He spun and bolted, deciding for the both of them that it was time to flee. Zehiya regained her balance, aiding him in their escape. She whistled loudly, for Kartal to follow. He circled high above looking down at the struggle below. Horse and rider flew out of the maze. Zehiya sighed in relief when she heard Rinzen's hoof beats behind her.

On they went at a full gallop, gaining distance from the ambush. Feeling Kimizi begin to flag and hearing only Rinzen behind her, she slowed to a trot, then a walk.

"We got away from them," she gasped, turning to Jangbu at the sound of Rinzen trotting up alongside her.

She froze, in shock—the saddle was empty.

24

General De-guang was a Khitan warrior and the leader of the forward scouting party of Yelu Khan's great army. He strode up to Jangbu. Grasping the lasso, he yanked it, flipping Jangbu onto his back. Jangbu looked up, dazed.

"Well, you are an ugly cuss," De-guang snorted, leaning over and looking into Jangbu's face.

His gloved hand rested on the hilt of his sword in its scabbard at his side. He was fully armored as a horse soldier, in lightweight black leather lamellar armor; each lamellar square of leather was stitched together with red silk cord. A cuirass covered his chest and back. A polished bronze plate hung at the center of his chest embossed with the face of a dragon that shone with amber brightness reflecting the rays of the sun now washing into the canyon. Thick pauldrons were strapped to his wide shoulders. His forearms, roped with muscles from a lifetime of archery and battles, were encircled with leather vambraces; embossed with swirling designs. A leather corselet hung around his hips and down his thighs to his knees, over a padded dark-red undergarment.

His vision clearing, Jangbu stared up into the obsidian eyes of the warrior peering down at him.

"With a scar like that you must have been in many a fight," De-guang snorted, his laugh parting the black moustache and chin beard on his handsome face. His long black hair was tied in a top knot under a leather helmet, its edges decorated with square spirals.

"What is your name?" the General demanded.

Jangbu blinked the confusion away as he remembered where he was and what had happened.

"Well, speak up, man!" De-guang ordered, nudging him hard with the toe of his knee-high leather boot. "What is your name?"

"Jang…Jang," Jangbu coughed. "Jangbu, my name is Jangbu."

De-guang straightened. "Well, Jangbu, I am General De-guang and you have just been given the great honor of joining the army of the great Yelu Khan!"

De-guang peered down the road. "And as soon as my men catch up with your companion who got away, he will have this honor as well. When we capture your horse, who also escaped," he said, glaring at his men, one of whom held the lead rope of the now-docile pack camel. "Then, you will ride and fight."

To his men, De-guang ordered, "Get him on his feet."

Jangbu winced when the men yanked the lasso off him and then grabbed his arms. Cradling his right arm, he twisted away from the men as searing pain shot through him. Kneeling, he struggled to get to his feet, swaying a little.

"You are injured from the fall off your horse," De-guang said, shaking his head in disgust.

Turning and striding away, he called over his shoulder, "Bring him to camp. If he is not able to fight in three days, then you can use him for target practice. We will not feed a useless mouth."

25

Zehiya reached for the length of rope around Rinzen's neck that was dragging behind.

"I see that you put up a good fight, girl," she said, grasping the woven hemp then coiling the long length. "Jangbu must have been pulled off your back." Looking back at the way they had come escaping the canyon, she worried, "Will they be coming after us?"

A chill of fear scurried up her spine. Gazing around her, she felt herself grow cold. Fear froze her limbs and indecision clouded her mind.

"Think!" she ordered herself. "Shall I go back to find Jangbu?"

"No, you idiot," she cursed herself. "I mean—no, bad idea," she amended. "He is caught. We need to find a place to hide," she said to the horses. Looking skyward, she wondered, "Where is Kartal?"

About to whistle, she decided against it. "It will signal those men. He will find us on his own," she assured Kimizi. Though in truth, she feared he would not find them.

Urging Kimizi, they set off at a quick pace, westward, the way they had come on the trade route.

"They are going to come after us," she said, aloud. "Where can we hide? How can we hide? We are leaving tracks anyone could follow."

Then an idea struck her. "I know where. Come on, boy," she said to Kimizi, as she turned to look back in the direction of the hills, sure she would see riders bearing down on them. Yet the road was empty. Relieved, she booted Kimizi into a canter with Rinzen following at the end of the rope.

Soon the sand road turned to hard rock at the base of the first group of hills they had passed before entering the maze of canyons. Here they would leave no hoof prints that showed their turn off the road up into the hills.

Head held high, Kimizi's ears were pricked forward, feeling Zehiya's concentrated gaze, as she searched the barren hillside, planning her route up and over the shoulder of the ridge.

"Will they see that our tracks do not continue on the road beyond this point?" she worried. "We will have to hope they are assuming we fled west and are not checking for tracks."

"There," she said, to Kimizi, deciding on their route to their destination.

Attuned to her intent, Kimizi broke into a trot, without even a squeeze of her legs, up the rock-strewn hillside. Zehiya guided him with a light touch of the reins on his neck. Rinzen kept close at their heels. Soon they were up and over the ridge, dropping down a steep hillside into a depression, hiding them from sight from anyone on the road. Few tracks could be seen over the hard stony ground. Fastening the end of Rinzen's lasso rope around a boulder, Zehiya secured the mare. She then tied the end of Kimizi's reins to a large rock on the ground.

Suddenly both horses' heads shot up, their ears forward. Zehiya froze, listening. "Wait here and not a whicker!" she commanded the horses in a whisper.

Silently as she could, she hurried up the hillside to the lip of the ridge they had just passed over. Near the top, she dropped down onto her belly, sharp stones poked her soft stomach through her robe and under-tunic as she crawled to the edge. Slowly, she raised her head to peer over. At the sight of three horseman cantering along the road below, she jerked her head down. She swallowed hard as her pounding heart leapt into her throat. Slowly she raised her head again and was relieved at the sight of them farther down the road heading west.

It worked, she thought, triumphantly. *Yet, they may come back, we should get away, further into these hills to hide.*

She looked around, at Kimizi and Rinzen. They were napping contentedly, their heads hung low. They were exhausted from traveling all night and then the struggle with the ambush and the hard run to escape.

"They need rest," she whispered.

Looking toward the road, she decided that she would wait and keep watch, in case the men came back. Removing several offending sharp rocks from underneath her, she made her perch more comfortable as she settled down to wait. With the hot sun on her back she kept the road in her sights.

Worries returned to her: *What happened to Jangbu? Did they kill him?*

Shaking her head, "No, stup... No, they captured him for their army, that was what he had warned me might happen."

Gritting her teeth, she thumped her fist on the ground. "Bad luck, bad, bad luck!"

"What am I to do now?" She let out a long breath. "Well, first make sure that they do not catch me. Then...?" She sighed. "I will think on this later. I will just wait now and be sure that they think I am long gone. Then I can decide what to do."

As she tried to swallow, she felt the dryness in her throat. Her stomach growled. Looking at the horses, she worried. *We need water and food.*

"We lost the camel, our food!" she cursed.

When she spied Jangbu's saddle bags on Rinzen, she considered, "Perhaps Jangbu kept food in his bags. I will check them when it is safe," she decided.

Laying her head on her folded arms, she watched the road.

"Zehiyaaaa...!" A voice shrieked. Out of an ominous dark sky, wide open eagle talons appeared, enormous sharp claws, hurtling toward her.

Zehiya started awake. Her skin was slick with sweat under her clothes from baking in the sun. Groggy with the sleep, she lifted her head and looked around in confusion, then she remembered where she was. A shot of fear ripped through her as she heard the thunder of hooves below. She lowered her head and listened as the horsemen continued past. Slowly, she raised her head and saw the riders disappear toward the maze of canyons. Relieved, she returned to the horses and announced to Kimizi, "We are safe."

Untying the flask from her saddle, she pulled the cork out and upended it to her lips; there was not even a drop.

"We need water," she groaned,

She opened the flap of Jangbu's saddlebag as Rinzen slept with her head hung low. Zehiya pulled out a wrapped bundle. Hopeful it was food, she unwrapped the silk to find a thick stack of parchment papers with a board on top and a board on the bottom holding the stack together. Curious what this was, she set it on a flat rock and knelt before it. Lifting the top board, she considered the first page. She could not understand the markings that filled it. Lifting the page, she looked at the next, to see another page covered with markings.

"This is like what Pema had in her cave," she said, in wonder.

Her stomach growled as she wrapped the bundle and put it back in the saddlebag, continuing her search frantically now, finding no food.

"Drat," she cursed. "He was probably going to refill his bag from the stores on the camel."

"Where is his flask?" she wondered aloud.

She noticed the leather cord hanging from the saddle, realizing the bag had been ripped from it. She shook her head. "The ambushers must have grabbed it to stop Rinzen from escaping."

Scanning the sky she saw a dark shape, flying high above.

"I hope that is Kartal."

She knew she could not whistle for him, even now.

Her thirst becoming more urgent, she sat on the ground, draping her long arms over her knees.

"What am I to do about Jangbu?" she asked herself. "I should return to Kavya and go back to Turpan. No, it is too far. I should go back to Hami then, and tell Ozturk. He will send men to rescue

Jangbu," she rasped, her throat growing more dry and tight. "I need water now! How will I find water? We cannot go back; the last watering hole is so far away."

She buried her head in her hands.

"What am I to do?"

26

Thirst was like sand in her throat, her lips were swollen and cracked. Hunger was a tight fist in her gut. Rising fear began to paralyze her. Her limbs felt heavy and weak. Tears began to well in her eyes. She lay back on the ground, unconcerned of the sharp stones jabbing her. The tears grew more insistent. Sadness and futility rose in her chest.

"Why?" she whimpered. "Why can I not find peace? Why must bad things happen to me?"

She rolled onto her side bringing her knees to her chest, pulling them tightly to her as she moaned.

Then, like a gentle sweep of a bird's wing, understanding settled over her.

Why do I think I must have peace?

Why do I think bad things must not happen to me?

Who says that which occurs is good or bad?

She sat up, contemplating these thoughts coursing through her mind.

"Who? Who is deciding these things; these ideas?" she asked aloud. "These are simply thoughts. I do not need to let these thoughts make me sad and weak!" she declared. "I will not be a leaf, helpless and blown about on the winds of my mind!"

Looking around at the barren landscape, Zehiya gazed up at the blue sky. It was so blue, so intensely blue. She felt the solidness of the rocky ground beneath her. Taking in a deep breath, she tasted the aroma of the dry earthy air.

Then the need for all to be as she desired fell away. Her concern for being beautiful, for being loved, for having lost so much.

It simply did not matter anymore.

"I am alive," she declared. "I am young and strong."

Taking out the medallion from under her robe, she gazed at the gold form of the Griffin, a lion and an eagle combined.

Power and wisdom, she thought.

The sound of Kimizi pawing the earth brought her out of her reverie. She watched quizzically as Kimizi raised his nose into the air and then lowered his head and pawed the ground, insistently. Then he repeated the gesture.

Realization dawned on her and she rose to her feet.

"You know, my boy. You know the truth but I never listen; I never see you or hear you because I am always lost in my thoughts."

Buoyant at the revelations that had freed her, Zehiya untied Rinzen and Kimizi.

Taking Rinzen's bridle off, Zehiya tied it to the saddle, freeing the mare of the bit. Then she lifted the lasso over Rinzen's head and stroked the iron-grey neck of the mare as she declared, "You do not need this rope, we are a herd and you will stay with us."

Rinzen nuzzled Zehiya's arm with her lips.

Coiling the long rope, she tied it to Kimizi's saddle, and then swung onto Kimizi's back, letting his reins hang loose.

"You know where there is water, of course you do—show me, my boy."

Kimizi trotted up the next rise and over the top. Rinzen followed as Kimizi made his way down the rocky slope into a wide canyon. When they arrived at the bottom of the canyon they stopped before a small gully lined with rocks. Kimizi lowered his head and gave a snort. All was silent, then Zehiya heard something very faint—a trickle. Kimizi followed the rocky depression and then stopped. To Zehiya's amazement and delight, out of the ground water trickled over rocks, making a small pool, then flowed out of sight again, back into the ground.

She slid off the saddle and staggered to the pool with Kimizi and

Rinzen on her heels. She dropped to her knees, filling her cupped hands with the cool sweet spring water, gulping handful after handful. The cool wetness was life itself coursing down her dry throat. Kimizi and Rinzen sucked contentedly from the pool, their eyes closed.

Satiated, Zehiya sat back on a rock, panting in relief.

"My boy," she sighed, "from now on, I will listen to you."

Hunger gnawed at her.

"Now, all we need is food," she said. Then noticed Kimizi and Rinzen were nibbling on tufts of grass growing between the rocks of the hidden spring.

"Well, I need food," she amended, as she rose to take Kimizi's bridle, off freeing him of the bit while he ate.

Just then she heard a familiar high-pitched "Kak, kak, kaaak."

She swung her head up to search the sky when a form shot toward them from the ridge. She ducked as Kartal swooped over her and flew to the other side of the canyon. Riding on an eddy he circled high into the sky and hoovered there, fluttering his wings, searching the canyon below.

She watched in fascination when he folded his wings to his sides and, like an arrow, plummeted toward the ground. As she had seen so many times before, right when it seemed that he would crash into the earth, he opened his wings and his talons grasped his prey. Clouds of dust rose around him as he tussled with something writhing on the ground.

Zehiya ran to him arriving when all was still again. Kartal pulled at the meat of a snake; as thick as her forearm and as long as she was tall. Looking up at her, Kartal gave a "Kak!" Then he stepped off his kill offering the remainder to her.

"Kartal!" She stooped before him. "My good friend, you found us!"

Looking at the sand-colored scales with darker spotted patterns, making it blend completely with the earth, she said, "A snake. I have heard of eating snake. We will share it, my friend."

Lifting the heavy reptile, she trotted back to the spring. Kartal soared ahead of her, landing by the pool. Dipping his head, he filled his beak again and again with the cool water.

Breathing heavily, Zehiya arrived at the pool, dropping the limp creature onto the ground.

Looking at Kartal, who was now sitting on a rock, she said, "I am glad you are back, my friend."

Crossing over the rocks to Kimizi she untied Kartal's leather hood from the saddle. Returning to the falcon, she stooped before him to place the hood over his head. Then, she stopped and considered her falcon. Sitting back on a rock with his hood hanging limp in her hand, she regarded it and then the majestic bird sitting before her. Looking into his savage dark eyes, the irises glowing brown in the sunlight, she marveled at their beauty and the intelligence she now perceived behind them. The realization dawned on her that in all the time she had known this beautiful creature, she had never once really seen him.

With a flick of her wrist, she flung the hood away.

"Obviously, you do not need this, my friend," she said.

Hunger becoming more insistent, she rose and stood over the snake, then she considered her surroundings.

"I cannot cook this snake. The men might see the smoke," she said. "Perhaps at night they will not see it?" With a shake of her head, she decided, "No, they may smell the fire."

Gazing at the rocky desolation around her, she sighed, "It matters not, there is no wood here and no dung to burn."

Drawing her dagger, she lifted the snake, slapping it onto a flat rock.

"I will eat it raw then. Feray and I never cooked snake, so how do I eat this? Do I skin it like a rabbit? Or just cut it into pieces?" she inquired, to Kartal.

He hopped over. Spearing his beak into the middle of the snake, he cut through the skin and drew it aside to reveal the bright red meat underneath. Then he took a bite, swallowing a chunk of the flesh.

Zehiya watched, transfixed.

"Oh, I see, I shall skin it and cut the meat from the bones. Do snakes have bones?"

With her sharp dagger she got to work slicing along the belly of the snake. She spread the skin, then cut underneath, separating the skin from the meat. She cut a small piece of raw meat and placed it in her mouth. She grimaced at the small rib bones, pulling them out of her mouth with her fingers.

"They do have bones," she said. "Not a bad taste though, it is not horrible," she declared, as she chewed the flesh, now free of bones.

She felt the effect of the nourishment immediately—a surge of energy rose in her. Looking up at the sun and then at the remaining meat, she considered.

"The day is hot. If I cut the pieces small, there will be enough time to dry the remainder," she explained to Kartal, who sat watching her with interest.

Busily, she cut the meat from the small bones and laid thin pieces on a flat rock, popping pieces in her mouth as she worked. The energy enlivened her body, making her feel optimistic. After placing the last piece on the drying rock, she cleaned her hands and her dagger in the spring. Untying her flask from Kimizi's saddle as he stood snoozing, she squatted by the spring to fill it with the clear water.

Looking at Kimizi, Rinzen and Kartal, she wondered aloud, "Now that we have water and food, what should we do?" With a sigh, she sat on the ground, then lay back to rest and think, looking up at the clear blue sky.

"We could go back to Ozturk's home. He would send men to help Jangbu, then we could join a caravan and I could return to Kavya."

Zehiya sat up, draping her arms over her knees.

"Then what of Dunhaung and Pema? It will take days for me to go back to Hami. Ozturk will need time to gather men and provisions and return."

She shook her head. "Too long. Jangbu is in danger. It may be too late if I go back to Hami."

She stood up and began to pace.

"When I was in need, Kavya, Sahin and Jangbu came to my aid—especially Jangbu!" she said, storming around her little camp.

Her medallion swung out of her robe.

Grasping it in her fist, she declared. "I am a warrior! I have the blood of an ancient tribe of formidable women warriors in my veins. I must no longer be as a child, looking for others to care for me. Now! In this moment I am a woman! I turn away from the world as a child!"

In a ritualistic action, Zehiya turned to face the opposite direction as she declared, "I turn now toward the world as a woman, as one who is the giver."

Squeezing the medallion hard, its solidness and weight feeling good in her fist, she promised, "I will find a way to get Jangbu out of the clutches of those men. I will save my friend and we will continue our journey to find Pema!"

27

"Yet, how?" Zehiya asked, as she climbed the side of a steep hill, slipping on the rocky scree. "How will I save Jangbu?"

Reaching the top of the peak, she gazed around her at the impossible maze of hills beyond. Black ominous clouds paraded across the sky.

"How will I find where they took him?"

"I will show you the way," came a voice from the sky above.

Zehiya searched above her for the source. The dark clouds dissolved away revealing a brilliant blue sky where a piercing bright light appeared. Zehiya shielded her eyes as the orb grew larger and larger; finally taking form as the Spirit Eagle. Her huge wings of light flapped lazily as she flew in a circle above Zehiya.

"Come with me," she called.

Without hesitation, Zehiya bounded into the void with her arms held wide transforming into long feathered wings. A gust of wind lifted her high above the hilltops. Catching up to the Spirit Eagle, she flew beside the bird of light; her feathers sparkling gold and brown and black.

Soon they were descending toward two peaks. Zehiya could see that there was a wide canyon between them, and there she saw men and horses.

"There is the camp where Jangbu is held as conscript," the Spirit Eagle said.

"Where is this camp?" she asked. "How will I find it?"

"You will find this camp by looking for the smoke rising out of the canyon from the cooking fires," the Spirit Eagle replied.

Zehiya nodded in understanding.

Circling above the canyon she spotted Jangbu who was sitting at the base of one of the hillsides that bordered this hideout. He was a distance away from the main camp. She could see, even from this high in the sky, that he was bound at the wrists with a rope and secured to a rock.

A warrior walked up to him with a bowl of food and dropped it in front of him and then turned and walked away. Jangbu reached for the bowl slowly, and in evident pain.

Zehiya watched, feeling something was wrong—then it struck her.

"He is not reaching equally with both arms outstretched," she said. "He is holding his right arm stiffly, trying not to extend it."

"He is injured," the Spirit Eagle said.

Alarmed, Zehiya said, "They captured him to fight for them. If he cannot…"

"…they will most likely kill him for sport," the Spirit Eagle finished the sentence.

The Spirit Eagle veered away from the canyon toward some distant hills. Zehiya followed her. Settling on one of the hilltops, the Spirit Eagle waited for Zehiya. Zehiya settled near her and looked back toward the canyon that they had come from.

"How will I free him from those warriors?" she asked.

"First," the Spirit Eagle began, "you will find this canyon hideout, then you will approach it from above. You must get to the rim of the canyon and with great stealth study the camp and a way down to it from above."

"I can get to the camp but how will I rescue him from all those men?" Zehiya asked.

"You," the Spirit Eagle replied, her intense gaze boring into Zehiya, "have all the talents and the abilities necessary to rescue Jangbu. Follow my instructions to find the camp, then trust yourself."

Zehiya started, awaking from a deep sleep as Kimizi nuzzled her arm. Reaching toward him she stroked his muzzle as she sat up. Her dream flooded back to her.

"Find the smoke," she said, aloud.

Getting to her feet, she picked up the blanket that was on top the saddle that she had been resting her head on. Flinging it over Kimizi's back, she recited, "My boy, we must find the smoke, that is where the canyon is, then we must study the camp to figure out a plan to get Jangbu out of there."

Shaking off the fear that constricted her chest, she assured herself, "I can do this. If I could not, the Spirit Eagle would have told me."

She tightened Kimizi's girth and settled the saddle bags behind the cantle and tied them securely. Then she saddled Rinzen, cooing to her, "Follow us, my girl. Your friend, Jangbu, will be with us again soon."

As she mounted Kimizi, she called to Kartal, who was perched on a rock, "Come, my friend."

With a gentle guide of the reins she turned Kimizi toward the hill top. She booted him to a trot heading up and over the hill. Rinzen following at their heels.

"Time to go my friend," she called over her shoulder to Kartal.

Kartal spread his wings and with one powerful stroke, he took flight after them.

28

Zehiya observed the expanse below her from the rocky top of the highest hill she had climbed to get a view of her surroundings. Looking back the way she had climbed she considered Kimizi and Rinzen who were tethered below.

"They will need more food and water, how long can I search?" she wondered aloud to Kartal, who sat perched on a sharp rock near her.

She had spent all day climbing hilltop after hilltop and she had seen no sign of smoke from anywhere amongst the hills beyond. The sun was past its zenith. Uncertainty began to gnaw at her.

I cannot do this, the thought nagged at her. *Even if I find him; I cannot fight all those warriors!*

The memory of her teacher, Pema, in the cave, came to her. In her mind's eye she could see the old woman, sitting on her meditation cushion, tapping her bony finger against the side of her head as she said, "You must learn to win battles from here now. With your wits, your mind. And to do that you must understand your mind. You must become master of yourself."

Breathing in a lungful of air, Zehiya let it out slowly, summoning her resolve. "Patience, I must…accept that this is not going as easily as I had envisioned it would."

She slumped against a jagged boulder in defeat. "It is too hard to have patience. I cannot find the camp," she whimpered.

Then she shot up in defiance. "No! I must not be weak. I must not give up. I must…think!" she commanded herself.

Kneeling, she cleared a patch on the ground free of stones. Picking up a pointed rock she stabbed the dirt with it saying aloud as she drew, "Here, is the road into the maze of hills, and here is where we escaped and hid, over the rise." Closing her eyes, she tried to picture it in her mind.

"Where was the sun?"

She brought back the memory of when she fell asleep on the hill by the road watching for the men that first day, and the realization came to her.

"At my back," she said, "then we went up this hill and over to the spring. Where was the sun when we were at the spring?"

"Over this hill," she said, as she drew the locations on her map, making all very clear now.

"It should be over there," she said aloud, gazing in the distance. "Yet there is no smoke."

As she scanned over the hills in the distance, the dark form of a large bird rose up and soared away from between two hills. Something about the sight of it nagged at her.

"That morn, when we first entered the hills," she said aloud, "Before the ambush, there was an eagle. I watched it rise up from its perch."

Gazing at the bird as it circled higher and higher the shards of memory coalesced.

"After it flew over us, we traveled further east into the hills. Then we were attacked."

She shifted her attention to the hills further east.

"If it had been that eagle's nest and not just a temporary perch," she mused, as she studied the hilltops, "and, if this is indeed the same eagle…"

Then she saw it, just a faint smudge of discoloration between two hills much further to the east, lit by the low afternoon sunlight.

"Smoke!" she said, triumphantly.

29

Jangbu winced as he bent to pick up the sword that was tossed to him.

"Come and fight, you ugly cuss!" the Khitan warrior goaded, as he paced in a circle around Jangbu, weaving his sword like a cobra ready to strike. His hard face split into a sinister smile, revealing discolored broken teeth.

Pain screamed from Jangbu's right shoulder down through his sword arm, making it useless. Grasping the sword in his left hand, he parried the blows struck by his attacker clumsily, the pain in his injured shoulder becoming unbearable with the effort.

The warrior turned away in disgust.

"He is useless!" he moaned. "A useless barbarian."

Then, he spun around with a kick to Jangbu's stomach which sent him hurling backwards, falling onto the hard ground with a thud. Curling into a ball on his side, Jangbu gasped for air. His hair came loose from his leather tie, spilling around his face.

"Enough!" De-guang ordered, striding toward the two men.

The warrior sheathed his sword, and with left fist in right hand he bowed to his commander.

"Take his sword," De-guange ordered the warrior. "Tie him. And leave him alone to heal, if he can."

Looking down at Jangbu, he growled, "I give you one more day. If you are still unable to fight, we will make sport of you."

Jangbu slowly got to his feet as De-guang strode away, then eyed the warrior who was retrieving his fallen sword.

The man looked back at him coldly.

"One more day and you are a dead man," he said.

Then he stomped up to Jangbu. Within inches of Jangbu's face he hissed, "Nothing will please me more than to feed your corpse to the crows."

Jangbu turned his head to the side reflexively at the stench of the man's breath, which was hot on his face.

Grabbing Jangbu's hands, the warrior cinched the rope tightly around his wrists, enjoying Jangbu's shudder of pain.

"You Tibetans are no longer the warriors you once were. You have no King. Your people have become weak and useless barbarians."

With a shove, he forced Jangbu back to his place by the boulders. "You will not even make that good of sport," he laughed, "we will find a way to make you entertaining."

Jangbu sat down against a rock and angrily watched the warrior march away. He looked up at the high walls around him with an urgency to get out of there. His heart sank. Not a chance, he could never climb out because they would see him. His arm cannot bear his weight in any case.

Zehiya, he thought with a sigh. *She got away from the men that went after her. But where did she go?* He could see their camel with its packs unloaded. *She has no food or water. Can she make it back to Hami?* The realization hit him like a bludgeon. *She is going to die out there.*

30

Zehiya crept on her belly to the edge of rim overlooking the canyon below. She rose her head up slowly just enough to peer over so no one would see her. There was the camp. She watched as Jangbu was kicked to the ground by one of the warriors then tied and shoved to the boulders to sit.

The same place he was sitting in my dream, she marveled.

She counted ten men, ten horses and four camels.

Our camel! She cursed in her thoughts when she saw him tied with the rest.

Forget the camel! She reprimanded herself.

So, she thought, *Jangbu is the only captive there now. He must have been the first. These men have not been here that long.*

Zehiya studied the steep hillsides down into the camp. Most of the slope was scree or steep rock drops. If her plan was to work, she needed to get down quickly and quietly, and back up again with Jangbu.

She shook her head forlornly as she studied the drop into the canyon. There was no clear route all the way down. There were possibilities, but they ended in drops too far to climb down or up. She lay gazing at the rocky terrain, trying to devise a route down. Committing all of this to memory, she scurried backward and away to where she had hidden the horses. Sitting with a flask and some dried snake meat, she considered what to do. She took in Kimizi and Rinzen as she chewed her meat.

"You both are losing weight. I have to get this done this night, before dawn," she explained, "so we can move on to some grazing ground."

"But how?" She thumped her knee.

The rope tied to her saddle caught her eye. Jumping to her feet, she untied it and rolled it out to its full length as she pictured the different possible routes that she had memorized. An idea began to take form. She hurried back to the overlook again, and lying on the edge, she studied the terrain with the possibilities having a rope offered.

"I think it will work," she whispered to herself. "No," she corrected, as she looked down at Jangbu and thought of what was at stake, "It must work!"

"You both must stay here," Zehiya instructed Kimizi and Rinzen.

The half full globe of the moon hung low in the sky, its reflection shone bright in the horses' large eyes. Kimizi nibbled nervously on Zehiya's bare arm with his lips. She wore only her tunic to aid her climb. Gently, but firmly, she held his muzzle, speaking quietly, looking from him to Rinzen.

"I will return," she whispered.

As she tethered their reins to a large rock, she urged, "You must be silent, not a murmur."

Taking the coiled rope from the saddle, she slung it over her head, resting the loops across her chest. A cold breeze caused her to shiver. Willing the cold away, she silently scurried to the edge of the rim and looked over the cliff that was to be the first leg of her way down to the camp. She felt for her dagger at her side. It hung securely on her belt which was cinched tightly around her waist. She closed her eyes and fixed the image of the route of footholds and handholds that she had memorized from across the canyon.

At the edge of the cliff she laid down on her stomach and

shimmied backwards, letting her legs drop over the edge, as she held tightly to the rim of the cliff. Immediately her foot found purchase, then her other foot found the next foothold. Relieved, she lowered herself to the one below that, then to the next one on the map seared in her mind's eye.

When she was at head level with the lip of the cliff, Kartal came hopping up to the edge.

"Kartal," she hissed, "go back and wait on your perch, on the saddle."

With a "Kak," he leapt over her head and soared silently away.

"Oh, it matters not," she groaned, in a whisper.

The dawn was not far off. She had picked this time knowing that most of the men would be out of the camp on the road waiting to ambush unsuspecting travelers.

Slowly, methodically, she made her way down the rock face, easily finding her way. At the bottom of this first leg, she stood still and listened. The camp was silent. She found the large rock she had spied from her observation perch. Lifting the rope coils over her head, she looped the middle to the rope around the rock. Grasping the doubled rope, she nimbly and silently belayed herself down the scree slope, using the rope to keep her from sliding and dislodging rocks. On the way back, the climb up would be possible without the rope, though the sounds of the rocks slipping would be heard. By then that would not matter as they would be far enough away from camp to evade capture, or so she hoped.

When she reached the bottom of this first leg, she slowly pulled on one end of the rope which slid effortlessly around the rock high above. Soon, she had the entire length coiled in her hand. She found a boulder and tethered the end of the rope securely to it. Then let the rope fall down the steep rock face. Taking a breath, she steeled herself for this last climb down which would put her at the bottom; in the camp. Fear gripped her.

I can't do this. I am just a girl, she thought, as a wave of nausea rose up into her throat and her stomach clenched. She held onto the boulder to steady herself as she took in slow, deep breaths. Reaching for the leather thong around her neck, she pulled her medallion out from under her tunic. The gold felt smooth and cool.

"Grandfather," she whispered in prayer, grasping the talisman tightly. "Be with me. Make me strong and sure."

Remembering Pema's instruction she added, "I will control my fear, my mind, and focus on my task!"

These prayers, and her iron will, pushed fear and doubt aside so they would no longer have control and create uncertainty and confusion.

Returning the medallion to its place near her heart, she took a couple of deep calming breaths and made herself feel the soles of her booted feet on the hard rock.

"I can do this," she assured herself, in a whisper, "I just need to focus on the task."

Grasping the rope, she turned and walked backward down the steep side of the rock face. Soon, she landed silently at the bottom. Leaving the rope for the return trip, she ducked behind a group of boulders. Jangbu was just the other side of these massive rocks. Drawing her dagger, she deftly made her way to him; sure the pounding of her heart could be heard in the entire camp. Then she saw him, leaning against a boulder.

Sleeping? She wondered.

Suddenly, she felt a grip on her arm; the force wheeled her around. The stink of his breath hit her before she saw the man's face. Zehiya thrust her blade up to stab him. Quick as a snake, he slapped it away and slammed her back against the boulder. Then suddenly, her attacker released her and dropped, like corpse.

31

Jangbu, holding a large stone in his two hands with his wrists tied together, looked down at the unconscious warrior then at Zehiya in disbelief.

"Zehiya!" he hissed. "What are you doing here?"

"Saving you, what else?" she hissed back. "Now let's go!"

"Cut these bonds," Jangbu whispered as he set the stone down quietly.

Zehiya glanced around frantically for her knife which had been slapped out of her hand by the warrior. There was no time to search for it now.

Jangbu pulled on the knots at his wrists with his teeth, finally the bonds came loose.

"I would have chewed them loose before, yet there was nowhere to go. They would have beaten me for it," Jangbu whispered. "How did you get here? Where are we going?"

"Follow me," she replied, while looking around in fear of any men from the camp who may be coming. All remained silent.

When they came to the base of the rock, she stopped and turned to Jangbu, who was right behind her. He was looking up at the rock and the rope that disappeared up it into the grey light.

"You are injured," Zehiya said. "Grab the rope. I will push you."

Jangbu shook his head. "Wait."

Sitting down, he whispered, "Pull my arm to put the shoulder back in place. It is not seated correctly, that is the cause of the pain," he explained.

Zehiya looked around the two of them, then quickly up at the pink hue in the sky. Dawn was here. She knelt beside him and thrust her hand under his robe feeling for his shoulder. She could feel that it was not right. Grabbing his upper arm, she pulled it away from his side and twisted his forearm out until she felt the pop of his shoulder go back into place.

Jangbu grunted, gritting his teeth so as not to make a sound. The pain was sharp, but then it subsided.

He looked at her in dismay.

"Where did you learn how to do that?" he whispered, feeling a wave of dizziness as he stood up.

"We must go, now! You go up first," she hissed urgently.

Rubbing his shoulder, he shook his head. "No, you go first."

Zehiya grabbed the rope and began to climb, walking up the rock face. Jangbu waited until she was at the top and then took hold of the rope. He gritted his teeth against the pain in his shoulder. It was not as severe as before but it weakened him. Gripping the rope with his good arm, he pulled himself up and walked up the rock the way Zehiya had, using his injured arm sparingly. When he reached the top his foot slipped and then gave way. He slammed hard against the unforgiving stone wall yet he held fast to the rope. His feet scrabbled to find purchase against the rugged surface.

Peering over the edge, lying prone, in an effort to keep out of sight from any in the camp who might see her, Zehiya reached for Jangbu, who was right below her just inches from her grasp. Zehiya grabbed the rope and stood up, pulling it with all her strength. It was enough. Jangbu pitched his arm over the edge and his fingers found a raised sliver in the rock to hold on to. Zehiya grabbed the back of his robe, falling backwards with the effort, pulling Jangbu with her. Jangbu levered a leg over and pulled himself over the top.

Rolling onto his back, he gasped to catch his breath. Zehiya coiled up the rope.

"Look!" A shout echoed from the camp. "There, on the bluff, they are getting away!"

Zehiya froze at the shouts, then saw men running toward them. She slung the coiled rope over her head, letting it fall across her chest.

"Come on!" Zehiya shouted, as she ascended the hill.

Jangbu jumped to his feet just as an arrow pinged off the rock a hands width below him. He bounded after Zehiya, following in her wake as she scrambled on all fours up the scree slope. More arrows landed only a footfall from the climbers. Zehiya braced herself for the one that she was sure would find her. She looked back to see Jangbu further behind her, scrambling up the slope, the loose rubble slipping away from each of his frantic footfalls, making his climb excruciatingly slow. An arrow struck him in the arm, yet it only pieced the fabric of his sleeve. Ignoring the shaft, Jangbu pressed on. Zehiya was almost to the top. Jangbu watched her climb effortlessly up the slippery slope. Then his heart fell. The top was not the summit at all, but another wall of rock. Arrows fell from the sky—a rain of daggers.

The archers were hampered by their position at the bottom of the canyon, the tall rock bluff an obstacle to a direct shot at the fleeing pair. The archers sent their arrows high in an arch, so they would drop onto the moving targets.

Despite the aching of his shoulder, Jangbu forced himself onward. Then intense pain bit through his leg. He grunted and turned to see that an arrow speared his right calf, the spike having pierced through his trousers at the top of his felt boot. He grabbed at the shaft, then thinking better of it, forced himself to leave it and continue onward. He looked up at Zehiya seeing the urgency and fear working on her face as she peered down at him from the top.

"Can you make it?" she called out, preparing to descend to help him.

He shook his head indicating for her to stay. Using every ounce of strength, he willed himself to ignore the vicious pain in his leg and continued onward. His hands were becoming cut and bloodied as he grabbed at the loose rocks to pull himself up. He pushed with his good leg, against the rocks falling away underfoot.

Finally, he reached Zehiya. She bent down to help him stand next to her at the base of the cliff.

"You have been hit," she said, kneeling down to inspect the arrow through the rip in his blood-soaked trousers. Its razor point was imbedded deep in Jangbu's calf.

Jangbu crumpled and sat down hard.

"Pull it out," he said.

Zehiya shook her head. "We must break the shaft. Best to leave the arrowhead," she said, as she gently separated the torn legging where the arrowhead had sliced through. "It will need to be cut out."

Looking around her, she grabbed a triangular-shaped rock. Resting its wide end on the ground next Jangbu's leg, she lay the wood shaft on the narrow sharp edge.

"Hold it steady, this is going to hurt," she said, raising another flat rock high above her head.

Jangbu, took hold of the arrow-shaft at his calf with a tight grip. Zehiya slammed the rock down onto the anvil, breaking the wood clean away with a loud crack. Jangbu gasped and sucked in his breath with the shock of pain at the blow. He lay on his side as the roiling waves of nausea crashed over him. Now there was only a hands-width of wood protruding from the wound

"Can you climb?" Zehiya inquired.

Jangbu sat up forcing the nausea and dizziness aside. He looked up at the wall disappearing into the sky. His leg was on fire and his heart was pounding hard. He felt very weak.

He shook his head. "Not a chance. Even with the pain in my shoulder, I might have been able to climb, but not with this injured leg too."

Zehiya looked down at the men far below and then her heart stopped. "Oh, no," she exclaimed.

Jangbu followed her gaze.

De-guang and his warriors, with several bound captives, came thundering into the camp.

"We have no time," Jangbu said. "They will climb up here soon." He grabbed Zehiya's arm, forcing her to look into his eyes. "Forget me. Get away. Go back to Ozturk's estate. Tell him to keep my horses as payment for your safe return to Kavya." He released her and closed his eyes with a shiver of pain. Then he opened them and continued. "You can wait there and visit with Sister Sonam. Someday Pema will return to her friend."

"I am not going to leave you here to die," she vowed.

In frustration, she searched the cliff face, as though it contained the answer to her dilemma, then an idea came to her.

"I will get you out of here. Wait for the rope," she urged as she sprang to her feet and began the climb up the cliff.

Jangbu watched in awe as her agile form disappeared up and out of sight. Then he looked down to see De-guang dismount his horse, his men bow to him and then point up at Jangbu.

32

Zehiya pulled herself over the precipice onto the plateau and scrambled to her feet. She sprinted to Rinzen and pulled her reins free from the boulder they had been tied to. Rinzen followed obediently, sensing urgency, as Zehiya led her near the cliff, then turned the mare to face away from the ledge.

"Jangbu needs your strength, girl," she said, as she tied one end of the rope to the saddle.

"Stand," Zehiya said to Rinzen, with a gesture of her hand, then she stepped to the ledge and hoisted the remainder of the coiled rope over it as she called out, "Jangbu! Catch the rope."

Jangbu looked up to see the rope slither in the sky and then strike the rock face near his head.

He grasped the rippling hemp line in his fist.

"I have it," he called out.

"Tie it around you. We will pull you up," Zehiya explained.

With a quick glance down, he saw that men had topped the bluff and now were beginning to ascend up the scree slope. He fastened the rope under his arms, around his chest and secured the knot.

"Ready!" he called out. "Hurry, for they are near."

Zehiya hurried to Rinzen and took her bridle in hand. Urging the mare forward the slack in the rope begin to tighten. When it grew taut, the mare balked at the unfamiliar tug on her saddle.

Zehiya slapped the mare on the rump.

"Come on girl, go forward!" she commanded.

Rinzen moved a step forward, then another.

"Good girl," Zehiya encouraged, praising her as they took step after step.

Jangbu felt the rope cinch tightly around his back. He held fast to the line as his feet lifted off the ground. His body began to spin, scraping his shoulder against the stone. Releasing his grip he grasped at the stone wall pulling himself around to face it as he rose, seizing any hand-hold he could find to aid his ascent.

Suddenly, there was a clamp on his leg. Pain racked through him. The rope tightened as he looked down into the face of a warrior who held fast to his blood-soaked boot.

Zehiya felt a strong tug on the rope. Rinzen strained at her task yet the rope would not budge. Something was wrong.

"Jangbu, what is wrong?" she cried out, fearing to release Rinzen to look over the edge to see what was the matter. She was trapped.

She slapped Rinzen's rump again.

"Common girl. Pull!"

Jangbu kicked at the warrior, connecting with his face. The man grunted, yet held fast. The rope buried deeper under Jangbu's arms and around his chest, squeezing the air from his lungs like a python. Hearing Zehiya's calls, yet unable to answer, he struggled, kicking to free himself of his unwelcome passenger. The man held fast to his boot at the ankle, his battle-hardened hands as strong as alligator jaws. He looked up at Jangbu, a determined grimace carved into his face.

Suddenly out of nowhere, a dark shape appeared overhead. With a high-pitched shriek, Kartal struck the warrior's upturned face and raked across his eyes with razor talons. With a bellow, the man released his grip falling to the earth, covering his bloodied eyes. Now blind, he stood and staggered, tripping on a rock that sent him tumbling backwards down the scree slope.

Shaking off his shock at the appearance of Kartal, Jangbu called to Zehiya. "Pull! Pull hard, I am free!"

Zehiya and Rinzen felt the rope ease. Digging her hooves into the barren ground, the mare pushed forward with her powerful hindquarters.

Jangbu felt himself lift now, and quickly. In moments, his head, then his shoulders were at the top. Flinging his arms over the cliff edge, he pushed himself up and over landing on the flat ground. Rinzen dragged him until he was a good distance away from the precipice.

"Whoa," Zehiya commanded.

Releasing the bridle, she ran to Jangbu and fell to her knees by his side as he pushed himself up. She helped him stand, his left leg taking all the weight. He pulled at the knot, his bound chest heaving, as he tried to gulp in air. The knot had grown so tight that they could not unravel it. Zehiya reached for her dagger but her hand grasped at empty space. Perplexed, she looked down at the scabbard and then remembered losing it when she had struggled with the warrior below. She sprinted to Kimizi and drew her sword from its scabbard on the saddle. Carefully, she slid the blade under the rope, its razor edge sliced through the woven strands effortlessly. The rope fell away, freeing Jangbu. He bent back, feeling his chest free to breath in the sweet morning air. Kartal swooped in and circled around them so close that they could feel the breeze of his wing strokes.

"There you are," Zehiya said to Kartal.

Then to Jangbu, "What happened down there?"

Jangbu shook his head. "No time. We need to go. Now."

They both looked at the cliff edge, fearing a swarm of warriors would come boiling over in any moment.

Zehiya took his arm as he limped to Rinzen's side. Stroking the mare's strong neck, he felt a surge of strength.

"I thought I would never see you again, my beautiful girl," he said.

"Lift your leg, I will hoist you up," Zehiya said.

Gripping the saddle to take the weight off his right leg, Jangbu bent his left leg. Zehiya grabbed it and lifted up as he swung into the saddle. He groaned as the arrowhead chewed and cut inside his calf. His boot was soaked with blood.

Zehiya ran to Kimizi and felt inside the saddlebag for her long turban. Wrapping the end of the cloth around her thigh to secure it, she pulled a length of it taut. Her sword sliced through it effortlessly, sending the ends fluttering away on the morning breeze. Returning to Jangbu, she wrapped the cloth around his leg to bind the wound and to

163

keep the arrow still as they rode. Sweat dripped down her back underneath her tunic. Her bare arms felt the heat of the sun. The morning was growing hot.

Retrieving her robe from the saddlebag, she slid into it as a movement caught her eye. Jangbu shouted a warning. She wheeled to see a man's hands then his head rise up over the edge of the cliff—a warrior. Zehiya slid her bow and an arrow from its quiver on the saddle. Having strung the bow before her decent down into the canyon hours earlier, she need only load the arrow onto the string. She raised the bow to aim at the man now rising to his knees, the hilt of his sword in the scabbard at his back could be seen above his right shoulder. She felt herself rushing to shoot, her arm was shaking. She steadied herself forcing herself to calm down.

If I miss, we are dead, she thought. "Slow and steady. Breathe," she counseled herself in a hiss.

Her arm went still as she took in a slow breath and aimed for the center of the man now rising to his feet as his hand reached backward, drawing his sword. Time seemed to slow down. Zehiya felt the string slip away from her bare thumb as she exhaled slowly. The arrow took flight, impaling the warrior through his right shoulder. The impact threw him off balance; he stepped backward, disappearing over the edge.

"Magnificent shot!" Jangbu grunted in praise.

Zehiya reached for another arrow.

"We should go, now!" Jangbu urged.

Zehiya looked to see that Jangbu was pale and slumped in the saddle. She bound into Kimizi's saddle still holding onto her bow and swung him toward Jangbu.

"Can you ride?" she asked.

Jangbu nodded. "Yes. You lead the way, go east."

Kartal soared above their heads as they galloped over the plateau and away.

33

De-guang watched his men climb up to apprehend Jangbu as he tried to make his escape.

He shook his head in awe as his warrior lost his grip and fell away and then Jangbu rose up the cliff side and disappeared over the edge like a Jinni; those supernatural beings who come from the mystical emerald mountains and wander about causing mischief.

Soon after the man had fallen bloodied and blind, two more warriors hurried past him to climb up the cliff. The first man was a strong and wiry man.

Deguang nodded in approval as this warrior swiftly made his way up the rock; leaving the second climber far behind him. When he made it to the rim and lift himself over the top, they all watched in anticipation as he reached for his sword at his back. Then, inexplicably, he was sailing backwards into space. His body collided with the man climbing up behind him, taking them both crashing onto the rocks below.

A gasp of shock rippled through the gathered throng.

"Shall we go after them on horseback up the road and around, Commander?" his henchman asked with a bow.

Looking back at the captives they had acquired in that morning's ambush, he considered. "The Tibetan was of no use. Yet, I would like to have his partner, the north-man, with fire-colored hair. He would be a valuable addition to our ranks."

A warrior near him stepped forward. With left fist in right hand he bowed. "Commander, that is not a man, that is a woman."

De-guang stared at him, then shot his gaze up at the now deserted cliff top. "A woman? How do you know this?" he demanded.

"I grabbed her while she was attempting to free the captive. She tried to cut me with her blade. I disarmed her," he replied, holding out the dagger. "The Tibetan must have struck me from behind with a rock," he added, rubbing the knot at the back of his head.

De-guang shook his head in amazement.

"A woman! A warrior woman of the northern tribes? Or perhaps... they were both Jinn. The Tibetan was as ugly as a Jinn," he said.

The men shuffled and murmured uneasily at this revelation.

"We all saw that winged demon attack our man, hurling him from his hold on the Tibetan!" one of the warriors exclaimed, pointing upward in consternation.

"And what else than a Jinni could have forced our second warrior off that precipice with such power?" another man asked.

Sharp claws of fear scurried up De-guange's spine as he gazed up at the cliff; those two may well be supernatural beings having taken the forms of a Tibetan and a north woman.

"Let them go," he scoffed feigning disinterest, to hide from the men the fear that was tightening its grip. "We need not waste our time."

Looking to their captives of four men that were huddled together kneeling on the ground with their hands tied, he continued, "We have a good catch this morn. We will need to add more in the coming days. Yelu will arrive with his army soon. Then we will be off to Hami."

34

Zehiya held her flask out to Jangbu when they were a good distance away from the canyon. He took it gratefully and sipped the cool sweetness.

"Where did you find water?" he asked in amazement, feeling instantly revived.

Keeping her grip on her bow, looking warily the way they had come, she said, "I...Kimizi found a spring. We need to find a place to remove that arrowhead and tend to your wound and the horses need water and fodder," she explained.

Jangbu looked around him at the hills in thought. Kartal swooped in from the sky, landing lightly on his saddle-perch in front of Zehiya.

Jangbu considered the falcon and waited for the hood to appear to cover his head, yet Kartal sat with eyes wide open, his head swiveling to take in all around them.

"I know of a hidden canyon with water and grass off the trade route; it is a day's ride from where we were ambushed," Jangbu said. "We must find our way out of these hills to the trade road, once there I can get my bearings."

Looking back the way they had come, he added, "I do not know if De-guang will send men after us. In any case we must be very cautious. Yelu is on the march with his army, heading this way. Should we run into them we will not escape. If we can make it to the hidden canyon then we can hole up there and rest."

"In my saddlebag there is a small bundle of oiled cloth," Jangbu said.

His leg which was now free of the boot with his trouser cut and rolled up over his knee, he continued. "We cannot wait until the morrow; we shall do this now."

The arrow-shaft protruded from his leg, like a broken branch growing from a bloody tree trunk.

They had found their way out of the maze of hills onto the empty trade road in the hottest part of the day. With no shade to shelter them, they continued on until nightfall. The horses stumbled along, fatigued beyond their limits. Zehiya dismounted many times, continuing the journey on foot, leading Kimizi to rest him. Rinzen carried Jangbu faithfully the entire way. Finally, they arrived at the hidden canyon where Jangbu would sequester himself and his horses on this route.

The moon was high in the sky coursing along its ancient track. Although it was merely a half moon, its light was as bright as day. Jangbu's gaze settled on the horses as they grazed on sparse grass that grew along the small spring that gurgled in the bottom of the gorge. Their bare backs were stained with dried sweat marks where their saddles had been. He leaned back against his saddle on the ground with Rinzen's sweat-soaked blanket cushioning his back. The horsey aroma of the wool calmed him as images of what had just happened this day reeled backward in his mind's eye.

Zehiya knelt next to him rummaging through his saddlebag.

He turned his attention to her, marveling at what this young girl, well in fact not such a girl any longer, had accomplished all on her own.

"Thank you for saving my life," Jagbu said, "It was truly remarkable. It took courage and...it was well done. How did you...find me? How did you...figure out how to get me out of there?"

Zehiya looked up from the saddlebag. "You need not thank me.

Your life would not have been in danger if you had not been helping me find my way to Dunhuang to find Pema. How I…it is a long story…" she hesitated, then added, "In time I may be able to tell of it; I too am amazed I succeeded."

Kartal sat on the pommel-perch of Kimizi's saddle, which lay across from Jangbu. The falcon eyed Jangbu.

"That was masterful how you sent Kartal to take that man off me at the cliff," Jangbu sighed. "I do not think I would have made it if you had not sent him. And what happened to his hood, is it lost?"

Mystified, she asked, "Sent him? Sent him where?"

Jangbu looked disconcerted. "When I was being held in the clutches of that warrior on the cliff who was holding tight to my ankle." He shivered at the memory of the pain.

Zehiya sat back on her heels. "Oh, when we could not pull you up. A warrior was holding you down? I could not let Rinzen go to see what was happening and then you just came free and it was easy pulling again."

She looked at Kartal and asked, "What did Kartal do?"

"He flew in and took the man's eyes out," Jangbu said.

"He did what?" she asked, looking at Kartal in amazement. "I had nothing to do with it. He had flown away when I started down the cliff. I had forgotten about him and did not know where he had gone."

They looked at each other, incredulous, and then at Kartal. A long moment passed as comprehension dawned. Shaking her head in wonder, she marveled, "He did that on his own."

Returning to her rummaging, she added, "It is a good thing I threw his hood away."

Jangbu placed his hand on her arm, stopping her.

"You threw his hood away?"

She looked into his eyes. "A lot happened while you were held captive," she explained. "I may be able to tell of it as time passes."

Jangbu released her and lay back. Dizziness overtook him and his leg was ablaze.

"I will wait to hear of it," he said, swallowing back the bitter taste rising from his roiling stomach.

Ignoring the long, silk-wrapped bundle that held the parchment pages that she had found two days before at the spring, she pulled the small roll of oiled cloth out of the second saddlebag. Untying the leather thong that secured it, she unrolled it to expose a sticky paste with a pungent aromatic scent that was dark in the moonlight.

"What is this?" she asked.

"Turmeric and honey," Jangbu explained. "It is good for wounds. I always carry it with me. Once we get the arrow head out, you will cover the wound with this paste, then bandage the leg tightly to close the cut flesh."

Zehiya looked at the bloody arrow shaft, then at Jangbu.

"This is not going to be easy. We have no dagger," she sighed, feeling queasy by the knowledge of what they were about to do next.

Jangbu nodded. "I know, yet you are strong; you can do it. It is good that the arrow entered the side of my leg rather than the back so I will be able to help you."

Zehiya stood and reached for her sword. The sharp blade whispered as it slid from the leather scabbard.

"I will guide it as you push. We will cut this wretched thing out," Jangbu instructed.

As he bit down hard on Rinzen's leather rein Jangbu nodded. His hands wrapped in turban-silk around the tip of the sharp blade, he flinched at the pain as the cold steel pressed into the wound alongside the arrow. Zehiya pushed slowly on the sword as he guided the blade. He grunted as he worked, the leather rein becoming soaked with saliva as he clenched his teeth in agony. He kept working, never succumbing to the searing pain. Finally, hand trembling, he grasped the broken end of the arrow and pulled. The arrowhead slid free from his flesh. Jangbu fell back onto the saddle, gasping, with the bloody thing held tightly in his fingers.

Zehiya laid her sword aside and knelt beside Jangbu's leg. Holding the water flask over the wound, she cleaned the blood away. With her fingers, she inspected the wound gently, feeling for any remaining pieces of wood or cloth that would prevent it from healing, causing it to fester if they remained inside. When she was confident it was clean, she applied the paste over the gash and then wrapped it tightly with her turban cloth.

Jangbu held up the bloody arrowhead. Inspecting the point, he could see the base of the steel tip swept back into barbs at its base which was why the arrow held fast in his leg.

Then, he tossed it aside and fell into a deep sleep.

The moon lay low in the east, like a curved sword-blade of shining silver hung from a belt of stars. It illuminated the road before them as it ascended into the night. They rode out of the protection of their gorge and onto the trade route after spending five days there.

They both felt stronger after the rest. Zehiya and Kartal had hunted each day, bringing in snake and rabbit. Zehiya laid strips of the butchered meat over the hemp rope she had strung between two boulders. The wind and hot sun dried the meat quickly and soon they had filled their saddle bags with enough to feed themselves for the trip to Anxi, the trade post at the crossroad to Dunhuang.

"This is the last time we travel by night," Jangbu said. "On the morrow after some hours of rest, we will travel by day to Anxi then onward to Dunhuang."

"Kimizi and Rinzen are too thin," Zehiya worried.

"In Anxi we will buy grain to fatten them," Jangbu assured her.

Zehiya looked at him, incredulous. "Buy grain? With what? They stole everything we had. I saw no coin in your saddle bags."

Jangbu smiled. "You forget. I hide caches of coin along the way just for this situation."

A smile brightened Zehiya's sour expression. "Where?"

"Just outside Anxi," Jangbu replied. "It is still far. We must pass through the desert. The wind blows the great dunes making a new landscape every day. This is why we must travel by day, to follow the way east and not become lost. The horses will make it," he assured.

"Water?" Zehiya asked.

"There is an oasis along the way called The Spring of Wild

Horses. The horses will be able to eat their fill of grass there. We will not stay long enough to fatten them, but they will have enough to keep them alive," Jangbu said.

"How is your leg?" Zehiya inquired.

With a grimace, Jangbu shook his head. "It remains painful. The wound does not fester, it will heal in time."

They fell silent as the hours and miles wore on. Zehiya dismounted Kimizi and walked with his reins held loosely in her hand. When she grew weary, she mounted once again and they continued on in what seemed like a timeless realm. They trudged onward as the moon cut its way across the sky, finally disappearing over the western horizon, replaced by a soft pink glow, then yellow, and finally white as the fiery globe of the sun made its majestic rise over the sand dunes with rays like molten steel.

"We will rest there," Jangbu said, pointing to a high dune in the distance. Its base was in the early morning shade.

"It is cool there now but will get hot soon enough," he said, as he urged Rinzen onward.

Jangbu dismounted and hopping on his good leg, he unsaddled Rinzen. After tending to Kimizi, Zehiya tied the horses, one at each end of the long rope, giving them room to wander. Yet, there was no grass. She took off her robe and Jangbu handed her his Zhuba. Placing the saddles apart and her sword secured in the sand as a middle pole, she fashioned an awning, draping each robe from saddle to sword, to protect them from the sun. Kartal swooped in from his early morning flight and landed next to Zehiya who had crawled under the robe tent as she held fast to the middle of the rope that was fastened to the horses.

"How did you know the method to correcting my dislocated shoulder?" Jangbu asked.

Lying on her side, her head resting on her arm, Zehiya murmured sleepily, "Feray taught me how. My father would do that to his shoulder at times. She wanted me to know how to move the shoulder back in place in case she was not there when it happened to him."

Jangbu nodded. "It is a good thing," he replied.

Pushing away the pain of the memory of Feray, Zehiya tumbled into a deep sleep.

Jangbu pulled the flask under with them and lay on his back with his head resting on Rinzen's saddle blanket. With a sigh, he listened to Zehiya's deep breathing. He gazed up at the robes above him, the fabric undulating as the morning breezes began to grow stronger. His leg felt as if scorpions were marching along its length stabbing it with their poison spears with each step. He would not tell Zehiya of the pain. With his many seasons of practice, he was able to sequester the pain in a chamber of his mind and close the door, not allowing the sensations to cloud it nor bring rise to his emotions.

He looked over at Zehiya's still form, the gentle rise and fall of her breathing. He marveled at her intelligence and her fortitude.

Kartal nested in the sand beside her with his head swiveled back, beak burrowed in the soft feathers between his shoulders, in contented sleep.

35

Secluded on the top of a sand dune, Zehiya and Jangbu watched as two hundred leather-armored men mounted on horses passed them in the distance. Red and black banners fluttered in the wind as the procession passed. Behind the main body of warriors a caravan of camels and their drivers followed, packed with weapons, food, water, fodder for the horses and with armor barding for the horses when the time came for battle.

"Who are they?" Zehiya hissed.

Squinting, Jangbu said, "That must be the advance party of Yelu's army. I think that is Yelu himself riding at the head."

"And, there…" He jutted his chin in the direction of the procession, "is most likely the remains of the caravan we would have been a part of, all seized for Yelu's army. It is a good thing we did not join that caravan after all," he marveled.

"Not the entire army?" Zehiya asked.

"No, they have come from the spring of the Wild Horses oasis. His entire army is massive and slow. Yelu will want to be in the lead to scout the route. They will assemble on the steppe, allow the horses to regain their condition, then continue on to Hami, then to Kashgar."

"How far is the remainder of the army behind them?" Zehiya asked.

"Probably several days," Jangbu replied as he slid backwards off the top of the dune. "Come, let us get the horses and proceed in a roundabout way to the spring. If we are lucky, the army will be gone by the time we get there."

After hours of trudging up and over sand dunes, they spied the oasis from a distance. It appeared empty and silent under the hot sun. They approached warily ready to turn and flee if they were mistaken and more warriors remained there.

Zehiya was amazed by the contrast of desert, its high shifting sand dunes dry and colorless, with the green oasis before her. In the center was a large pool of still water, shinning bright like a mirror. The only inhabitants here now were a few camels, lying about, skinny and worn. They watched the arrival of Janbu and Zehiya with indifference.

Seeing that their way was clear, they hurried to the shoreline. Jangbu dismounted and limped as he lead Rinzen over the uneven ground, churned up in pits and mounds from so many men and livestock. Zehiya followed him, leading Kimizi. At the water's edge she released her hold on the reins and fell to her knees. Her trousers became damp from the wet ground as she scooped up handfuls of water. Her dry throat felt at first a barrier to the wetness, then it became a greedy organism of its own.

"Slow down," Jangbu warned, "you will make yourself sick. Small sips, then wait, then small sips again."

Zehiya repressed an urge to scowl at him. He was right, after all. She sat back on her heels, breathing hard. The wetness felt both good and strangely painful too. Taking up a small handful of water, she sipped it slowly, letting it slide down her throat. She noticed the songs of birds, something she had not heard for a long time, she realized.

What if the world had no birds, the thought came to her, *how empty, how strange.*

Standing, she scrutinized the shore line to the trees. Detritus was strewn about everywhere, like palm fronds after a wind storm. Leaving Kimizi, she wandered toward the items, finding a torn turban-cloth which was a faded and dusty indigo. Zehiya shook it out and taking off her shortened one, replaced it with this one, weaving it around her head, she was grateful for the greater protection from the sun.

"I am amazed there is still any green here at all after that horde. Come, let us unsaddle the horses and let them graze and rest, then we can inspect the leavings. Perhaps there may be items of value to us," Jangbu said, as he led Rinzen away from the water's edge to the shade of the trees.

Jangbu started awake at the sound of Zehiya releasing her armload of findings and then dropping to the ground to sit cross-legged in the sand. Resting back against his saddle, he rubbed his dry eyes. With a yawn, he stretched his arms and arched his back. His leg was swollen, he could feel the pressure inside the bandage.

"Well, here is a dagger," Zehiya said, holding up the weapon, its blade broken a third the way from the tip.

Handing it to Jangbu, she went on. "It will serve, even though the blade is broken. Better than none."

Jangbu inspected the blade. The handle was made of ivory.

"We may be able find a metalworker in Anxi to grind a new point," Jangbu said. "Until then it may be useful indeed."

Holding up several torn turban cloths, Zehiya said, "I will wash these for bandages."

Kneeling, she walked on her knees to Jangbu's leg.

"I will unwrap it and let it have air, then I will clean it and apply fresh medicine and a clean bandage," she declared, as she reached to unbind his leg.

Jangbu shot his hand out to stop her, not wanting her to see the condition of the wound. "Perhaps we should just leave it as it is until we get to Anxi," he said.

She stared at him, uncomprehending.

"Anxi? Why? We need to tend to this now," she said as she began to unwind the bandage.

Jangbu tried again to stop her.

"There will be a healer there," he said.

Reflexively, Zehiya slapped his hand away.

"I have tended many a wound on our horses and watched when Feray treated wounds of my father and brothers. We need to see if it is healing or if it is festering," she said, glaring at him. "This could cause your death if we do not treat the wound correctly," she added.

Jangbu lay back in resignation as a wave of dizziness overtook him.

The stench hit Zehiya before the wound was even exposed, causing her to gag. When the final wrap was undone, Zehiya gasped at the red and purple swollen leg. Jangbu sucked in air as Zehiya prodded the angry flesh.

Shaking her head in dismay, she asked, "Why did you not tell me? You must have known this was in such a state; the pain must be terrible."

"To worry you would achieve nothing," he replied.

Grabbing the flask, Zehiya began to clean the crusted tumeric paste away from the hot gash. Gently, she squeezed the last of the medicine out of the wound and washed it away as she poured water over the area. Gingerly, she separated the incision to peer inside and then began squeezing and manipulating the flesh, urging the puss to exit the wound. The sickening rancid smell hung around them as she worked. With their new-found knife, she probed the yellow goo.

"There," she said, triumphantly holding the knife up. A tiny thread of Jangbu's trousers that had ridden into the wound on the tip of the arrowhead, lay across the metal edge. "We did not get everything out of the wound."

Jangbu stared at the knife. "Well, that is the folly of not inspecting the wound in the daylight. We just left it wrapped since the night we removed the arrowhead."

Without a word, Zehiya rose in one smooth motion with the flask and bandages in hand. Jangbu watched her disappear toward the lake to get more water and wash the bandages. He lay his head back with a sigh, shaking his head.

"Jangbu," he said, with a chuckle. "Sometimes you are such a fool."

Zehiya felt a lightness in her step. Removing her boots at the shoreline, she waded into the water feeling the cool mud ooze through

177

her toes. When she was waist-high in the water, she unfurled the bandages, dunking them and pulling them through the water, watching absently as the grime, herbs, and blood that had soaked through the silk were released.

She was stunned. "I am not in paralyzing pain," she marveled aloud in a soft voice to herself. "I remembered my home, our horses, my father and brothers and Feray. I just spoke to Jangbu of tending their wounds. There was no pain in the memory. I am remembering them and I am not curled up in agony."

Letting her head fall back, she spread her arms wide opening her chest to take in a long full breath. Releasing it slowly, feeling the sensation of the warm air leave her, she gazed into the blue sky in wonder.

"My heart is healing," she said.

36

They rested at the oasis for three days. Four days later, traveling over the shifting waves of sand as the sun washed the land in morning light, the terrain transformed into a flat and hot barren landscape.

Zehiya looked up to watch Kartal high above, his dark form circling in the clear blue sky, then pulled the end of her turban across her face, shielding her skin from the sun.

Feeling optimistic, now that he was free of the burning pain in his leg, Jangbu rode with his back straight and relaxed as he chewed on a piece of dried rabbit meat from their supply. The horses had put a bit of flesh on from the days of grazing on the oasis grasses, yet they remained thin.

"What do you think happens when one dies?" Zehiya asked, breaking the silence.

Jangbu unwrapped his turban and considered the question as he shook out the cloth, releasing sand and dirt that hung suspended on the still air.

"There are many beliefs about what happens when we die, when our bodies die," he began, speaking as he rewrapped the linen around his head. "How can we really have an answer that is not simply a belief?"

Zehiya urged Kimizi alongside Rinzen.

"I guess it is a question that cannot be answered since no one comes back from death to tell us what lay beyond," Zehiya pondered aloud.

"Well, in fact there have been those over the centuries, a very few, that have been said to have died and come back to tell of their experience. In Tibet they are called Day-loak, yet I have never met one. There are also enlightened beings, like the Buddha and Padmasambhava, and others who speak of what happens to our consciousness when our bodies die," Jangbu said.

"Day-loak? What do they say lay beyond this life?" Zehiya asked in wonder.

"They say we enter a place, more like enter a journey, meeting beings and seeing lights. We Tibetans call it a bardo. It is the place we go before we are reborn into a new life as a sentient being. The choices we make in the bardo, along with our karma created in life, determine what we will be and the circumstances we will be born into in our next life," Jangbu said.

Zehiya stared at him, taking it all in. "Do you believe this?"

"There it is—we always come back to what we believe," Jangbu chortled.

Reaching forward to pat Rinzen's strong neck, he continued, "When I was in that Khitan camp I thought more seriously about death, because I thought I was surely headed for it. Before that experience, I had been confident in my belief about death and what lay beyond. In that camp however, with death hovering near, I felt it as a visceral reality, no longer a concept or idea. Now, despite that I had in the past felt secure in my knowledge and understanding of death, I am no longer so sure."

He looked over at Zehiya, who gazed at him in interest.

"Now, I find, that I am very afraid of death," he said, turning his gaze to the way ahead. "I have to come to terms with this, it is a meditation for me."

"Maybe it is better to be more concerned with life and on living, rather than on dying," Zehiya mused aloud, "since when we die we can do nothing about it. It comes and we are powerless. Maybe it matters not what happens at death. Maybe it is better to focus on living a good life; a long life."

Jangbu laughed and nodded his head. "Words of wisdom, yet not to be heedless in a life lived, to pay attention to one's karma and lead a good life, a worthy life."

"Kar...ma?" Zehiya asked.

"Karma is the result of one's actions. Your karma follows you in this life and determines the next," Jangbu explained. "You must pay attention to your actions."

They both fell into silence at this and rode on as the sun crossed the sky and the day grew hotter. Kartal sat on the pommel of the saddle, in contented slumber. Zehiya's bow and arrows in their quiver made a soft shuffling sound as they tapped against Kimizi's flank with each step. Zehiya untied the flask and took a small sip.

Handing it to Jangbu, she asked, "Who is Pad...Padma..."

"Padmasambhava?" Jangbu asked.

"Yes, Padma...sam...bhava," Zehiya said.

"He was a great master, a fully enlightened being, a Buddha who lived and taught in Tibet long ago. They call him the second Buddha, though I am very sure there where others—other buddhas," Jangbu said.

"I thought the Buddha was... I thought that was his name... Buddha," Zehiya said.

Jangbu shook his head. "Buddha is a description, it means awake, one is awakened to reality. The Buddha you are speaking of is Shakyamuni Buddha. He was a prince in Nepal. His name was Siddartha Gautama of the Sakya clan. He became enlightened, awake. His teachings of wisdom spread through Nepal, India, Tibet, and China and all along the trade route far to the West."

Zehiya gazed into the distance, considering. Jangbu took a sip from the flask, then held it out to Zehiya.

As she was tying it to her saddle, the sky suddenly became dark.

Zehiya pulled up on Kimizi. Jangbu halted Rinzen. They stood frozen in confusion. Suddenly, a strong wind surged around them. The horses whinnied in fear, prancing to flee. Zehiya and Jangbu kept them circling to control their primal urge to bolt.

"It is a black storm," Jangbu shouted, above the increasing roar. "We must get the horses to lie down and take cover next to them."

Taking the end of his turban, he wrapped it around his face, leaving only his eyes exposed.

"The winds will become very strong," he yelled.

Zehiya dismounted as stones carried on the wind pelted her. Jangbu urged Rinzen to her knees. Trained to lie down, she complied with alacrity. Zehiya prodded Kimizi, he sunk onto his knees, then his hind quarters followed. The wind increased in a blast. Zehiya screamed as Kartal tried to take flight, watching in horror as he somersaulted away on the gale into the roiling gloom. Releasing Kimizi, she flung herself after him into the darkness.

"Zehiya! No!" Jangbu shouted, grabbing Kimizi's bridle, keeping him from rising where he lay next to Rinzen. He could not let the horses run away into the storm in a panic, for they would surely perish as many before had in these storms. Holding tightly with both hands and all of his might to the bridles of the prone horses, he knelt helpless, unable to shield his eyes from the bombardment of sand and stones.

"Zehiya!" he called out blindly, his eyes shut tightly, his words snatched from him in the roar.

Zehiya sprinted after Kartal who was a dark blur in the distance before her. The wind pounded her back as she ran with all of her strength, fixing her gaze on that blur, determined not to lose sight of the falcon as the shrieking gale took him away. As she gained on him, a powerful gust sent her flailing and she hit the ground with a thump. Gravel in her mouth, she stayed focused, reaching out for Kartal. She felt the tip of a wing feather, then it was gone from her. Rising against the squall, she launched herself forward, grasping for him. Finally she felt his wing in her grip and dragged him to her as he squawked and squealed in pain and fear. Kneeling, braced against the torrent, stones and debris whizzing by, she folded his wings to his sides. Untying her belt, she struggled with her flapping robe, holding him to her as she wrapped the robe around him. Cinching her belt tight, he was protected in her makeshift pouch. He struggled, then relaxed, as she tried to stand. Yet she did not know which direction she must go to return to Jangbu and the horses.

"Jangbu!" she called out. Her shout to him was a mere whisper on the thundering wind.

Staggering in the direction she thought might be correct, she stopped. If she went the wrong way, she would be further from Jangbu and the horses. A blast of wind sent her sailing backward onto her seat. She wrapped her arms around the bulge that was Kartal under her robe. She knew she must stay close to the ground or the wind would carry them away.

"Jangbu? Jangbu!" she cried out, in growing terror, shielding her eyes as she searched sightlessly into the black barrage of pelting stones and sand.

She must find them so she could take cover next to the horses, or she and Kartal would surely die; they could not survive long unprotected. Curled up on the ground, trembling, she buried her head in her arms as the storm grew even stronger.

"Zehiya?" a soft voice in her ear. "Zehiya."

Shielding her eyes, she looked up. There, standing before her, was a shimmering white light unaffected by the black gale.

"Grandfather?" she whispered, raising her head.

"Come, Granddaughter, this way," Grandfather said, beckoning with a silvery outstretched hand.

Zehiya rose to her knees and forced herself to her feet, bending low against the wind as she followed, in amazement, the white ghostly form of Grandfather walking ahead of her, leading her. She struggled after him for what seemed like only moments.

Then he stopped and gestured beyond—there she saw the dark shapes of Jangbu and the horses.

She looked up at Grandfather.

"Grandfather...how?"

"I told you, Granddaughter, my love remains always," he said. "I am so proud of the woman you are becoming."

His eyes filled with love as his body of light expanded. Zehiya watched in awe as wide shimmering wings grew out from his form, transforming him into the Eagle Spirit. It rose high into the sky and then dissolved into the blackness.

Lurching forward, Zehiya fell next to the hunched form of Jangbu. His robe covered both Rinzen and Kimizi's heads, protecting their eyes and allowing them to breathe.

She flung her arm around his hunched back, feeling his strong muscles under his thin cotton tunic.

"Zehiya," he said, in relief, lifting his head to meet her eyes.

"Jangbu," she gasped.

Holding tightly to him as the storm roared over them, threatening to pull them up and away into the darkness, she wept.

37

"**H**is wing is broken, and some of his flight feathers are gone—others are broken—yet, he is alive," Zehiya said, with a sigh of relief as she inspected Kartal, who sat on the ground with one wing hanging away from his body and the other wing having wide gaps where there were once feathers. The falcon looked up at her, his eyes blinking.

"How do we splint a broken wing?" Jangbu asked, as he shook out his robe. The thick layer of sand caked on it flew away on the breeze. The black storm had lasted for hours when finally it subsided, it left them all covered in a thick layer of dirt, stones, and sand.

Zehiya looked up at Jangbu, his back turned to her. She stood in alarm. "Your back is bloodied, are you in pain?" she said, reaching for the back of his tunic showing splotches of dried blood.

"It hurts some. Without my robe, I had little to protect me from the storm. Until you returned and shielded me with your arm," he said, glancing over his shoulder. Turning his attention to the horses standing with lowered heads in a snooze, a thick coating of sand covering them and the saddles, he smiled. "My robe was better used to cover their eyes and nostrils."

Zehiya reached out to touch his back. Remembering the feeling of his strong muscles under the tunic she pulled her hand away, disconcerted at the flush of heat that surged through her.

"We will need to soak it to free it from the wounds," she said, turning to get the flask.

Jangbu turned, "No, we need the water to drink. You will have to free it dry, slowly; but we will do this later. First, we need to tend to Kartal. Do you know how to splint the wing?"

"Yes, I have watched it done once. I remember how."

Looking at their turbans caked with sand, she shook her head.

"We need thin clean material, like silk, to set the wing. Everything is caked with sand and dirt."

Struggling into his robe, Jangbu flinched at the pain as it settled on his back. "I have what we need," he said.

Crossing to Rinzen, he opened the saddlebag and took out the wrapped bundle. Holding it aloft, he unwrapped the silk covering it, then returned the boards and parchment pages into the bag.

"Here," he said, holding the silk out to her.

"I will need to cut it into strips," she said.

Jangbu nodded. "Do what you must."

Shaking out the silk to full length, Zehiya took the broken knife they had found at the oasis and cut the silk in half making three, two finger-wide strips. Jangbu knelt to hold Kartal as she gently folded the wing against his body, feeling the broken bone ends align. Gently, she wrapped the thin strip of silk around the folded wing to hold it bent properly in place.

"Fold the good wing and hold it next to the body so I can match the two," she instructed Jangbu.

Lining up the top of the wrapped wing with the good wing, she took another strip and wrapped the broken wing against Kartal's body and under the uninjured wing, leaving it free. She was careful to wrap all snuggly, yet not tight, so he could breathe easily.

Sitting back on her heels, she said, "He can ride on his perch. I will have to hold him if anything should cause him to fall."

"How long will it take to heal?" Jangbu asked.

"A fortnight," she said, stroking Kartal's back. "Yet, he needs those lost feathers replaced and the broken ones repaired or he will not be able to fly until his next molt, which is moons from now."

Looking into Jangbu's concerned face, gray with a coating of dirt, she marveled that she no longer saw his twisted scared face as a defect. She simply looked upon her friend—a true friend. It was Jangbu. Her heart lurched as she recognized in him a rugged and rare beauty.

Clearing her throat, she asked, "Is there a falconer in Anxi?"

Jangbu thought for a moment.

"I do not know for sure, yet Anxi is a busy crossroads town, there must be a falconer there. We shall look for one—why?"

"A falconer will have what we need to repair his broken feathers," she said.

Rising, brushing the dirt from the knees of his trousers, Jangbu said, "We must be careful not to run into the remainder of Yelu's army or perhaps a scouting party in advance of the main army. They may be on the trade route coming from Anxi. We will skirt the main route. I know the way. It will take a day longer, yet it should be safe."

38

A day later, Zhiya sat mounted on Kimizi, holding Rinzen's reins as Jangbu went behind a grouping of rocks. She watched the sun, dim and hazy in the thick hot air, fall beyond the horizon, the sky turning yellow, then fading to pink.

Soon he returned, dusting off a wrapped bundle of silver coins, the cache he had buried outside Anxi. After placing it inside the fold of his robe, he swung up onto Rinzen.

"We will settle the horses in the livery, then go to the inn," he said.

The back streets were unusually quiet as they wove their way through the block houses of Anxi, an important garrison town at the edge of China. Here, travelers from China stocked up on what they would need before embarking on the long journey across the sands of the northern route through the Gobi desert to Hami then along the base of the Tien Shan mountains, skirting the Taklamakan, the killing desert, the way Zehiya and Jangbu had arrived from. Or travelers could proceed to Dunhaung and stock up there if they were traveling the southern trade route that skirted the southern edges of the great and perilous Taklimakan desert from oasis to oasis to Khotan.

Zehiya smelled the aroma of hay and manure before she saw the livery, a group of small corrals holding horses that were contentedly munching on piles of hay. They rode up to a low building and dismounted as a stocky Chinese man came to stand at the open

188

doorway.

"Master Jangbu!" he hailed. "You have returned!"

"Shang," Jangbu called. "You are well, my friend?"

Nodding, Shang hurried to them. With a bow, he took Rinzen's reins from Jangbu.

"I am well, yet you look like you have seen the black demon," he said, taking in the dirt-covered group.

"We have indeed," Jangbu said.

Looking down at Jangbu's bandaged leg, he frowned.

"You are injured?"

"It is healing," Jangbu said.

Searching over Jangbu's shoulder, he asked, "Is Norbu coming with the horses you brought back from Fergana?"

Jangbu placed his hand on Shang's shoulder.

"Norbu is...is...Norbu was killed. His horse fell. We were being chased by bandits."

Shang froze in shock. Wiping his face in disbelief, he said, "Dead? Norbu is dead? And they stole your horses?"

Shaking his head, Jangbu said, "No, my friend, the horses are safe in Hami."

Shang looked quizzically at Jangbu. "Hami?"

"I am helping my friend Zehiya travel to Dunhuang," Jangbu explained, gesturing toward Zehiya.

Shang watched with interest as Zehiya lifted Kartal from the saddle, cradling him in her arms.

"You are going back to Dunhuang now?" he asked.

Ignoring the question, Jangbu asked, "Is there a falconer in Anxi?"

Shang peered at Kartal, resting in Zehiya's arms.

"A falconer?" He scratched his head in thought. "Yes, there was one I heard of on the outskirts of town to the east. Ask at the inn; someone there should know."

With a wry smile, Shang said, "And you avoided Yelu's scouting party, I see. They rode through here gathering men to fight for Yelu. Lucky for you."

Jangbu chuckled. "We did not, as a fact," he said.

Shang looked at him in surprise.

189

"Then how is it you are here?"

"I escaped, with help," Jangbu said. "I will tell you the story one day, my friend, yet now we are tired and starved. We need to get to the inn."

"Very good, I await that day. Be assured there will be more of those warriors riding through here soon. I have heard word the main army is only a few days to the east. You will have to leave Anxi before they arrive. Come, I will put your horses up and feed them. Take your saddle bags and I will store your saddles," Shang said, as he led Rinzen away.

Jangbu took Kimizi's reins from Zehiya, freeing her to carry Kartal, and followed Shang around the house and hay storage to the corrals.

The streets were dark in the moonless night as they made their way to the inn. Zehiya's legs felt leaden as fatigue draped over her and each step was an effort. Kartal felt heavy in her arms. She licked her cracked, dry lips. The night was turning cold as the wind rose up, on it rode the smoke of the many cooking fires in town.

Finally, they pushed through the heavy wooden door of the inn which was a low building made of brick. Zehiya's stomach rumbled at the cooking aromas wafting from the kitchen. Not realizing how hungry she was previously, she now felt she could not go another minute without food.

All eyes fell on them as they entered the large room, filled with patrons eating at low tables surrounded by cushions, the stone floor covered in carpets. A haze of smoke from pipes and hookahs filled the air. Jangbu lead the way to a table in a corner. Zehiya settled Kartal on a cushion next to hers, then lay her bow quiver down and removed her sword-belt, lying it next to her as she sat cross-legged on the cushion. She stared at the hazy forms of the diners, who, having lost interest in them, had gone back to puffing on their pipes, eating and murmuring their quiet conversations.

A woman appeared at their table. Her deep brown eyes sparkled above high cheek bones. Her black hair hung in a plait down her back to her waist.

"Master Jangbu," she said, in a quiet tone with a slight bow. Eying Zehiya, she asked, "So glad to see you have returned from the west. Norbu is dining too?"

"Good to see you as well, Tashi," Jangbu said. Then placing his hand on the young woman's arm and cleared his throat. "Tashi, I have sad news. Norbu was killed when we were attacked by bandits."

Tashi's eyes widened, then went narrow with anger. "He was a good man," she said, bowing her head, anger turned to grief. "I shall...he will be missed."

"Yes, he will," Jangbu agreed.

"What is Huang making in the kitchen?" Jangbu asked, feeling strange in changing the subject.

"Noodles and vegetables with goat meat," Tashi answered.

"Very good, we are starving. Please bring us tea as well. Do you have two rooms for the night?"

Tashi shook her head, holding one finger up. "Only one left." With a glance over her shoulder, she said, "It is a busy night."

Jangbu glanced at Zehiya. "We will take it."

With a slight bow, Tashi turned and disappeared into the kitchen.

"I will sleep on the floor," Jangbu said.

Zehiya gazed with interest at a group of men in a corner of the room. They passed a small pipe from man to man. A wave of sweet-smelling smoke added to the aromas of the room.

"What are they doing?" she asked, nodding toward the group.

Jangbu looked at the group nonchalantly, so as not to attract attention, then turned his attention back to Zehiya.

"Opium. They are smoking opium," he said, shaking his head slowly. "Bad for the mind, bad for the spirit, bad for karma."

"Opium?" Zehiya said. "What is opium?"

"It comes from a poppy plant. It is used for medicine, but also for pleasure."

"Why do they smoke it if it is bad?" Zehiya asked.

"They are bored or sad. Once they begin smoking it, they can never stop. It is a demon. It destroys lives," Jangbu said, with a grimace.

Just then, Tashi appeared with a large tray. She set down two ceramic bowls filled with noodles, goat meat, carrots and onions in a yogurt curry sauce, a plate of flat unleavened bread and a pot of tea and two cups and chop sticks.

"Your room is the last one, on the right," she said, setting down a large key. "I am glad you made it safely, Master Jangbu," she said. Then she turned and was gone.

Zehiya dove into the meal greedily. She could not remember the last time she had eaten cooked food. This savory dish was a far cry from the dried meat on which they had been subsisting. Jangbu controlled the urge to devour the food, eating slowly.

Finally, Zehiya felt she could slow down. She took a small piece of meat in her fingers, wiped off the curried sauce, then offered it to Kartal. He snatched it in his beak, swallowing it in a gulp. She gave him another, then turned back to her meal. Between mouthfuls of food and sips of hot tea, she asked, "What is so pleasurable about opium?"

"It causes a dreamy state. It takes away pain," Jangbu said. "People who take it want to escape from life. People who feel their lives are difficult or meaningless, or if they have a tragedy happen to them and cannot bear the pain, try to escape into a pleasurable state with the drug, but then when they wake up, their lives remain the same but now worse—because they need the opium or they will experience much discomfort without it. They become trapped."

Zehiya nodded, as a wave of fatigue washed over her.

Jangbu pushed his empty bowl away with a satisfied sigh.

"Let us get some sleep. We will find the falconer on the morrow," he said, rising to his feet, slinging both their saddle bags over his shoulder.

Just then Tashi appeared, a small lantern in her hand. With a bow, she handed it to Jangbu.

"Best of rest, Master Jangbu," she whispered.

"Can you have someone bring a floor mat?" he inquired.

With a fleeting glance at Zehiya, she nodded and silently was away.

Zehiya stood and put her sword-belt on, slung her bow quiver over her shoulder, and took Kartal into her arms. Then she followed Jangbu, weaving through the maze of seated people, exiting through a back door.

The night air was cold and fresh.

"Privy?" Zehiya asked.

Jangbu nodded, taking her to a small building made of stone. He set the lantern on the ground and gently took Kartal into his arms. Zehiya took the lantern and ducked inside. A bench made of stone sat against a far wall. A hole was carved in it that opened into a deep pit dug in the ground below. The stench of waste filled the room.

She breathed in the fresh air when she came back out into the night, taking Kartal from Jangbu, who then ducked into the privy. She looked up at the river of stars, feeling Kartal's warm body next to her. She shuddered at the thought that she almost lost him.

Finding the door to their room, Jangbu struggled with the large padlock, wiggling the key until it finally twisted, opening the bar. They stepped inside, their lantern casting a soft glow. Zehiya placed Kartal on the bed.

"I will sleep here tonight, but on the floor on the morrow," she declared, then lay down next to Kartal.

A tapping came at the door. Jangbu opened it to a young boy holding out a rolled bamboo matt. Jangbu took it and closed the door. Rolling the mat out, he settled down cross-legged, opening his saddlebag to bring out the loose boards and stack of parchment pages. Reverently, he placed them on top of the saddle bags, making a table for them.

Zehiya watched with interest as he turned the first page up and gazed at it. She wondered at the black markings on it.

"What is that you are doing?" she asked.

Jangbu looked up at her. "I am reading."

"Reading?"

Jangbu sat back, hands on knees. "You know what reading is, do you not?"

Zehiya shook her head.

Craning to look closer, she said, "What are those black markings? Are they paintings, like those I have seen on rocks in the Barskoon gorge, by our homestead?"

"You do not know what letters are, what writing is?" Jangbu asked. Yet, he knew, many women, especially a young girl, knew nothing of reading and writing if they were not exposed to it or taught it.

"Your father did not keep ledgers for his sales of swords?" Jangbu inquired.

Zehiya thought for a moment.

"Ledgers?" she asked. "What are ledgers?"

"They are books one records information of trade, of business transactions," Jangbu explained.

"If he did, I never saw him," Zehiya said.

"Well, these are scriptures," Jangbu said, gesturing toward the stack of parchment. "They are the writings of the Buddha. Writings are letters. Letters are drawings of sounds. Letters are combined to make words, drawn on parchment. Ledgers use numbers, drawings of numbers, accounting for silver, gold, or trade goods. Reading is understanding the meaning of the drawings."

Zehiya nodded in understanding.

"Can you draw these letters? Make these words on parchment?" she asked.

Jangbu nodded.

"Can you teach me how to…do this? How to draw the sounds and read them too?" she asked.

Eyebrows raised in surprise, Jangbu said, "Yes, I can teach you. On the road to Dunhuang we will begin. Now get some sleep. We have much to do on the morrow."

Zehiya settled back on the hard cushion. In a moment she was fast asleep.

Jangbu stared at the scripture, not reading a word. Hearing her soft breathing, in deep slumber, he looked at her, her body curled protectively around Kartal. She was a remarkable young woman, he thought. Eager to learn, never letting fear dissuade her from…from…anything, he marveled.

39

"Restrain him," the falconer, Gerel, requested. "Where is his hood? Is it lost?"

Zehiya held Kartal gently, but firmly on the table in Gerel's home, which was a stone building on the outskirts of Anxi.

"He has no hood," Zehiya said. "He no longer needs it."

The Mongol falconer looked at her quizzically, then let go of the subject, as he gently extended Kartal's good wing.

"Mmm," Gerel murmured, holding the wing out with one hand as he stroked the length of his wispy moustache that grew down to his thin beard with the other.

His long black hair was twisted into a top knot. His threadbare hemp robe was spotted with dirt and grease. He wore faded felt boots.

"We must replace these three flight feathers," Gerel said. "Hold the wing."

Jangbu stepped in and took hold of the wing as Gerel cut the damaged feathers free with a small knife, leaving a length of the quill from each still attached to the wing.

"Keep hold of the wing," Gerel said as he turned to his workbench to study his collection of feathers that were harvested from dead falcons found in the wild as well as those from Gerel's own falcons when they had molted.

"My son, Ganzorig, would be here to help with this, but he ran off to join Yelu's scouting party when they passed through, just days ago," he said.

"Why not wait for the army?" Jangbu asked.

Gerel turned to look at him, taking in the scarred and twisted face before him. Far from looking strange and foreign, Jangbu's face looked very familiar, like that of many a warrior from his Mongol clan.

"He is young, all of his life he has heard the legends of our warrior tribes to the north. Anxi is not an exciting place for a young man. Ganzorig wanted to fight the Mohammedans—he was anxious to go."

With a sigh, he turned back to the feathers laid out in a row on the bench.

"Perhaps it is for the best, they need all the men they can muster. If the Mohammedans succeed in taking city after city along the trade route, trade will cease, China will close its gates and we will be paupers or die under the invader's sword unless we convert to their religion."

To Jangbu, he asked, "You are Tibetan? Are you Buddhist or Bonpo?"

"I follow Buddha's teachings," Jangbu answered.

As he picked up feather after feather and held each to the spaces in the wing, Gerel said, "I and my people do as well. I could never convert to a religion such as the Mohammedans profess."

"It would be difficult under their rule," Jangbu agreed.

Shaking his head, Gerel said, "Why can they not simply let people choose their own path and enjoy this life?"

"I have never known why people cannot allow others to choose their own way. I can only surmise that is simply the ego," Jangbu answered.

"True," Gerel agreed. "If they come, I will return to my homeland to the north with my son—pray he survive the fighting."

As the men talked and Gerel measured feathers to the spaces in the wing to find the ones that would fit alongside the good feathers, Zehiya gazed at the three falcons and one eagle sitting, silent and hooded, on their perches along a wall of the one-room abode. The aromas of sweat, cook-fire smoke, birds and their droppings under their perches, mingled in the room. The wooden window shutters were open, allowing fresh air and shafts of sunlight in.

"You can release the wing now," Gerel said, having chosen three feathers.

He cut the quill tips off them and then he shaved small pieces of bamboo to fit snuggly inside the hollow quills of the ends of each feather. Zehiya and Jangbu watched with interest as Gerel, a stocky muscular man, meticulously fitted and shaved and fitted the bamboo again and again. When he was finally satisfied, the falconer took a small piece of oiled silk and lay it on the table under Kartal's wing as Jangbu extended it again. Kartal chirped and struggled. Zehiya cooed for him to settle.

"You are good with birds," Gerel said, watching as Zehiya calmed Kartal. "My sister is a falconer. She is good with birds too."

"Where does she live?" Zehiya asked.

"Far to the north," Gerel jutted his chin, "On the steppe at the foot of the Khangai Mountains."

Now with Kartal still, Gerel dipped one end of the bamboo into a ceramic jar of fish glue. Though his fingers were thick and callused, he slid this into the hollow quill end on the wing with the dexterity of someone with small and sensitive hands, and then with a very small horsehair brush, he painted the glue onto the exposed end. Finally, he slid the matching feather onto the exposed bamboo to meet the end of the cut quill.

Zehiya nodded in approval.

"It is perfect," she said.

Repeating the process twice more, Gerel finished by wiping away any exposed glue.

"The glue will take time to dry and harden, so keep the wing still. I cannot repair any feathers on the broken wing—you did a good job setting that. It should stay bound for a fortnight," he said.

"What is his name?" Gerel asked, as he put his supplies away.

"Kartal," Zehiya said.

"Kartal? That means eagle, does it not?" Gerel said.

"Yes," Zehiya said, "I have always wanted an eagle. I once had an..." she trailed off, not wanting to tell of her loss.

Gerel gazed at her with interest. "You look like you are of the Kyrgyz people. Good falconers, your people."

Gesturing to his eagle, he beckoned Zehiya. "Come see my

beauty. This is Batzorig. His name means 'strong courage'."

Zehia stood before the powerful bird, its head tilting, feeling her presence.

"It is a male eagle?" Zehiya asked, looking at the bird with admiration.

Nodding, Gerel said, "Yes, he is smaller than the female of his type, but he is a formidable hunter."

Gazing at Batzorig, he said, "You both are traveling to Dunhaung, you said?"

"Yes," Jangbu said, who was now standing alongside them, admiring the bird.

"There are cliffs to the west of the Dunhaung caves; in those cliffs you will find eagle nests," Gerel said.

40

The frigid wind blew fiercely as Jangbu and Zehiya made their way toward the oasis of Dunhaung, a three day journey. Zehiya felt better now, clean after spending time at the public bathhouse in Anxi and washing her clothes. She wore a new sheepskin coat that Jangbu had bought for her, as now the days and nights were growing quite cold. The aroma of the gamey hide filled her nostrils.

Jangbu, too, felt renewed after the same experience, and secure as he held the lead rope of the pack mule, loaded with food and water, that they had hired from Shang. It would be returned when Jangbu returned, or sent back with a trusted traveler. Kimizi and Rinzen, though still lean, had their strength back. They would have a long rest in Dunhuang.

It would not be long now, Zehiya mused, until she would sit before Pema and resume her place before this teacher. To meditate with this woman and feel the peace she had experienced in the gorge near her home, before... She brought her thoughts firmly back to Pema, someone who is familiar, someone who she knows in this world of strangers. Try as she may to keep it at bay, the pain of loss returned, and wrapped tightly around her core. She was overcome with a profound feeling of emptiness; her family no longer existed in this world

Yet, I have Kavya and Asrila, Sahin and Jangbu in my life now, she thought. That knowledge eased the constriction around her heart.

She wondered about Jangbu, how long would he stay in Dunhaung? As the image of his saying goodbye and riding away played in her mind, her heart clenched. Turning in the saddle, she looked at him. So familiar now, and his scar? His disfigured face? What scar? She saw only this kind and good friend who risked all to bring her to Dunhuang. Not only that, she saw a handsome man, for he would be if not for the knurled skin along the one side of his face. The memory of the feeling of his strong body close to her in the black windstorm returned, causing a stirring in her.

Jangbu smiled, noticing her gaze, and then a question worked on his face.

She pulled up on Kimizi's reins allowing Jangbu and Rinzen to come alongside her. "How long will you stay in Dunhaung?" she asked, above the wind.

Jangbu pondered for a moment while he pulled the front of his sheepskin coat closed.

"I have been thinking the same thing. I do not know. I must return to Amdo to get more coin for the return trip to Hami for the horses. My brother will have to come with me to help drive them back to Amdo," he said. "That is, if the horses are still in Hami. Yelu may have taken them for his army."

Zehiya shuddered. "All that way again; and they may not be there?"

"If I know Ozturk, he will have hidden them from the army, if he could," Jangbu said, feeling more assured by the idea.

They rode in silence as the sun crossed over the sky, the ends of their turbans wrapped around their faces. Zehiya rested her hand on Kartal's bandaged back, dusting off the sand that accumulated there. Thoughts of the falconer's words drifted into her mind; the cliffs, baby eagles, and the pain of the loss of her eagle, Neylan.

"You would like to capture a baby eagle to raise?" Jangbu asked, breaking the silence between them.

Zehiya looked at him, surprised.

"How did you…? Yes, I have longed for an eagle since I lost Neylan. Will you will help me find one?" she asked, hopeful.

Jangbu considered. "I will help you. We will travel to the cliffs the falconer told us of," he said. "You know how to locate a nest?"

Nodding, Zehiya beamed. "Yes, I can."

"Very well, we will find you an eagle after we find your teacher Pema and before I leave for Amdo," Jangbu said.

They stopped to make camp for the night, grateful that the wind eased a bit as the sun fell over the horizon. Making a windshield of the saddles, they huddled down to eat the dried meat, walnuts, dried apricots and drink from the flasks. Jangbu fed the horses and mule grain from collapsible oiled cloth buckets, then gave them each water from the water bladder that the mule carried. When this was completed, they settled down to meditate together, Jangbu reiterating the method before they began, so Zehiya would not forget. Afterwards, Jangbu would answer any questions Zehiya had.

"When I am settled and following my breath, I begin to grow sleepy, I can't keep my eyes open. How do I keep from falling asleep?" Zehiya asked.

"That is a very common obstacle to practice," Jangbu began. "One method I use is to visualize a white lotus in my heart. On the lotus are small bright white lights, like bright stars in the night. I visualize these bright stars rise up from the lotus into my head. Another method is to get up from the cushion and resume in walking meditation."

The next two days passed in silent monotony as they traversed over the sea of sand dunes. Zehiya used this time to practice meditation and keep herself from falling deeply into daydreaming. At first spending so much time in meditation was boring and her mind wandered into endless stories to entertain her. With her strong will she persisted in ignoring the dance of imagery in her mind and remained concentrated on her breath as the tether to stay in the present moment. Finally her thoughts fell away. She could hear the grains of sand fall away from each of Kimizi's foot falls. The desert air filled her lungs and she could detect many separate aromas and scents. The blue of the sky and all the tones of the sand dunes took on a luminous glow.

The thought of her stepmother, Feray, came to her. The scene of the murder of her father and brother played in her mind. She did not ignore these thoughts nor try to push them away, but instead she contemplated that her family could no longer experience life—death had come to them. She knew that death will come to her too. This profound realization rocked her.

"This is why I must be here in this life, not live in daydreams," she whispered to herself. "I do not want to miss this life, what is really here."

She looked back at Jangbu, seeing that he was in deep meditation as he sat straight in the saddle, and she could see by the movement of his lips that he was quietly chanting mantras.

She looked up at the sky and around her. "Life is magnificent and at the same time horrible," she considered, speaking softly to herself. "I am alive, my life is a gift, I will not squander it," she vowed.

They passed a tall watchtower manned by Buddhist Uyghur warriors, the new controllers of this route. Control, protection and fee collection of this trade route had changed hands many times over the centuries. The warrior at the gate, dressed in leather breastplate, trousers, and tall boots, armed with a sword, collected a fee from Jangbu. Zehiya noticed his bow, in its quiver with arrows, leaned against the gate post, at the ready for speedy use.

They followed a trail of posts, driven deep into the sand to be seen even as the landscape changed with the ever shifting of the sands in the wind. Remnants of the ancient wall built by the Chinese rose out of the sand here and there.

Shrieks and whistling rose and fell in volume from the high dunes as the cold wind blew steadily.

"What is that sound?" Zehiya asked, calling out to be heard over the wind.

"They call that the Singing Sands," Jangbu explained. "It is caused by the wind."

Zehiya began see the forms of men, dressed in white shimmering robes that flowed around them on the wind, appear in her peripheral vision. But when she turned her head to look closely, they were gone.

"Those are the desert Jinn," Jangbu explained, when she told him of the phenomena.

"Jinn?" Zehiya asked.

"Spirit beings," Jangbu explained.

"They are real?" she asked.

"Some believe them to be real," he said. "Some believe they are mischievous beings that delight in causing trouble."

Up ahead, they saw forms materializing over a high dune. First one figure riding on a camel, crested then tromped down the dune, wisps of sand were kicked up with each hoof beat. Then another appeared and another after him.

"Caravan," Jangbu said.

Soon a line of camels, loaded with packs, snaked over the dune and down its side. Clouds of sand rose up around them, then were blown away on the wind. Jangbu and Zehiya looked on as the line continued longer and longer, as if it would never end.

"Dunhaung is the meeting of the northern and southern trade routes," Jangbu explained, jutting his chin. "They must be coming from Khotan and are heading for China."

Zehiya and Jangbu waited until the string of travelers came close. The headman undulated on his magnificent Bactrian camel, decked in a luxurious red and gold carpeted saddle. Long silk tassels at the corners swayed with each fluid step of the creature.

"As-Salaam-Alaikum," the man greeted, pulling on the reins of his camel, stopping before them. He looked only at Jangbu, averting his eyes from Zehiya.

"Wa-Alaikum-Salaam," Jangbu replied, with a nod of his head. "Do you speak Turkic?" Jangbu asked.

"Yes, I do," the leader said.

"How far have you come? What is the news from the West?" Jangbu asked.

The string of camels behind the man passed around him, continuing eastward as he answered, "We began in Khotan and are bound for Chang'an. There was fighting in Khotan when we left."

"Fighting?" Jangbu asked, in surprise.

Nodding, the man continued, "Yes, Prince Satuq Khan's nephew, Ali Arslan, has proclaimed jihad in Khotan, to convert all the Buddhists to Allah; peace be upon Him. The Buddhists have taken up the sword to resist. I have not heard any further word. We are the last to arrive from the West on the southern route."

"So, Satuq's nephew has converted," Jangbu said, understanding the portent. With a nod Jangbu said, "Ma'a salama, many thanks for the news. May your journey be safe."

With a gesture of his hand and a switch of his camel-whip, the leader called, "Ma'a salama," over his shoulder as his camel trotted away.

Silence fell over Jangbu and Zehiya as the caravan disappeared into the distance. Jangbu rubbed his chin, musing over the news from the west. A feeling of foreboding washed over him. He looked at Zehiya who studied him.

"Where is Khotan?" she asked.

His face grim, he said, "Khotan is to the west, a long way, six thousand Li." Then considering, he said, "It is probably the same distance from here to Aksu."

Zehiya nodded her head slowly, remembering the small oasis town that she and Asrila had passed through, nestled along the base of the mountains beneath the pass from Lake Issyk Kul, so long ago.

"Buddhists are fighting the Mohammedans?" she asked.

Jangbu urged Rinzen onward; as the lead rope tightened on the mule, it threw its head up in protest, then followed.

Kimizi fell in next to Rinzen as Jangbu explained, "Khotan is an ancient Buddhist city. The Mohammedans wish to convert all in Khotan—all in the world—to their own religion, so they have attacked the city. If the Buddhists do not fight and win, the Mohammedan warriors will destroy all the Buddhist temples, scriptures, statues, and monasteries. These new overlords will require conversion to the religion of Mohammed. If one wishes not to convert from their Buddhist faith and practice then they will be required to pay a tax to the Mohammedan overlords or be slain. The Buddhists will be second class citizens in their own city, so they must fight to remain free and to save their city and their way of life."

Zehiya fell silent. An ominous feeling settled over them as they traversed over the churned path of the caravan.

"Will they come to Dunhuang?" Zehiya asked.

"If they conquer Khoton, then yes, they will come. Yet, it will be a long time until the Mohammedans send warriors here; a full circle of the seasons or two until they arrive," Jangbu said.

Night had fallen when they arrived at the entrance of Dunhaung. Two high towers, along the broken remnants of the great wall that ended on this spot, stood as entrance on the ancient route. They were manned by four garrison guards. At the base of the towers another guard, seated on a rough wooden bench, gazed at Zehiya and Jangbu as they approached. With a yawn, he waved them through, then sat back and leaned against the stone wall of the tower as they passed.

Soon they came upon a temple, its roof swept up in graceful curves to meet the starry sky. Below it, a crescent shaped lake shimmered reflecting the moon that was now rising over high sand dunes. Dismounting, they led the horses and mule to the lake shore to drink. The temple glowed with the soft light of oil lamps. Zehiya felt transported by the chanting of the monks inside.

"Beautiful," she said, in a whisper.

"Yes," Jangbu agreed.

"Where will we stay?" Zehiya asked as they lead the horses away onto the road.

"I have a friend who has a cave abode among the many caves carved into the cliffs in Mogao, thirty Li beyond the city. He is not there now and will not mind if we stay in the cave. We will not go into the city, we will go directly there," Jangbu said.

"What about the horses?" Zehiya asked.

"For tonight they can be tied outside the cave. On the morn, we will secure them in the corrals by the stream. It is a safe place, with space for them to move about," Jangbu assured.

41

Rays of sun, cascading through the entrance of the cave, bathed Zehiya's face, and awakened her from a deep sleep. With a groan, she rolled away from the bright morning light, and covered her face with her turban. For a moment she did not know where she was. Then as the haziness of sleep cleared, she remembered. Sitting up on the carpet that softened the stone floor, she took in her surroundings. The cave had been lit by only an oil lamp when they arrived the night before.

Jangbu was gone now, his saddle bags lying nearby where he had slept. A low table stood in front of a cushion against one wall of the cave. A stack of parchment pages lay on the table. Zehiya rose and studied them. They were Jangbu's, from his saddle bags. An altar at the other wall stood under a painting on cloth, hung between two wooden dowels attached to the wall. The rich colorful imagery depicted a woman seated on a lotus with the Buddha in the clouds above her head and dancing women at each side of her. A bronze statue of the Buddha was placed in the middle. Seven small silver bowls, each filled with water, were lined up before the statue. Unlighted oil lamps were placed at each end of the small altar.

A curtain hung at the back of the cave. Zehiya peered behind it to see a chamber-pot. With a sigh of appreciation, she stepped behind the curtain. Moments later she exited the cave and stood transfixed by the sight that greeted her. The entrance of the cave was high on a narrow ledge. Stairs carved into the cliff-side led down. A wooden banister was attached to the rock. She marveled that she had gotten up here last night and had not remembered this. There was a forest below of trees swaying in the morning breeze. This sea of green infused her with the sensation of peace and refreshment. Beneath the leafy canopy, a procession of monks and nuns in saffron and red robes walked peacefully, hands folded. Hearing the sound of chanting, Zehiya leaned out to view the length of the cliff-side and could see there were other caves, many other caves in these cliffs.

"Pema?" Zehiya wondered aloud. "She could be in one of these caves."

Remembering the horses, she looked to where they had been tied the night before, but did not see them. Then she saw the familiar form of Jangbu striding along, with a bag slung over his shoulder. In moments, he was bounding up the steps toward her.

"Tashi de ley!" he greeted with a bright smile.

Standing next to her, taking in the view, he said, "Beautiful, is it not?"

"It has been so long since I have seen trees, it is truly a marvel," Zehiya replied.

Raising the bag, he said, "I have tea and cakes. Come, let us feast!"

Zehiya followed him, eager for the promise of these delicacies.

"Where did you get these?" she asked, as Jangbu busied himself beside the fire pit inside the doorway of the cave.

"In the market, it is on the other edge of the forest," he explained, jutting his chin in the direction. "At sunrise, I settled the horses and the mule in the fenced pasture by the stream, then headed to the market."

Placing the teapot on the fire, he asked, "Sleep well?"

Nodding, Zehiya said, "I see that there are other caves along the cliff. It should be very easy to find Pema, if she is here."

Breaking off a chunk from the pressed tea brick, Jangbu plopped it into the heating water, then closed the lid.

"Not so easy. There are hundreds of caves along these cliffs," he explained.

Surprise working on her face, she exclaimed, "Hundreds? How? Why?"

Jangbu rummaged in a deep shelf carved in the cave wall, bringing out two silver cups and wooden bowls.

"The caves have been carved in these cliffs for centuries," he explained. The aroma of fresh baked almonds, honey and flour filled the cave as he unwrapped the cloth that held a round loaf. "Long ago they were carved in the cliff for meditation practitioners and for use as temples, with painting and carved statues, by patrons of Buddhism. As time went on, many merchant travelers had caves carved and painted, honoring the deities as a guarantee of safe travel west and back over the Taklimakan desert; a truly arduous and dangerous journey."

He smiled as he handed Zehiya a cup of tea and a bowl of cake.

"It is almond cake," he said. "We will find Pema, if she is indeed here," he assured, settling cross-legged, his cup of hot tea cooling and bowl of moist cake on the carpet before him. "It will take time though."

Zehiya set her bowl on the carpet and blew on the hot tea. She swooned at the woody and flowery aroma. Taking a sip, she marveled at the taste.

"What tea is this?" she asked. "I have never tasted such a tea."

"Jasmine. They mixed jasmine flowers with Chinese tea," Jangbu explained.

Zehiya bit into the cake, closing her eyes at the exquisite taste of almonds and sweet honey. Taking a sip of the fragrant tea, she marveled how long it had been since she had such tasty food and good tea. Even Anxi did not have these delicacies.

Lovely, she thought.

For a week, Jangbu and Zehiya searched through the market and temples, asking if any knew of Pema. Zehiya stood in awe at the caves she was invited into. Many had large stone statues of the Buddha carved into the rock wall of the cave. Colorful paintings of round Mandalas or of Buddha, deities and mythological beasts flying in the sky or sitting in clouds adorned the walls of the caves. Some had paintings depicting historical scenes of patrons or great masters of the Buddhist lineages.

She looked over the shoulders of monks sitting at low tables in some caves translating and copying texts from those brought from India or China. She tried to understand the writing, but, alas, could not read well enough yet.

"Keep studying and practicing," Jangbu encouraged. "You will be able to read and write within a turn of the seasons."

All who they met or passed on the road looked in wonder at this tall young woman with long red hair, her falcon sitting on her gauntleted hand, blinking and swiveling his head, taking in all around him. Zehiya's green eyes, once intense and challenging, had grown soft, her practice of meditation relaxing her mind and allowing her emotions to calm.

Zehiya felt no need to carry her sword here, leaving it resting in the cave with her bow and arrows. Each morning, after their meditation practice and reading and writing lessons, Zehiya and Jangbu would head out, away from the caves to a spot where Jangbu had set up a target for archery practice. After that, they would spend the remainder of the day searching and talking with all they met. With Kartal's wing healed and with the broken feathers replaced, in the early evening, as the sun settled in the west, Zehiya would step outside the cave and release him into the sky, to spread his wings and hunt. When he returned with a limp rabbit or other small animal in his talons, Zehiya gave all of it to him to eat. She had lost her taste for meat, enjoying more the nuts, vegetables, fruits, and cakes from the market. Her body had changed too. With rest and good food, her tall boney frame was filling out with lean muscle and full breasts.

After the passing of a full cycle of the moon, Zehiya sat dejected in the morning sun on the ledge at the entrance of the cave, her feet dangling over the edge.

"She is not here," she declared. "We would have found her by now."

"There is another set of caves, west, a hundred Li, they are more remote," Jangbu said, as he sat on a bench cut into the rock at the entrance. "We have exhausted our search of Mogao caves. If she is in the Dunhaung area, then she must be there," he said, massaging his calf.

The wound was now fully healed, yet still it ached in the mornings. He had a slight limp to his step but in time this would disappear.

"No one has even heard of her. How is that possible after speaking to so many people here?" Zehiya asked.

Nodding in agreement, Jangbu said, "She has done a good job of secluding herself, yet, since she is a lay practitioner and not a nun in the monastic order here, it is not strange she is known by only a few. We have simply not been able to find those who know her. There are many practitioners in this region who remain in seclusion."

"Come," he said, rising to his feet. "Let us gather the horses and the mule. We will fill the flasks then go into Dunhaung city and stock up on food and supplies. We have one more place to look."

42

The gates in the thick walls surrounding Dunhaung city stood open and inviting as Zehiya and Jangbu entered becoming surrounded by the flow of travelers into the city, a shocking contrast to the serenity of the Mogao caves. Kimizi and Rinzen were filled out and strong after their long rest and daily feed. It felt good to be astride Kimizi again, Zehiya thought, as they made their way through the throng of people, carts, rickshaws, horses, and camels. The crowd dispersed upon entering within the protective walls of the city. The smells of cooking food, burnt grain, spices, unwashed bodies, and dung mingled in the air. The day was growing hot as the sun rose high in the sky.

"We will get barley flour and butter to make tsampa," Jangbu said, as they made their way to the market. "No need to cook tsampa. And we will buy more tea."

"Almonds?" Zehiya asked.

Jangbu nodded. "There are dried apricots, too. There is some grazing by the river there, yet we will need grain for the horses and mule."

"You will need a gift," Jangbu added.

Zehiya looked at him quizzically. "A gift?"

"For your teacher—for Pema," Jangbu said.

"Oh, I had not thought…You are right, I need to give a gift."

Then with a feeling of foreboding, she asked, "What if Pema does not want to teach me, and does not want a student? What if she does not want me to disturb her practice?"

Jangbu considered. "This is possible, yet I think that considering your effort to find her, she will accept you and guide you. You will be required to practice on your own. She will instruct you and you will practice. You will not be with her constantly."

Looking at Zehiya, Jangbu added, "Had you considered this; that your meditation practice will be a solitary thing?"

"I only know that when I was with Pema, when I learned and practiced meditation with her, I felt at peace. The world was bright and beautiful," Zehiya replied. "I had not considered what it would be like when I found her again."

They grew silent as they rode through the streets. Arriving at the edge of the market, they dismounted and led the horses into the maze of market stalls. At one stall Zehiya stopped and picked a length of cloth from a stack of silk piled high. She inspected it, longing to replace her turban, now faded and tattered, with this beautiful silk of radiant green.

"It is beautiful," Jangbu agreed, walking up next to her, leading Rinzen and the mule. "However, we must conserve our coin."

"I need to find a way to make money," Zehiya said, placing the shimmering cloth back on the pile, remembering Kavya's promise of wealth if Zehiya became her protégé.

"When you are proficient at reading and writing you will find many who will pay for your skill," Jangbu said.

"Truly?" Zehiya asked, eyebrows raised.

With a nod, Jangbu answered, "Indeed—for correspondence, copying texts and other needs."

"Are there not enough monks and nuns who can do this?" Zehiya asked.

"Not all of them can read and write. There are many texts that need to be copied. The patrons of the Buddha dharma here will pay for copies to be made." Looking at her with a smile, he said, "You can stay here in Dunhaung, practice with your teacher and support yourself copying texts. With the added benefit of learning the scriptures as you read and copy them."

The idea that she could become independent lifted Zehiya's

spirits.

"I can have an eagle too," she mused.

"If you like," Jangbu said.

The mule's packs were now full, and the sounds and smells of the city fell away behind them as they traveled west up and over sand dunes. After a time they came to the Dang river and followed the worn path along its shore. The day was hot. They were grateful to be so close to water for the journey, thus only needing to carry their personal flasks, giving the mule a reprieve from the added weight.

By day's end, the flat earth began to rise upwards. The river wound its way along the base of cliffs rising high on its northern bank. Jangbu and Zehiya felt instant relief from the hot Gobi desert as they entered a forest of huge willow trees. The long soft limbs swayed in the breeze, caressing the pair as they passed through the forest. The last rays of the sun sparkled through the umbrella branches before it sunk low, then was gone far into the west. The sky turned pink, then lavender as Jangbu halted under the trees in a sandy spot by the river.

"We shall make camp here, then proceed to the caves in the morning," he said as he dismounted Rinzen.

After unsaddling the horses, they staked them with a long line of rope so they could nibble grass and drink. They then lifted the paniers and thick under-pad off the mule. Once it was free, it trotted to the shore to take long sips of the cool water. No need to stake the mule as it would never leave its herd of Kimizi and Rinzen.

Jangbu busied himself with pulling the pot, tea and food from the bags as Zehiya searched for wood.

Soon they were sitting by a small fire holding cups of tea and munching on balls of tsampa, barley flour rolled in butter.

"What if Pema travels again? To the cave where I first met her, in

Barskoon gorge?" Zehiya wondered aloud.

Jangbu considered.

"I would suggest that you find Pema, practice your writing and reading, becoming very good at both, then notify the monastery of your skills. When you are settled and are given employment as a scribe, you can plan your meditation practice. You will not meditate all day. At first you will meditate a part of the day, then you will study the teachings of the Buddha for more understanding of the purpose of your meditation and of life." Smiling, Jangbu continued, "After all of that, if she leaves, you will be better able to decide what to do. All will become clear when you find Pema."

The moon rose high, making the night as bright as day. Jangbu lay back against his saddle, studying Zehiya.

"Do you really want to practice Buddha's teachings; or was your motivation just to find Pema?" he asked.

Zehiya held her third cup of tea in her hands as she leaned back against Kimizi's saddle. She gazed up at the bright globe in the sky, then answered, "At first it was just not to be alone. Pema was the only person I knew, I felt close to, after... after the murder of my family," she said, gulping back the tears, then composing herself. It was becoming easier to do. "Since I have been learning to read the teachings with you, I find that I am truly curious. I am interested in learning more." Sitting up, she said, "When I was with Pema, and now meditating with you, I have experienced the power of mediation and understanding my own mind. As Pema taught, I find with practice, that I am not so much a leaf on the wind of my thoughts. Now, I find myself wanting more, to travel to where these teachings lead," she said.

Jangbu looked at her and nodded. "Very well then. I am glad that you are inspired. This practice will become difficult, but considering your natural tenacity, I think you will progress well on the path."

"Path?" Zehiya asked.

"Path to liberation from samsara, from suffering. Practicing the Buddha's teachings is to be on the path," he explained.

Zehiya settled back and pulled her thick coat over her.

"I just hope we can find Pema," she said, her eyes growing heavy with sleep.

43

T he Tibetan yogini, dressed in a long undyed hemp tunic that reached down to her sandaled feet, was crouched next to the river when they rode up early the next day. She rose as the two riders approached. The blazing red hair of the woman on the red horse was easy to see even from afar. As the day was still cool, the woman had no head-covering. The man though, had the end of his turban wrapped around his face; only his dark brown eyes could be seen.

"Pema?" inquired the young woman.

The Tibetan raised an eyebrow, looking the woman up and down as she dismounted her horse and handed the reins to the man. Pema then noticed the falcon sitting on the saddle.

"Pema? Do you remember me?" Zehiya asked, as she slowly walked up to the woman by the river.

With a lift of her chin, the woman answered, "I do remember you and your falcon; yet you were just a girl when we last met. In Barskoon? It was at the cave in the gorge, correct? What is your name? Zehiya, if I remember correctly."

With a gasp, Zehiya rushed closer, "Yes Pema, in the gorge. It is I, Zehiya."

Glancing up at the man sitting silently on his horse, Pema said, "What are you doing here, Zehiya?"

"I have been searching for you since I left you in Barskoon," Zehiya said.

215

"Searching for me? Why?" Pema asked, incredulously. She then held her hand up. "Wait, let us go to my cave. I think this is a story better told over a cup of tea," she said, reaching for her water jug.

"Let me carry that," Zehiya said, stepping forward.

Pema acquiesced and looked again up at the man as Zehiya lifted the heavy jug. "What is the name of your companion?" she asked.

"Jangbu. This is my friend Jangbu," Zehiya said.

"Jangbu?" Pema asked, her eyes narrowing as she scrutinized his covered face. "You are welcome for tea too, Jangbu."

"Thank you for your generous offer, Lady," Jangbu replied with a slight bow. "You two go on; I think you have much to talk about. I will water the horses and set up camp by the river," he said, indicating west. "Zehiya can come find me after you have spoken. I will not be hard to find."

Jangbu leaned against the trunk of a large willow tree sipping his tea and gazed at the river that lazily slid by, while Kimizi, Rinzen and the mule snoozed in the shade. He sat upon a saddle pad with rough tree bark at his back. Kartal sat atop his saddle, his head swiveled back nestled in his feathers, fast asleep. Absently, Jangbu rubbed his calf. The sun was sinking low, it would not be long until dark. At the sound of footsteps he turned with a start at the same time that Kimizi and Rinzen raised their heads and nickered. Kartal awoke flapping his wings.

"There you are!" Zehiya exclaimed, appearing through the trees.

"Ah, you have found us," he replied, watching with amusement as she plopped down on the sandy ground near him. "Did you have a nice visit with your teacher?"

"I told Pema everything," she responded, with delight. "She agreed to take me as student, but I must find my own cave because I cannot live in her cave with her. She needs solitude for her meditation practice. She did say she knows of a cave here in these cliffs that is not being used and will show me on the morrow."

Zehiya reached for the saddle pack and began digging inside.

"Have you eaten? I am starved," she said as she pulled out a bag of barley flour and oil skin of butter. Then the bag of almonds and apricots.

"I did not want to eat her food," she added.

Jangbu rose pouring himself another cup of tea from the pot on the fire. He raised the pot in a gesture to her and she nodded.

"Yes, tea would be nice."

"I have not eaten," Jangbu said, as he filled her cup.

"Pema told me that there are many people living and meditating in these caves. I would never have known it, is so quiet here and no one is outside walking about like at Mogao caves. I am lucky a cave has been vacated recently, so I can use it," she said as she hungrily prepared balls of tsampa. Then she continued, "Pema spoke of the Mohammedans possibly coming here. I was amazed she had heard this. She said she does not know how long it will remain safe to practice here. She also said that the monasteries and practitioners will need to hide the sacred Buddhist texts, so the invaders do not destroy them."

Zehiya set a bowl of tsampa before Jangbu and then flung a saddle pad at the base of a nearby tree and sat, placing her bowl on her knees as she leaned back. Jangbu considered her words.

"I suppose that news travels here easily," he said. "Where will she go if this is true?"

"She did not say," Zehiya replied, between mouthfuls. Then changing the subject, she said, "I do not know how I will take care of Kimizi if I live here." Concern working on her face, she asked, "Do you know how I will feed him?"

Jangbu scratched his scared chin. "And an eagle? Do you still wish to find an eagle?" he asked.

"Yes, that will be easy because my eagle can live in the cave with Kartal and me. I can train the eagle and Kartal and I can hunt every day," Zehiya replied.

"Well," Jangbu said, "Bring me to your cave after your visit with

Pema on the morrow. When I see the location we can discuss the care of Kimizi."

Zehiya looked up as she wolfed down the last ball of tsampa from her bowl.

"You are welcome to come with me; Pema can show us both," she said.

Jangbu demurred, shaking his head, "You show me after your visit."

Zehiya looked at him quizzically and shrugged, "Very well, I will come get you after my visit."

Looking around at the camp, Zehiya said, "This is a nice camp you have made. I like it here better than Mogao. It is quiet and peaceful here."

44

Two moons had passed since Zehiya had moved into her cave and the days fell into a routine. This morning, like every morning of her stay here, she awoke and marveled at the colorful murals that covered the walls of the cavern. One painting depicted a female spirit dancing in the clouds. Another depicted many seated Buddhas and mythological beings. There were also symbols and animals and other creatures; Zehiya never grew tired of studying these paintings.

She stepped outside the entrance of her cave onto a ledge that jutted out from the steep cliff. Kartal hopped off his perch, made from a thick willow limb that sat next to her bed, and followed her out, flying up into the sky. She watched him disappear, and then turned her gaze below to the corral she and Jangbu had built inside a circle of trees, using willow branches to span the spaces between the trunks, forming a sturdy enclosure. Kimizi, Rinzen and the mule stood quietly together. She could see a curl of smoke rise into the sky from Jangbu's camp just beyond, which was hidden from view under the canopy of trees. She climbed down the wooden ladder that was attached to the cave ledge, to the bottom of the cliff and went to the corral. The horses whinnied at the sight of her, jockeying to be the first to receive a bucket filled with a few handfuls of barley grain. Satisfied that they had enough water in the large pail that was secured to the trunk of one of the trees, she left them and strode along the path that wound through the willow forest between the river and the cliffs. The air was thick with the aroma of the morning cook fires from the other caves; the inhabitants of which she rarely saw. Soon she arrived at Pema's cave for her morning meditation instruction over a cup of tea, which Pema always had ready. Pema's cave was entered by way of a ladder as well. Inside were statues of Buddhas carved into the stone walls. Brightly painted murals depicted scenes from the ancient stories of the Buddha Shakyamuni's life.

Pema was solicitous of Zehiya's questions and wanted full reports of her experiences when meditating alone in her cave. Pema never tired of her student; who was bright and studious. When the morning instruction with Pema was over, Zehiya returned to her cave for a meal of tsampa and tea made in the fire pit which was placed just inside the entrance, to allow the smoke to escape outside. It was cool in the cave, a relief from the growing heat of the day. Kartal glided in and landed on the ledge of the cave, flapping his wings before settling. After her meal she slung her bow and arrow quiver over her shoulder and went to gather the horses and mule. Placing a halter rope over each one's head and then with three lead ropes in hand, she slid open the gate of limbs and led them to Jangbu's camp. Kartal glided over the tree tops after her.

"Tashi de ley," Zehiya called in greeting when she entered the camp.

"Good day," he replied, taking the mule's lead rope from her. "Your Tibetan is getting better."

"Where should we go to find grass for the horses today?" she inquired

Securing the pack frame onto the mule's back, Jangbu answered as he tied their bows, arrows and a target of woven willow branched to the frame, "North, father up river. I think we will find good grass there."

They traveled a league when they found a large green meadow shaded from sun by a tall cliff. Jangbu set up the target for their daily archery practice while the horses and mule grazed. After shooting practice and when the horses had enough to eat for the day, they made their way back to the camp, allowing the horses to drink their fill of water in the river, then they put them back in the corral. After their midday meal in the camp, Jangbu instructed Zehiya in reading and writing under the cool shade of the willow braches that waved in the afternoon breeze, as they sipped cup after cup of jasmine tea.

"Why do you avoid Pema?" Zehiya asked, looking up from her writing practice.

"Avoid—what do you mean?" Jangbu replied.

"Both Pema and I have invited you for tea in her cave and you always refuse—why?" Zehiya retorted.

Jangbu shrugged, "No reason, I wish to remain in solitude, except for visiting with you. Pema is your teacher, I need not interfere."

"Pema has questioned me about your aloofness," Zehiya said.

"What do you tell her?" he asked.

Zehiya sighed. "I tell her that I know not why. That you are usually very friendly to strangers, but now for some reason, you wish to remain in your camp alone."

"This is true, what does Pema reply to this?"

"She just nods and says we must not force you; to leave you be," she replied.

"That is good advice," he said with a chuckle. "Tell her I am on retreat, except for my time with you for archery and reading and writing instruction."

After dinner with Jangbu, Zehiya returned to her cave. Kartal glided in and settled on his perch. Exhausted from her busy day, she blew out the flickering flame of the butter lamp and lay on her bed made of a saddle blanket and sheepskin robe. Though sleep beckoned to her, she lay awake for a long time in the darkness of the stone cavern wondering how long Jangbu would stay here. More importantly, how would she feel when he departed?

She sat up with the sudden clench of her heart.

Surely he would come back to visit me? she assured herself as the pain in her chest became more persistent. She took in deep breaths, feeling as though she was suffocating.

But how long? What if he is killed on the road and I never see him again?

She lay back, hugging herself and breathing slowly, taking in deep breaths to calm her mind as she struggled with her feelings. Little by little the tightness in her chest eased with the admission she was trying to keep at bay.

"I do not want him to leave," she whispered in the darkness.

Zehiya was awakened by a bright light shining before her. She sat up and gazed into the undulating light as it grew larger and then it transformed into the Spirit Eagle with its wings spread beyond the cave walls. In a rush, Zehiya found herself beside the Spirit Eagle flying into the night sky, circling above the cliffs. She looked down to see Jangbu's camp, the dying fire sending a wisp of smoke spiraling up, disappearing into the night. The river shimmered silver as it snaked along the edge of the forest.

"Zehiya, you are at an important crossroads in your life," the Spirit Eagle said, her golden eye sparkling in the darkness.

The two of them flew higher and higher until they were surrounded by the stars. The sparkling reflections of light coalesced into a road before them. Zehiya looked down in amazement as they glided along this shimmering path. They came to a fork in the star road and stopped, fluttering in the air. Zehiya considered the two options disappearing into the void.

"Which road do we take?" Zehiya asked.

The Spirit Eagle flew ahead of her and glided around in a circle, then stopped above the division of the sparkling road and faced Zehiya.

"You are to be presented with a choice," the Spirit Eagle replied, as she transformed into two beings, each one hovering above a path. On the right side was the Spirit Eagle, on the left was a beautiful Goddess, her robes made of shimmered gold, green and red light. In her left hand she held a stack of gold parchment pages of a sacred text, in her right she held a sword high in the air, ready to cut through any obstruction in her path.

"The direction you choose will determine your spirit guide and your future," said the two voices in unison.

Zehiya stared in dismay at the two beings before her. The

Goddess was so beautiful and inviting. She longed to read the text that she held in her sparkling hand of light, to understand what secrets it held. The Spirit Eagle was so familiar, Zehiya felt safety and freedom in her presence.

"How do I choose?" she asked.

"Trust yourself, Zehiya, and listen to your heart. Use the sword of discrimination to choose between childhood desires and your growing wisdom. You have enough skills now to decide which is which," the two beings chorused, as they dissolved into one large a ball of light, then shrunk back into a candle flame.

Zehiya opened her eyes to see the lamp flame flickering before her eyes. She lifted up on one elbow and rubbed her face. She was certain that she had blown the flame out before she had lain down to sleep. Blowing it out now, she reviewed the images and message of the powerful dream that was vivid in her mind. She considered its meaning, but the pull of sleep overtook her.

45

Zehiya was crouched before the fire making tea the next morning when a call came from outside, "Madam? Madam, it is I, Deshi, I have come with a message from Mistress Pema."

"Come up the ladder Deshi," she invited. "What is the message?"

The boy, who was tall and very thin, appeared at the doorway. He was dressed in a faded tunic and trousers, with worn felt boots.

Bowing to her, he recited, "Mistress Pema bids you good day and requests you not come to her cave this day. She is engaged in solitary practice and must not be disturbed. You may come to her in three days hence."

"Very well, Deshi, thank you," Zehiya said.

She stepped out of the cave and watched as the boy scurried down the ladder and then disappeared into the forest. She was startled to see Jangbu appear out of the forest heading her way. Her joy at seeing him surprised her.

"Tashi de ley," he said, bounding up the ladder to her entrance.

"Tashi de ley. What are you doing here so early?" she asked, with a laugh.

"I have heard that you do not have practice with your teacher this day," he replied.

"How did you know this? I just found out not a moment ago from Deshi."

"I saw him by the river on his way here and asked him where he was going and why," he said.

Lifting the teapot, she inquired, "Would you like tea?"

With a nod, Jangbu said, "Please."

They sat on the ledge looking out over the trees, enjoying the tea and each other's company, now so familiar.

"Since you are free this day, we should find your eagle," Jangbu suggested.

Zehiya's eyes widened. "I am free for the next three days. This is the perfect time to search for my eagle. If we find one, I will have time to get it settled in the cave before I go back to instruction with Pema in the morns," she said, excited at the prospect.

Jangbu got to his feet as he drained his cup.

"Very well, get your flask and saddle pad, I will carry your saddle. Shall we leave Kartal here?" Jangbu asked.

Considering Kartal, sitting on his perch, Zehiya said, "If the mother eagle sees him flying around the nest she will be alerted and surely kill him. But, we need him with us to hunt a rabbit or some other small animal to leave as gift for the mother eagle, in trade for her chick. While I am climbing to the nest he can stay tethered to Kimizi, on the saddle. It will be well, we will make sure he is safe."

It was midday by the time they arrived in view of the eagle cliffs that rose high into the clear blue sky. They both looked in wonder at the maze of lofty peaks, with many nooks and ledges made by a millennia of pummeling sand storms, wind and rain, that had broken the rock away, sending boulders tumbling down to rest in a scatter on the ground far below.

From this distance Zehiya could see a ledge she was sure would have a nest. She and Jangbu looked for landmarks and decided the best way to ascend the cliff to the ledge. He must memorize the way up because he would be her guide from below.

They wove through the large boulders on the approach to the base of the cliffs, and found a shady area to tie the horses and tether Kartal securely to the pommel by his tresses.

At the base of the cliff Zehiya sat on a rock and removed her boots and her robe. She slung the bag with the rabbit offering over her tunic across her back. In the bottom of the bag she had stuffed cloth to spread out the soft walls in order to carry the eaglet back down safely.

"I will find a perch with a view and call to you should you lose the route up," Jangbu said, as he turned to go.

Zehiya started up the cliff face, easily finding hand and footholds. She was halfway up when Jangbu climbed to the top of a large boulder, giving him a view of the entire side of the cliff. He watched in awe as she climbed effortlessly up the rock face. In fact it was an easy climb for her with many lips and flanges to hold to. Then she stopped with her legs and arms spread clinging to the cliff, searching for the route up. He could see that the next hold on the route was too far for her to reach.

"Zehiya," he called out, "the next handhold is too far from you. Back up the way you came and there you will see a rim that will allow you to step up. The holds are closer that way; that is on the route up."

Jangbu watched anxiously as Zehiya moved back, then up. He let out his breath in a gasp of relief when she found the route.

The climb became easy now as she headed for the ledge. Now and then she instinctively glanced at the sky, fearing the dark shape of the mother eagle. Thankfully all was clear. Finally reaching the ledge, she slowly lifted herself to peer over and was satisfied to see two young eaglets in a nest of branches built in a crevice set back against the wall. Climbing up slowly, so as not to cause the birds to panic and call out to their mother, she settled herself next to the nest and ever so slowly lifted the strap over her head and set the bag next to her. She looked down at Jangbu who was waiting on the bolder far below.

What a true friend, she thought.

She studied the eaglets, her dream now come true, as their black eyes observed her intently, and was struck by an odd feeling.

If I take one of these eagles I will be bound by the care and training of it for the remainder of its life, she considered.

Gazing down at Jangbu, she wondered aloud in a whisper. "Would it not be better to be free? Free to study, to practice meditation—to travel? Be free to go and do as I wish?"

Her heart clenched with an overpowering realization as she gazed down at Jangbu. "I do not want him to leave. I want to go with Jangbu when he goes back to Hami, and then, wherever we wish to go beyond that. I want to meditate with Jangbu and study the texts and write," she declared aloud.

The birds stirred uneasily at her voice.

The memory of Kavya's question to her when she left Turpan came to her. *"Do you love him? Will you marry him?"*

Her heart ached with this realization as she gazed down at him far below.

"I do love Jangbu. I cannot think of a life that I would want to live without him," she declared, in a soft whisper. "What of Pema?" She answered her own question. "Pema may leave anyway. I have found her and I have received instruction from her; I can arrange to meet her again." With a feeling of exaltation she proclaimed, "This world is both large and small. Pema travels the great trade route as I can. I can continue my study and practice with Pema too."

She was suddenly struck with dread; what if Jangbu was tired of her and wanted to be on his way, be free?

Looking at the eagles, their wings held out and mouths opening and closing in agitation, expecting food, she remembered her dream.

"This is the crossroad," she whispered. "The Spirit Eagle is one of you little ones; my old life." As she looked down at Jangbu and beyond him, she said, "A life with Jangbu, and freedom to travel and to practice meditation and study the texts is the way of the Goddess I saw in my dream." With a thump of her fist on her knee her choice was crystal clear.

Deciding that it was best not to have any trace of her being there which might alarm the mother eagle, she decide not to leave the rabbit. She stood up, placing the bag over her shoulder and settling it at her back.

Gazing at the sky, she made a prayer. "I thank you, great Spirit Eagle for all you have shown me. I have made my choice to continue on this new path." Looking down at Jangbu, she continued, "I will go with Jangbu, if he wants to be with me. If he does not want me? Then I will study and stay to practice with Pema without him."

Zehiya turned with a parting gaze at the eagles now chirping and squawking at her. She hurriedly began her decent. She was a good distance from the nest and making her way down the stone wall when she heard Jangbu calling a desperate warning to her. A shadow passed over her. Her heart leapt. She shot an instinctive glance up as the huge winged form passed over her again. Jangbu's words were drowned out by the shriek of the mother eagle as it circled and plunged with huge razor talons spread wide to strike.

Zehiya ducked her head just as the strike hit her back. She gasped for air as the power of the blow slammed her chest into the rock, knocking the wind out of her. Then, the strap across her chest snapped tight with the bag now in the vise like grip of the eagle's talons. Zehiya felt the strong tug and her body begin to leave the security of the cliff as the powerful raptor flew backwards, dragging her with it to a certain fall. Zehiya screamed as her grip on the rock began to slide away. She grabbed furiously at the rock to gain purchase as she slid down, the eagle pulling steadily on the bag.

Jangbu had watched Zehiya become smaller and smaller as she climbed higher. Now she sat on a ledge near the top of the cliff.

His heart sank as he wondered when he would leave this place and leave Zehiya behind with Pema. He had been staying, camped next to the river just to be near her. This eagle hunt was an excuse to stay with her longer; but what now? He had to get back to Amdo for money and then retrieve his horses in Hami. He had been too long gone from his brother who needed the new stock. And he had spent his and his brother's money, the money he had hidden outside if Anxi, just for the kind of situation that he was in, being robbed by bandits, on Zehiya.

Shaking his head, he chided himself. I could have gotten the horses home, to Amdo; instead I...

"I am in love with her. What a fool, I have allowed my feelings for this young woman to distract me from my duty and my practice. I have been swept away by desire," he scolded.

Then in defense, in this his personal tribunal, he declared, "What is wrong with helping someone I love? Does the practice of the Buddha's teachings mean that I stop loving, stop living?"

"No," he answered his own question. "I am not a monk, I took no vows. Life IS my practice, and what better challenge is there than loving someone, being honorable to them. This is not lust dictating my actions. I love Zehiya. I have learned and grown so much from this experience!"

Then he let his breath out, deflated, "It matters not that I love her. I am ugly," he said, rubbing his scar. "No one as beautiful as she will love one as ugly as me."

He looked up at Zehiya who was beginning her descent.

"Ah, so now she has an eagle," he said aloud to himself.

He then noticed a dark spot appear in the sky growing larger as it swooped over the top of the cliff.

"Eagle!" he declared to himself.

"Zehiya!" he yelled desperately, jumping and waving his arms. "Eagle! Mother eagle! Get out of there!"

Hearing a piercing screech from where the horses were tied, Jangbu saw that Kartal was flapping his wings and pecking at his trusses tied to the saddle. Kimizi danced against his rope, agitated by Kartal's display.

Remembering Zehiya's warning, Jangbu instinctively jumped off the boulder and ran to grab Kartal. He could not let Kartal get away. With Jangbu's grasp only a hand's width from the falcon, Kartal freed himself, and in one powerful stroke was up and away.

Jangbu ran back to the boulder and watched in horror as the mother eagle with Zehiya's bag in its talons, flapped her huge wings powerfully, flying backward, pulling Zehiya off the cliff.

Jangbu gasped, "Zehiya! No!"

She was going to fall and be killed right in front of him, and he could do nothing!

A deafening shriek filled Zehiya's ears—a new one that was higher in pitch. The tension on the strap released suddenly and sent her sliding down. Her fingers were cut and slashed as she grabbed at the rock face searching for purchase. Her right knee hit a protrusion sharply, the pain ignored as the primal fear for survival surged through her. Finally her hand found and held a rock lip, her bloodied fingers soaking the rock as her other hand and feet scrambled to find another hold. She felt a solid knob under her toe, then secured her foot to it. She hung, heaving with deep breaths, as her other hand found purchase. She gritted her teeth as the pain in her knee roared through her. Gingerly, she tried to move her free leg, her toes feeling below the quickly swelling leg to find the lip of rock. She put her weight on the leg when her foot secured a narrow ledge. The pain was intense. Even with the pounding of her heart in her ears, she heard the shrieks and squeals behind her.

Realization dawned on her.

"Kartal!" she yelled, trying to look back. "Get away! You will be killed!"

She needed to get down, off the cliff, and call Kartal to her fast. Commanding herself to be calm and ignore the pain in her knee, she took long slow breaths as she searched for another hold and inched her way down.

Jangbu heard the shriek before he saw the spear-like thrust of Kartal's dive strike the mother eagle's back between her wings. The eagle let go of Zehiya's bag and tumbled down and away from Zehiya. In moments the eagle regained flight and sped after Kartal, just as he was wheeling around to land another blow on the formidable bird.

Kartal dove under the huge mass of the mother eagle, and swooped up above her. With agility, he turned and dove, landing on her back, he clung to her with his razor sharp talons while ferociously ripping at her flesh with his beak. The mother eagle dropped, trying to shake Kartal off as he rode on her, the sting of his attack turning her rage into savage fury. She twisted upside down, causing Kartal to lose his grip and fall away. Not deterred, the falcon regained flight and persisted in hot pursuit on the eagle's tail feathers as she swooped along the cliff and, catching an eddy, glided up effortlessly into the sky. Kartal remained right behind her. Blood sprayed off her wings from her bleeding back with each powerful stroke. With the falcon relentlessly on the chase, the eagle's fury turned to fear as she struggled to flee from her attacker. Kartal stayed focused on his prey when he heard a sharp clear whistle. He shifted his attention, falling back from the eagle slightly. Then he heard the whistle again. He altered his course and broke away from his prey, turning back to the third whistle; the call of his mistress.

Kartal swooped in as Zehiya, bloodied thumb and forefinger in her mouth, completed her piercing call. She stood on one leg, her arm around Jangbu's shoulder for support.

"Kartal!" she gasped, as the falcon settled on the saddle perch; Kimizi stepped sideways with a snort.

"That was incredible!" Jangbu exclaimed. "He took on that eagle and saved your life!"

Feeling Zehiya go limp, Jangbu lowered her to sit on a boulder. Blood oozed from a gash on her forehead and she absently wiped it away from her eyes. Her tunic was torn and blood soaked from the scrapes and cuts on her chest and stomach. Jangbu handed her a linen cloth from his saddlebag and a flask of water. She took a drink then held the cloth to her head to stanch the bleeding.

"How is your leg?" he asked, as he knelt before her, gingerly feeling the swollen knee; her britches were stretched tight around the inflammation.

With a groan, she gritted her teeth. "It hurts. Bad."

He reached for the bag at her side and felt the limp mass inside.

"She killed the baby," he said, sadly.

"Baby?" Zehiya asked.

Then, realizing what Jangbu was thinking, she pulled the strap over her head, settling the bag down on the ground.

"No, it is the rabbit. I never took an eaglet," she said.

Confusion worked on Jangbu's face.

"Never took an eagle? Why?"

Zehiya groaned as the pain in her leg grew sharper and nausea roiled her stomach.

"Tell me later. We need to get you to Pema's and treat that knee and your wounds," he said.

"Pema is in retreat; she wishes not to be disturbed," Zehiya reminded him.

Jangbu led Kimizi to Zehiya. "She will just have to be disturbed. You need help," he said. "I will help you mount your horse."

Zehiya stood, holding onto the saddle. Kimizi swung his head around and sniffed Zehiya's injured leg, then let out a guttural groan. To their surprise, Kimizi dropped to his knees lowering himself to the ground, unseating Kartal who fluttered to a nearby rock.

"Thank you, my boy," Zehiya laughed.

She gritted her teeth as Jangbu took gentle hold of her injured leg and helped her swing it over the saddle and right herself in the seat. When she was settled Kimizi glided up to a stand. Kartal swooped back onto his perch.

"You saved my life, my good friend," Zehiya said, as she stroked the falcon's back.

Jangbu mounted Rinzen, and reined her around.

"Ready?" he asked.

Zehiya nodded and held onto the pommel, her throbbing leg useless against Kimizi's sides, as Jangbu and Rinzen lead the way.

Zehiya searched the sky and saw mother eagle circling high above.

"I hope Kartal did not injure the mother badly," she said, noticing the blood on Kartal's beak and head.

"It would be sad," Jangbu said, looking up at the dark shape in the sky. "Even if she had every intention of sending you to your next life. She looks strong up there; I think she will heal. I am still amazed by what Kartal did."

Jangbu pulled up on Rinzen's reins and turned in the saddle to Zehiya.

"Kartal means 'eagle' in your language?" he asked.

She looked down at Kartal, his majestic bloodied head swiveling to take everything in, as the realization hit her.

"Since I was a little girl I have been longing for an eagle, dreaming of an eagle and searching for an eagle. Yet, I have had my eagle all along!" she replied, shaking her head in amazement as she rested her hand gently on her Kartal.

46

Pema sat in deep meditation.

Scuffling sounds from outside entered her awareness.

"Pema?" a voice called.

Familiar sound, she thought, *Pema.*

"Pema? We have come for help."

She knew now that the voice was speaking to her, she is Pema, that is her name. A shadow filled the cave entrance. Pema watched in wonder as the large form entered the cave. Then she realized that it was not one but two forms. She stood.

"Zehiya?" she asked, watching the man, the man who had always covered his face when she was near, lower Zehiya onto the small carpet covering the stone floor.

The man rose and turned to Pema. She gasped in shock as she took in his twisted scared face.

"Pema, I am sorry to disturb you. This is my friend Jangbu," Zehiya said, leaning back on her hands with her leg outstretched.

Pema stared at Jangbu. "Friend?" she asked, perplexed.

"She needs care," Jangbu said, gesturing toward Zehiya.

Pema knelt down next to Zehiya.

"What has happened to you?" she asked, looking Zehiya over with her torn and bloodied tunic front, the scrapes on her arms, the bruise on her swollen cheek, the cut on her forehead, the blood now dried on her face.

"I fell while climbing the cliffs," Zehiya explained. "I have injured my knee very badly."

Pema lightly touched the tight trousers around her knee.

"We will have to cut these off," she said.

To Jangbu, she gestured to a bamboo bucket next to the fire-pit. "Get water; I will need to clean her and cut these trousers off. Does she have other clothes that you can get from her cave?"

"Yes," he said, grasping the bucket. With a quick look back at Zehiya, he disappeared through the doorway.

Pema busied herself, gathering a knife and her ointments, placing them next to Zehiya. She knelt and began cutting through Zehiya's trouser leg, the leather parting easily by the sharp blade. Her knee was twice its normal size, an angry red and purple. Zehiya grimaced, sucking in a breath in pain as Pema gingerly prodded the knee and the leg above and below it.

"I do not think it is broken," Pema declared, sitting back with relief.

They both started at the sound of a high pitched screech and whoosh of Kartal swooping in, and landing next to Zehiya. He jumped up onto a rock near the fire-pit.

"Kartal saved my life," Zehiya said. "On the cliffs."

"He saved your life? On the cliffs? What were you doing climbing the cliffs? How did you fall?"

Suddenly Zehiya felt dizzy. She lay back.

"You can tell me later," Pema said, rising to get her rolled sheepskin and placing it under Zehiya's head.

Soon Jangbu returned and set the bucket and robe down next to Zehiya.

"The leg is not broken. I will need to undress her and clean her wounds," Pema explained.

With a nod, Jangbu said, "I will come back on the morrow unless there is anything else you need."

With a long look at his face, Pema said, "Nothing now."

Days later Zehiya sat up against the wall of Pema's cave, on a bed made of her sheepskin robe and saddle pads, sipping tea. Her leg was raised on a rock softened with a folded tunic. Kartal sat on a perch set next to her.

"Hello the cave," Jangbu called from outside.

"Enter," Pema called back.

"Ah, you look better," Jangbu said to Zehiya as he seated himself on the carpet.

"I feel better," Zehiya replied.

"The swelling is down, it is almost normal," Pema said, looking intently at Jangbu. "She is lucky her leg was not broken."

Jangbu nodded.

Gazing at Zehiya, Jangbu asked "Can you tell me why did you not take the eagle? I have been wondering."

Pema looked at Zehiya, with curiosity.

"Did she tell you the story?" Jangbu asked Pema.

"She told me of the mother eagle and the fall, not of why she did not take the baby," Pema said.

Zehiya took her last sip of tea.

Looking fixedly at Jangbu, she said, "When I was up on the cliff, next to the nest, with two eaglets within my grasp, I realized I did not want the burden of the baby eagle, of the training and care that would be required. Instead, I want to be with you and learn to write and to read the scriptures."

Placing the cup down, Zehiya leaned forward to continue, but the pain in her leg forced her to settle back against the wall again.

"I do not want to watch as you leave this place; I want to go with you," she said earnestly.

Jangbu sat back with surprise and shock on his face.

"That is, if you want me with you," she added.

Jangbu smiled and nodded. "Of course I want you with me," he said.

To Pema, Zehiya continued, "I do not want to stop my training in meditation with you, Pema. You are my teacher. I can visit here to spend time with you for instruction and practice once in a turn of the seasons. And when I am traveling with Jangbu I can practice on my own between our visits. Would this be acceptable to you?"

Pema looked sternly at Jangbu.

"You have not told her," she accused Jangbu, "she has no idea?"

Jangbu shook his head, lowering his gaze.

Pema's lip curled, holding back a smile.

Composing her face to its usual solemn reserve, she said to Zehiya, "He has not told you."

Zehiya stared at Pema.

"Told me? Told me what?" Zehiya asked.

With a gesture toward Jangbu, Pema replied with a question, "Do you know who this is?"

Zehiya looked at Jangbu and then back at Pema. "He is Jangbu, a horse breeder from Amdo," she answered.

Shaking her head solemnly, Pema began, "Your friend Jangbu is a disciple of Atisa. Atisa is one of the greatest masters of Buddhism in Tibet." Gesturing toward Jangbu, she continued, "This is Master Jangbu Khenpo, most call him Master Khenpo. He is renowned as the Scarred-Face Master from Amdo; he is a much sought after teacher of Buddhist philosophy and meditation."

Zehiya looked from Pema to Jangbu in confusion.

Then she starred at Jangbu. "You are a master; a teacher?" Zehiya asked incredulously.

Jangbu nodded slowly, his gaze fixed on the floor.

"My dear," Pema said, to Zehiya, "do you remember when I said to you, 'When the student is ready, the teacher will appear'?"

With a grand gesture toward Jangbu, she concluded, "He has appeared."

"You knew?" Zehiya asked Pema.

Shaking her head, Pema explained, "I know him as Master Khenpo and I have received teachings from him in the monastery at

Magoa caves. He teaches to groups of monks, nuns and lay practitioners—such as myself. I have never had private teachings from him though. But now I understand why he has kept his face covered when he was near me; he did not want me to know it was he. When I saw his face for the first time, I knew, but not before. Since I know him as Khenpo and not Jangbu, I would have never guessed your friend was the great Master Jangbu Khenpo. Since the day I discovered that it was he I have kept quiet, waiting for an explanation," Pema said.

Zehiya stared at Jangbu.

"Are not masters and teachers many seasons old?" Zehiya asked Pema. "You are an older person, but Jangbu is young, not seven springs older than I."

"True," Pema agreed, "Most Buddhist masters have spent many seasons in practice and meditation, they have lived a long life before they are qualified as masters. The reason Jangbu is so young is because he began his training with the great Atisa when he was a very young boy."

"Is that not correct?" Pema asked Jangbu.

Jangbu tore his gaze from the floor and looked up.

"Yes, it is true."

"You are a warrior!" Zehiya protested to Jangbu. "You travel the trade route to Fergana. How can you be a Buddhist Master?"

"It is true that I am trained in fighting," Jangbu began, "but I am not a warrior in that I enjoy a fight or that I sell my martial skills to a lord or to a king. I am trained in the martial arts because, unfortunately, there are those that prey on the weak. I fight in self-defense and to defend my family and those who are too weak to defend themselves." he explained, "I also practice with sword and bow as a meditation. It is true that I travel for my brother to obtain horses; my family have been horse breeders for many generations. I combine travel along the trade road to Fergana, for horses, with teaching at the temples and monasteries I pass on the way. I have traveled and taught every three springs along this route since I was a boy, first with my teacher and then when I was ready, on my own."

"Why did you not tell her; who, what, you are?" Pema asked Jangbu.

"Yes, why?" Zehiya followed.

Jangbu shifted uncomfortably, rubbing his scar, he considered his answer.

Sighing, he replied, "I wanted you to be my friend, just my friend. I just wanted to be nobody."

Then to Pema, he said, "I am the teacher, yet she..." gesturing toward Zehiya, "has taught me much. About life, about love. The struggle of desire and the need for honor. She has shown me the truth of true friendship."

To Zehiya, he said, "I wanted you to see me as just a man, no one special, and I have grown to love you. You are a remarkable woman and my time with you has been a great lesson for me, to experience love and desire in the face of being no one special and with no expectation of my love ever being returned. You see, as a well-known master, women offer themselves to me easily, because they think that their association with me will give them power and prestige or they think that they will become enlightened simply by being close to me. They care nothing for me, they do not even seek to know who I am; they are caught in the trap of their ego and not willing to do the work necessary to reach their own enlightenment." Jangbu leaned forward and continued in earnest. "But you are an independent sort of person, you take responsibility for yourself and you diligently do the work—the hours of meditation and the daily self-examination that is necessary for growth. Zehiya, you cannot know what a joy it is for me to be just an ordinary man in your eyes."

Zehiya stared at Jangbu, a tear slid down her cheek.

Wiping it away, she said, softly, "I have come to love you as well."

Jangbu sat back. "You have?" he asked, in surprise.

Zehiya nodded. "I just want to be with you and share this life with you. I cannot imagine my life without you."

"Ah," Pema said. "A true love. Now that is rare."

47

THREE SPRINGS LATER
IN TURPAN

"**M**y adopted daughter has returned!" Kavya cried, as she hugged Zehiya tightly.

With tears rolling down her cheeks, she turned to Jangbu, and reached for the two springs old boy in his arms.

"My adopted grandson," she cooed, "let me hold you."

She took the squirming child in her arms. "What is his name?"

"This is Arif," Zehiya said, proudly looking on. "He is named after my grandfather."

"Jangbu! Zehiya!" Sahin called, as he strode in, arms held wide.

Zehiya stared at him. He was still the most beautiful man she had ever laid eyes on.

Looking at the two men hugging and slapping each other on the back, she thought, *I would not trade Jangbu for ten Sahins.* Gazing at Jangbu, her love for the man behind the scar filled her.

"Sister, it is good to see you so well and beautiful as ever," Sahin said, turning to Zehiya with a bow.

"It is good to be back, brother," Zehiya said, returning his bow.

"Sit," Sahin implored, "you must be weary from your travels."

"Sister!" Asrila cried, appearing from the kitchen.

She set the tray of tea on the mat, and ran to hug Zehiya.

"Look at you!" Zehiya said, hugging Asrila fiercely, then holding her by the shoulders at arm's length, to look her up and down. "You are as beautiful as ever. A little one comes?" She asked, looking at the slight swell of Asrila's belly.

"Yes," Asrila answered proudly. "My second child."

Everyone turned at the sound of, thump, thump, thump coming from the courtyard. A boy ran in.

"I brought her, Madam," he said, with a bow as Kavya placed a coin in his hand.

With a thud, thump, thud, the old woman appeared in the doorway. Shaking a finger at Jangbu, she scolded, "So you ARE the Master of Amdo, the Scarred-Face One!"

"Sister Sonam!" Zehiya greeted her, in surprise. "How good to see you. Please sit, have tea," she said as she guided the old woman to the cushions.

"I will, as well," said a familiar voice from the doorway.

Zehiya spun around.

"Pema! You are here!" Zehiya exclaimed, "What a wonderful surprise. Please come in."

The group all settled on the cushions around the mat before a feast of fresh baked bread, spiced mutton, rice, dates, and cakes.

Kavya beamed. "Please, eat and enjoy; this is a happy day. My daughter Zehiya and my new son Jangbu have returned with my grandson. My heart breaks with joy."

"Are you teaching here at the monastery?" Sahin asked.

Swallowing a tasty bite of spiced mutton, Jangbu nodded. "Yes, I will be teaching here and at several other monasteries on our route."

With a gesture toward Zehiya, he added, "Zehiya will be copying and transcribing scriptures for these monasteries during our stay at each."

"You can read and write?" Asrila asked, in awe.

Zehiya set her tea cup down.

"Yes, Jangbu taught me. I earn money from the monasteries, and I have the opportunity to read many texts."

Sister Sonam nodded in approval.

"You both are traveling to Fergana for horses?" Sahin asked.

"Not this time," Jangbu replied, taking Zehiya's hand in his. "We are going to Lake Issyk Kul, to Barskoon, Zehiya's ancestral home, to find out what the village did with her family's remains. We also are seeking any horses bred by her family that may still be in the area. If so we will buy what we can and bring them back to Amdo to improve our herd."

Holding little Arif in her lap, Kavya added, "My grandson is staying here with me until they return, it is not a trip for one so young."

Everyone talked and laughed while they shared stories of the time they had been apart.

As the day turned to dusk, Zehiya walked out to the stall where Kimizi contentedly munched his hay. Throwing her arms around his neck, she hugged him tightly and breathed in his scent. Kartal chirped from the beam where he was perched high above them.

She pondered her journey since that day, so long ago now, that her family was murdered.

"Well, my boy, you carried me all the way," she whispered to Kimizi.

He turned his head and nibbled on her thigh with his lips, and then, with a soft whicker, resumed his eating.

Kartal left his perch and landed softly on her arm. Stroking his back, she said, "My eagle. We have been good friends to each other, indeed we saved each other's lives."

Reaching into her robe, she grasped the gold medallion that hung around her neck, the one that Grandfather had given her. It sparkled in the last of the day's light. The sounds of laughter and talking from the house filled the night. There was a doom-teck, the melody from a drum, and the beautiful plucking sound of pipa strings. She could see inside the house through the window from across the courtyard. Gazing at the group inside, she remembered the horror and pain at the loss of her family in Barskoon. She marveled that now she had been given another family, and a son, a beautiful boy. She had learned to become a good friend—first toward herself, then toward others who were worthy of her. She had recognized her value and in turn, she was given the gift of true friendship and love.

Lifting her arm, she sent Kartal back to his perch on the high beam. Squeezing Kimizi's neck, she said, "See you on the morrow, my boy."

She walked out into the courtyard and looked up at the starry sky, then moved closer to the window to watch the festivities. Asrila, beautiful and elegant as a goddess, sat plucking the pipa. Handsome Sahin sat cross-legged on a cushion across from her playing a goblet-shaped ceramic drum which was cradled across his thigh, in complement to Asrila's brisk melody. She laughed to see Sister Sonam bouncing her son, Arif, on her knee to the music. Pema was dancing around the room! Pema dancing? Zehiya laughed—Pema had become light and joyful. Jangbu, her beautiful husband, her best friend, sat laughing and clapping his hands in rhythm. Finally there was dear Kavya, her adopted mother, with her face radiant as she danced, carried along by the joy of the music.

Zehiya threw her head back and her arms wide and danced to the rhythms herself. She whirled, sending the stars above spinning, her heart bursting with love and joy.

High above an eagle made of light circled. Her golden eye sparkled as she gazed down upon the dancing young woman in the courtyard.

THE END

.

Special thanks to my editors
Margaret Eldridge
and
Amy Farrell

My appreciation to
Jaclyn and Warren
for taking the time out of your busy schedules
to read the manuscript and give your feedback

CPSIA information can be obtained
at www.ICGtesting.com
Printed in the USA
BVHW040850010521
606269BV00020BA/242

9 780692 781821